THE
VALE

BEHIND THE VALE

BRIAN D. ANDERSON

First Published Longfire Press, March 2018

Cover Illustration and Interior Design by Gene Mollica Studio, LLC.

Printed in the United States of America

Second Trade Paperback Edition

ISBN-13: 978-0-692-04675-3

CHAPTER ONE

D rake swirled the pale brown liquid around in his glass and then placed it on the bar. Why did he even bother? Nasty stuff. Tasted like vomit. Hell, it didn't even get him drunk…it hadn't been able to for a long time now. The raucous laughter and inebriated voices at his back made him all too aware of this fact. The low-life dregs of Vale. No one else would even consider coming to a dive like this. Still, dregs or not, at least they were capable of having a good time. Which was more than he could say for himself.

From the ceiling hung dozens of pairs of boots, all of them ripped off the feet of unruly patrons who had chosen to take their fun a bit too far, which was really saying something in a regular rough house like this. These days boots were hard to come by; good ones, anyway. In truth, they were probably the only things in the place worth stealing. Not that anyone was stupid enough to try. Mack would have his shotgun out from beneath the counter before you could touch a single bootlace.

The thrumming music crackling from a speaker on the

1

BRIAN D. ANDERSON

wall darkened Drake's mood even further. It was an old tune from way back in his father's days. He couldn't recall the title, just hearing it playing over and over on the vibraplayer in his dad's home office.

"You drinking or not?" asked Mack, settling his elbow on the other side of the bar. The scowl on his face said clearly that this was not a friendly enquiry.

"What do *you* care?"

"This place is for paying customers, *hawker*."

"I paid."

Mack sniffed. "Sure you did. An hour ago."

Drake picked up his glass and very deliberately poured the contents onto the floor. "Okay. So give me another."

"You're a real piece of work. You know that?" Mack reached back and snatched a bottle from the shelf. "Why do you come here?"

Good question. But not one for which Drake had a good answer. He shrugged. "Maybe I like the atmosphere."

After shoving the replenished glass in front of him, Mack wandered off to the other end of the bar, muttering insults under his breath as he went. Drake picked up the whiskey and held it to his nose. For a brief moment, he actually considered drinking it. But good judgment quickly got the better of him, and he put it back down again. It might not get him drunk, but it sure as hell could make him sick.

He was still dwelling on this when the door swung open and a small mouse of a man in a well-tailored blue pinstripe suit slunk in. The nervous look on his narrow face as he clutched a leather case tightly under his arm was more than enough to earn him attention from some of the rougher characters present. After crossing over to an empty table near the far wall he took a seat, his eyes darting constantly back and forth.

"Dumbass," muttered Drake.

Guys like that came in from time to time. He was probably on some job that had taken him outside of Troi; and from the look of things, this was his first time so far away from the city. Now he was seeking to make the most of it. Out here in the provinces, secure in the knowledge that their wives couldn't possibly know what they were up to, many of them came to places such as this looking to live out some depraved fantasy they would never dream of being involved with back home. Mostly they were on the lookout for cheap women or drugs. Whatever it was, all they usually found was a whole lot of trouble.

A sultry beauty with auburn hair and olive skin sidled up beside Drake. Skin-tight black leather pants and a tank top accentuated her curves nicely. Flashing a seductive smile, she reached over and picked up Drake's glass.

"It's not like you were going to drink it, hawker," she told him in a playful tone. After downing the whiskey in a single gulp, she motioned for Mack to bring her another.

He gave her a sideways look. "I'm busy, Allie. What do you want?"

She leaned her head on his shoulder. "You, my dear. For the longest time."

"Stop messing around. I don't have time for your games today."

"I know, sweetie. That's why I'm here." She took the glass from Mack and waited until Drake slid some money across the bar before drinking it. "Your latest client is a real piece of crap. You know that?"

Drake sat up straight on his bar stool. "What do you mean?"

"He killed the poor guy you caught for him. Shot him twice in the head, right in front of the sheriff's deputy. Didn't

3

say a damn word. Just shot him and walked off, as cool as you like."

Drake shrugged. "So what?"

"Because you're next. That's *so what*."

Drake spun his stool around and ran his eyes over the bar's patrons. Regulars, mostly. A local *vash* dealer called Lenny had approached the newcomer and was whispering into his ear. The man quickly shook his head and gave a timid smile. He wasn't here for drugs, apparently.

He returned his attention to Allie. "I'm next? Why would you say that?"

"Because I hear things, sweetie. You charge too much. And the word is that your client has no intention of paying up."

"He'll pay," Drake assured her. He reached down and touched the handle of his P37 resting in the holster on his belt. "One way or another, he'll pay."

"Don't be a moron," she told him. "From what I hear, this guy is hooked up with some powerful people. Troians. And not the workers, either – the top dwellers. The *real* Troians."

"So?"

Allie shook her head in wonder at his casual response. "You really must have a death wish. Anyway, just so you know, I hear that he's hired someone to take you out. Someone very special. So just watch your back, okay?"

Drake waved for Mack to bring her another drink. "I'll do that. Thanks, Allie."

A slender girl in a low-cut red dress and high heels was now sitting in the newcomer's lap. But once again he began shaking his head, all the time still clutching nervously at his case. *So, he's not here for women either.* And if the girl was the wrong gender, the guy was most definitely in the wrong bar.

Even so, he wasn't showing any inclination to leave.

Allie gave him a light kiss on his cheek and sauntered off. Drake moved his gaze over to the door. If Allie was right – and she usually was – then he had come here for nothing. His client had known full well with whom he was dealing. Drake had a reputation for ruthless efficiency; that's why he had been hired in the first place. Now Allie was telling him someone special had been hired to take him out. That could only mean one thing: a mage.

He didn't like mages. Wielding magic made them unbearably arrogant. He had worked with them in the past, but found them to be far too dependent on spells and glamour. Take all that away, and they were usually no better than the scrawny little …

Drake glanced over to the table where the newcomer had been sitting. It was now empty. Instinctively, his hand shot to his gun. He slowly stood and moved toward the door, eyes scanning every part of the room. Where the hell *was* he?

A soft glow near a wooden support off to his left answered the question, and he dove hard to the floor just in time. A streak of blue fire shot from the assassin's hands, striking the side of the bar and exploding with an ear-splitting crack. Tiny flames rained down on Drake's back, burning holes in his jacket and searing his skin. Keeping low, he headed rapidly for the front door.

Elsewhere, customers were screaming and slamming into one another as they scrambled away from the assassin, most of them crowding toward the rear exit. The mousy little man was now grinning viciously, clearly reveling in the fear and panic he was causing.

Still on the move, Drake unholstered his gun. But with his torso facing away and at an awkward angle, he knew hitting his target would be nothing short of a miracle. He squeezed the trigger anyway. A ball of white light burst from the barrel to a mark just to his would-be killer's left. It was close enough. The light exploded with a chest-thumping thud, and the sheer force of the blast lifted the assassin three feet into the air and threw him almost completely across the room. With glass and broken furniture still slamming into the walls and ceiling, Drake rose to one knee to see flickers of light dancing around the assassin's body. A protection cloak, he thought. Clever…

He channeled his power into the P37, the heat in his chest growing more acute as he did so. But Drake had long since learned to ignore this. The more powerful the shot, the more pain was required to fire it. Right now the mage was dazed, but far from out of the fight. As if to confirm this, a thin stream of mana spewed forth from his opponent's fingertips, striking Drake in the left leg. Gritting his teeth against this new source of pain, he pressed his shoulder to the door and tumbled outside.

A few more seconds; that was all he needed. His shot was almost ready now. It was probably strong enough to penetrate the cloak, but it would be better not to take any chances. The parking lot was rapidly filling up with those bar patrons who had made it through the back door. Engines coughed into life, sputtering and popping like fireworks from cheap mana fuel and poor maintenance as the vehicles labored their way toward the street. Some were so slow, those inside would have been better off on foot.

Drake pushed himself up and limped toward a row of trashcans near the corner of the lot. Smoke was already rising from the building. Magical flame didn't usually spread very much, but old timbers caught easily.

A figure stepped out of the door, and the man's posture told him that the assassin had recovered faster than he had hoped. Drake flicked a switch just above the trigger and fired. A thin line of blue light streaked out and formed a circular pattern before striking the mage squarely in the right shoulder. The force sent him staggering a few steps back inside the bar. But he emerged a second later, arms outstretched and face twisted with rage.

Drake smiled. This one was powerful...but inexperienced; otherwise, he would have recognized what had hit him. And he sure as hell would have chosen a different spell with which to counter. As it was, just as Drake reached the cans, the assassin let loose a blast of highly focused mana, its blue light dazzling and radiating pure magic. It was a spell designed to utterly annihilate a foe. Not that it ever reached its intended target. The beam came to a sudden stop halfway between the pair before it split in much the same manner that Drake's earlier shot had and then headed directly back to the source. This time, though, the pattern was much more widespread, with the intention of surrounding and trapping its target rather than actually striking it. As feral screams flew from the encased assassin's mouth, Drake gave a tight smile. The mirror spells the P37 could fire were always useful against mages. Particularly inexperienced ones who allowed anger to get the better of them.

With the mage waving his arms wildly about, vainly trying to regain some of his power, Drake took careful aim and squeezed the trigger. The hiss of the P37 was accompanied by a recoil so powerful it felt as if it might rip his arm clean off, and the pain in his chest was nearly unbearable. The impact of the fist-sized projectile completely collapsed the building, piling fresh kindling onto the now raging fire. When the dust had settled, the body of the mage was little more than a smoking pile of ash and bone.

Drake dropped to his knees, clutching his chest. After

holstering his weapon, he allowed himself to slump the rest of the way to the ground, then rolled onto his back. *Mack will be furious*, he thought. *Assuming he's still alive.* As for Allie, he had already caught a glimpse of her in the car lot and knew she had made it out safely. She was a survivor. And in spite of her suggestive dress and flirtatious manner, she was not one of the prostitutes who practically lived in the bar.

By now, all of the cars were gone, and the roaring of the flames was the only sound to be heard. With the pain in Drake's chest receding, he felt anger rise up. The client should have just paid him. Now he would have to do something he hated – kill for free. If the man had been able to seek out and hire a mage to come after him, he was probably every bit as connected as Allie had suggested. Drake would need to move fast, before word of this spread and the client learned that his assassin's attempt had failed.

The crackle of tires on gravel had him reaching for his weapon again. He looked up, then collapsed back down, grumbling curses. The creak of a car door and the crunch of boots made him almost willing to risk facing a hangman's noose and put a hole straight through the man approaching. Almost...but not quite.

"What the hell, hawker?" The sheriff's gravelly voice raked at his ears.

"Leave me alone, Barnaby," he growled. "This isn't the time."

Needless to say, his request was ignored. "Have you lost your mind?" the lawman demanded. "You just burned down Mack's bar. You think you're special or something? I'm taking you in."

"You know damn well I didn't burn it down. Blasted it down, maybe. But it was already on fire anyway, so who cares?" He rolled up onto his elbow. "I heard about what happened to my runner. And if you think I'm just gonna let you take me away so the same thing can happen to me..." He began to chuckle mirthlessly.

The sheriff huffed. "I don't know what the hell you're talking about."

"Sure you don't." Drake pushed himself fully to his feet.

Barnaby was a bloated worm of a man, with narrow eyes and a balding head. The uniform he wore was old, tattered, and roughly patched after having been let out a dozen or more times. He was holding a revolver in his hand, though up until now he'd had the good sense not to point it.

Drake nodded at the weapon. "What do you think you're going to do with that? Piss me off?"

The caliber wasn't nearly powerful enough to do anything more than hurt like hell. Not that he wanted to put up with that either. Barnaby was one of the few people in the area who knew about his 'protection.' He'd had a report sent from Troi informing the sheriff of this the very first week Drake had showed up in the area. Things between the two men had changed from that moment on. These days Barnaby did all he could to avoid so much as a passing conversation. Which meant his being here now was almost certainly coerced.

Nonetheless, he continued to bluster. "Look here, Drake. You can either come with me until we can sort this out, or you can start running. And I can promise that the bounty they'll put on you will be big enough to call out every damn hawker in Vale."

Drake could see that the man was scared. He craned his neck and looked up at the overcast sky. "You know something, Barnaby? I was really hoping this would be a nice day. But look – it's cloudy as all hell."

"Are you going to come without a fuss or not?" The tremor in his tone was obvious.

Drake blew out a hard breath and met the sheriff's eyes directly. "You're not getting my weapon. Is that clear? And I'll take my own car."

He shifted on his feet. "You know that's not how this works."

"I'll tell you what I do know, Barnaby. I know you're about as honest as a starving vash addict. And *you* know damn well who sent that mage after me."

Barnaby opened his mouth to speak, but Drake's hand shot up to silence him. "I don't mind that you're a sorry waste of a man. Hell, I don't even mind that you're corrupt. I mean, who isn't on the take in some way or another around here? But I do mind walking into your station unarmed like a sheep to the slaughter. I mind that a lot. So, here's your choices. I can get in my car and drive down to your office with my weapon tucked snug and secure at my side. Or I can simply blow your head off right now and take my chances that no one will care about a bloated pig of a man who finally got what was coming to him."

Large drops of sweat were beading up on Barnaby's brow, and his eyes darted to Drake's gun. "Fine. We'll do it your way. But I promise that you'll regret this, hawker."

After putting away his gun, he got back in his car. Drake watched him go and then crossed the lot to the far corner where his own vehicle was parked. At the brief touch of his hand on a small mana pad, the lock clicked and the door opened.

The scent of leather and oil that greeted him as he settled inside brought a smile to his lips. He placed his index finger briefly on a pad beside the steering wheel and leaned back in the seat. In response, the engine hummed almost inaudibly into life. It was a true one of a kind. He took a long breath while listening to its even rhythm for a few seconds.

Perfection. Even the black paint was custom, sparkling with flakes of mana-infused silver. The car's sleek lines and sloped rear end made it look like it could actually take flight. And with what was under the hood...*no one* would ever stand a chance of catching her.

"Are you ready, Cal?" he asked, looking at the console. A yellow light blinked rapidly as if in response; a check of the fuel gauge then drew a groan. He had needed this payday. Quality mana fuel was rare...and expensive.

He glanced over his shoulder to where the sheriff was still waiting. A sinking feeling dug at the pit of his stomach. This was not going to end well. That much he could count on.

CHAPTER TWO

D rake lowered the car window and shut off the vibraplayer. Right now, he preferred to listen to the hum of the engine and the roar of the wind. He had been tempted to put the top down but decided against it. Should things take a bad turn, it might be safer to have it up. Besides, it wasn't all that hot today – a benefit of the overcast sky.

A pity the scenery wasn't better, though. Mile after mile of crumbling buildings and shabby houses covered the landscape. Everything was gray and dull; made more obvious by the mana streams flowing overhead in a seemingly infinite array of colors. The few shops scattered about were packed with hungry people scrambling to get what little food was available – though it was never enough. Children either darted about the streets pushing along carts filled with scrap metal to sell to the recycling trucks or dug through heaps of stinking refuse hoping desperately to find something of value that could be traded for food or money.

Yes, Aurora was about as poor a province as there was in Vale. Not that the others were much better; but Aurora was particularly sickly and run-down. Here, even the newer buildings were covered with a depressing coat of muck and grime, conveying all too clearly the depth of hopelessness felt by locals. Yet despite all this hardship and poverty, for a hawker at least, it was the best place to find business.

Runners often hid in the very worst areas, believing that they could blend in more successfully amongst the filth. But more often than not, it was the exact opposite. The inhabitants were invariably suspicious of strangers and kept almost exclusively to themselves. The last thing they wanted was someone with a bounty on their head bringing trouble to their door. They might not have had much, but what they did have, they were determined to keep. Half of the time, all Drake brought back was the runner's body after he had been killed by the locals for stealing food or clothes.

Lately, though, he'd been thinking it was about time to move on. He was becoming far too recognizable in Aurora, making it increasingly tricky to get in and out of places without attracting attention. Which in turn was making his job a damn sight harder than it needed to be.

A sigh slipped out. A former royal guard turned hawker was bound to attract extra attention anyway, wherever he went. And it wasn't like he could hide the fact. The local law enforcement was usually the first to find him out. Anyone new was automatically checked out with the archives in Troi, and the people there were not known for keeping such information confidential. Then there was his P37. If the archives didn't give him away, his weapon certainly would. Only members of the royal guard carried a P37. You couldn't buy one; each was custom made by its owner, and the secret of its construction was never divulged. He damn sure wasn't about to give his up just to blend in with the crowd, not when it had saved his hide so many times. No. Once he was finished with this latest mess, he would move on…again.

Barnaby kept them going at a fast click – showing off the fact that his car also had some muscle under the hood. Several times he blew by slower vehicles, sounding his siren as he passed and scaring the hell out of them. The third time he did this, he very nearly ran an old man completely off the road. Drake decided it was time to show the pudgy bastard a thing or two about speed.

"You ready, Cal?" he asked, a wry grin creeping up from the corners of his mouth. "Let's do it." He slammed his foot down on the accelerator and was instantly pressed hard back against the seat.

Barnaby must have seen him coming because he sped up and swerved left, attempting to cut him off. But Cal was way too fast. Drake pushed her to over one hundred and fifty before easing up. By then, Barnaby was just a tiny dot in the mirror. Drake laughed at the thought of the sheriff cursing and screaming that his prisoner had decided to run after all. Just to rub it in even further, he made sure that he was completely out of sight by taking a few hard turns at a speed he knew was sure to send Barnaby's car skidding off the road.

The sheriff's office was near to Vale's reservoir, an area where virtually all of what little commerce and infrastructure the town possessed could be found. Here, the mana strings could be seen glistening like a spider's web in the morning dew across the sky. For most people, this signified a place where power was abundant and life was good. But for Drake, it was just a harsh reminder of the past.

As he approached the sheriff's office, he saw a long red van parked directly outside. On the side of the van, the lion sigil of the royal court immediately caught his eye.

"What the hell are *they* doing here?" Drake muttered.

He pulled next to the van and waited for Barnaby to catch

up. This was no disgraced noble forced to serve the king as a lowly bureaucrat in some dilapidated outpost; someone like that would be driving a vehicle that was old and dented. This van was brand new. Fresh from the factory.

Maybe they're not here about me, he thought. *Yeah, right. And maybe I'm a high mage.*

He went over in his mind what they could possibly want with a disgraced guard who'd been exiled to the outer provinces. Nothing he would like, that was for sure. The only other time Troi had been interested in him was when they had wanted him to kill a civilian activist who'd been causing trouble up north. But Drake was no assassin. Sure, he killed. Quite often, in fact. But only when he couldn't bring a runner back alive.

Some hawkers didn't care. They would simply kill the poor bastard and move on rather than take the extra time and effort needed to capture someone alive. Dead bodies don't try to escape. Half the money, but also half the time and aggravation. That was not Drake's way. He had never been a cold-blooded murderer – regardless of what the royal court claimed.

Barnaby eventually screeched into the lot and parked directly behind Cal, clearly a tactic to block him in. Drake chuckled at the man's clumsy attempt to assert his authority. If he wanted to leave, this sure as hell wouldn't stop him. Cal could tear through the sheriff's car like it was made from wet paper. The mana-infused silver in the paintwork was more than just decoration. Drake got out and started toward the office entrance, the chirp of Cal's auto-lock sounding from behind after a few steps.

Barnaby hurried over to join him, puffing and wheezing as he took hold of Drake by the arm. Drake shot him a warning glance.

"We don't want this to get rough, do we?" Barnaby asked. From the nervous expression on his face it was clear that this was not intended as a threat. "At least do me a favor and close your coat."

Drake chuckled and nodded his compliance. "You got it, boss." He buttoned his coat to cover his weapon, though the bulge this created would still make it obvious to almost anyone that he was armed. "Lead on."

Barnaby opened the door and stepped inside, pulling Drake along with him, though taking care to use the very minimum of pressure.

The cool air felt nice, and though the outside of the building was in desperate need of a good scrubbing, the interior was clean and orderly. Chairs were lined up against the wall, and soft music was coming from a speaker overhead. The desk clerk, a thin, pale-faced man with round spectacles, was sitting behind a glass window at the rear of the lobby. To his right was a door leading to the rest of the station. He looked up at Drake, frowning.

"Still waiting for that promotion, Milton?" Drake asked with a smile.

The clerk ignored his jibe and switched his attention to the sheriff. "He's waiting in the interrogation room," he said. "And he's getting impatient."

"You plan to tell me what someone from the royal court is doing here?" Drake asked Barnaby.

"You think they tell me anything?" he replied, opening the door leading to the back.

Lights from overhead buzzed and crackled noisily as they passed along the hallway. The wall on one side was lined with holopics of past kings and the present ruler – though at some point these had been taken down and never put back in the correct order of reign. Whoever the court had sent was sure to have noticed this and would likely be giving Barnaby a severe reprimand. The black and white tile floor was clean, but had numerous cracks and blemishes and was badly in need of repair. In spite of this, overall it wasn't such a bad place to spend your working hours when compared to what was usually found in Aurora.

They continued down the hall and through a small conference room where three doors lined the wall to their left. The middle door was slightly ajar, and a waft of smoke drifted out, accompanied by the scent of tobacco. Tobacco was expensive, so this meant that whoever was inside was either very rich or very powerful. Most likely both. Drake hadn't had a good cigar in years, and the aroma was making old, almost-forgotten cravings return.

Barnaby opened the door fully and gestured for Drake to wait. From his present position, he could see only a pair of boots propped up on a metal table. Military boots. *This just keeps getting better and better*, he thought ironically.

"You can go," said a familiar voice. "I'll speak to him alone."

Without a word, Barnaby turned and started back toward the hallway door. Drake could see the fear in his eyes. And there was a good reason for it being there. He could feel his rage building as he continued staring at the boots.

"Do come in, Drake. Hasn't anyone taught you that it is rude to keep old friends waiting?"

The way he rolled the letter R and exaggerated each syllable only served to make Drake even angrier. Pretending to be a top dweller; that's all it was. Yet the man inside the interrogation room was as far removed as possible from one of the elites. More like the very lowest of bottom feeders, in Drake's eyes.

He unbuttoned his jacket and pushed the door fully

open. There, dressed in his finest white uniform complete with medals and ribbons, was Xavier Mortimer, captain of the royal guard. His black curls were oiled and pushed back in the fashion of the nobility, though contradicting this he had the angular features and deep-set brown eyes of the working class, which was why he tended to keep his collar turned up high. A cigar hung between a set of perfect teeth as he gave Drake a welcoming smile.

"It is so good to see you again, my old friend," Xavier said, removing his feet from the table. "How long has it been? Eight years?"

"Nine." Drake took a chair on the opposite side. "Why are you here?"

Xavier sighed. "I see that life amongst the rabble has robbed you of your courtesy."

"And I see that you are still trying to forget that your father was a cook."

Though Xavier's expression didn't change, Drake noticed a tiny twitch in the corner of his eye that made him suppress a satisfied grin.

"Ah, yes. Dear old Dad. He still asks about you when I visit. It broke his heart when you were convicted. He still thinks you were falsely accused, poor fellow. He just can't imagine the great Drake Sharazi could ever have become a… murderer."

"I'm losing patience, Xavier. Get to the point."

Xavier clicked his tongue. "Mind your temper. We don't want this to become unpleasant, do we?"

Drake sneered. "Oh, I don't know. Let's find out."

It was an invitation Drake knew for certain would be accepted. Both men reached to their side simultaneously. In a blur of motion, two P37's were drawn, each trained and ready to fire.

Xavier's smile never faltered. "You've lost your touch, old friend. I think this harsh environment is definitely starting to take its toll."

"I'm still fast enough to blow your damn head off."

Even as he spoke, Drake knew this to be a false claim. They had drawn their weapons virtually in chorus. Had they pulled their triggers, both of them would now be dead. But it had not always been like that. Had he really gotten slower? Or had Xavier gotten faster? Probably a little bit of both, he suspected.

Xavier holstered his weapon, then waited for Drake to do the same before continuing. "I have a message for you, one that I think you will want to hear. So perhaps you should stop acting like a child for a moment."

"I'm not doing any of your damn dirty work," Drake snapped back. "So unless you've come with a royal apology, you have nothing to say that I want to hear."

"A royal apology?" Xavier chuckled softly. "Now that *would* be a cause for celebration, I imagine. But alas, no. Still, you might be pleased to know that King Nedar still thinks of you fondly. So fondly, in fact, that he has sent me to deliver a personal message."

The hair on the back of Drake's neck prickled and his heartbeat increased significantly. *A message from the king.* Though he had long since learned to accept what had happened to him, in reflective moments he still dreamed about returning home. Not that it did any good. As the years passed, any hope of actually achieving this had all but disappeared. Home had become nothing more than a memory. And yet now, was it possible that this message was about to rekindle his long-abandoned dream?

"If you need a moment," said Xavier, obviously amused by the effect his words were having. "I can only imagine what life must have been like for you, living in filth for all these years. And then here I come, bringing a glimmer of hope into your tragic tale."

Xavier's smug expression quickly had Drake regaining his composure. "I'm fine," he responded. "I was just amazed that the captain of the royal guard would be reduced to the status of messenger boy. When *I* held the position, the king would never have thought to send me on such a mundane task."

"His Royal Majesty wanted to be sure you understood the importance of the matter," Xavier explained, though a bit too eagerly.

"Then why don't you get on with it?"

"He wants me to convey his deepest regret over how events transpired. And that he truly wishes circumstances had been different." He rolled the cigar between his fingers absently, watching the smoke rise from the tip.

"Is that all?"

"Of course not. He also commands you to come to Troi and report to the magistrate."

When Xavier did not continue, Drake leaned in, forcing him to make eye contact. "Nothing else?"

"What did you expect? A full pardon and a welcome home parade? Or perhaps reinstatement as captain of the royal guard? Feel fortunate that the king thinks of you at all. Your sovereign has a duty for you to perform. That should be enough."

The faint hope that had been rising inside Drake began to collapse, leaving behind only fury and resentment. Straightening his back, he forced himself to keep his expression impassive. "Please thank His Royal Majesty for his considerate message and kind words. Tell him I'm afraid I am otherwise occupied at the moment."

Xavier rubbed his cheek and groaned. "I thought you might be difficult. I even told the king as much. But he assured me that you would come."

Drake rose from his chair. "Then he was mistaken. And for once, you were right." He began to leave.

"They've taken Prince Salazar," Xavier said quickly. "I wasn't supposed to tell you that until you reached Troi. And you can't say a word to anyone. But that's why you've been summoned."

Drake halted, his hand resting on the doorknob. "*Who* has taken him?"

"We don't know. But we think they're from the outer provinces. That's why we need you."

Now things were different. Drake could hear the sincerity bleeding into Xavier's haughty tone. He drew several deep breaths before finally speaking. "Very well. Tell the king I'll be there."

He opened the door and strode out.

"Don't you want to ask?" Xavier called after him. "I know you do. Are you not even the least bit curious about her?"

Drake continued walking, pretending not to hear him. Barnaby was waiting just outside in the hallway, sniffing a cigar obviously given to him by Xavier – no doubt the bribe for bringing him in. He snatched the cigar from the man's hand as he passed by and shoved it into his pocket.

"Hey, that's mine," Barnaby shouted.

Drake called over his shoulder, "Not anymore it isn't. Now move your ass and get that heap of a car out of my way before I ram it."

Kicking open the lobby door, he quit the station. Barnaby followed close behind, hurrying as fast as his ample girth would allow. When the way was clear, Drake fired his engine and pulled back, stopping for a moment when he was parallel to the sheriff.

"Tell the guy who sent the mage after me that I'll be seeing him real soon."

Barnaby shot him a hate-filled look but said nothing.

As Drake pulled out onto the road, he tried to calm himself. The thought of returning home was exciting, but also terrifying. He was an exile. Everyone in Troi knew his name, and unless the king proclaimed him innocent, he was still a criminal in their eyes: a murderer. He would always be thought of as one. And something told him that a royal pardon wasn't forthcoming. They needed him; that was the beginning and the end of it. Once he had served his purpose, he would be cast out again. Even so, it was impossible to extinguish the tiny flame of hope that had been rekindled.

Slamming the accelerator to the floor, he focused his thoughts on Salazar. How could anyone have kidnapped the prince? For sure, whoever had been able to accomplish such a feat was not a foe to be taken lightly. Only the king himself had more protection. To overcome the numerous security measures preventing such an abduction would have taken large measures of skill and daring, not to mention considerable resources. On the plus side, those same resources would be very difficult for the kidnappers to conceal. In a land starved for the basic necessities, to a trained eye they would stand out like a beacon in the dark.

It was easy to understand why the king would send for him. Who better for the task than a hawker possessing the power of the royal guard? And one with a personal interest in the prince's safe return. He pushed Cal past one hundred and sixty, turning the landscape into a wretched blur. Frames of a picture he hated to see. But it had been his life for nine long years.

Are you not even the least bit curious about her? Xavier's words plagued him. Of course he was. How could he not be? But it didn't matter. By now he was nothing but a long-forgotten memory to her. He had to accept that. There were some hopes he could never allow to surface.

Some feelings would tear him apart, no matter how much time had passed.

CHAPTER THREE

D rake touched the light switch to the cramped apartment and muttered a curse. No power again. Nothing unusual. When this far removed from anything resembling civilization, one had to expect a bit of inconvenience. He shuffled his way through the living room to the kitchen and rummaged around the junk drawer for some candles.

After lighting one of these and placing it inside the ashtray on the table, he retrieved a bottle of water from the cabinet. It was a long drive to Troi – three days if the weather held. He needed to pack for the road. Not that he had a great deal to take with him; most everything in the apartment belonged to the landlord. When you lived the life of a hawker, it didn't pay to burden yourself down with too many possessions. He thought back to his apartment in Troi. At night, he would regularly walk out onto his balcony and stare at the mana streams crisscrossing the city. It was never dark up top, but at night the light was so different... almost spiritual, like rivers of pure magic bringing life to the entire world. And all of it spawned from the great power station of Troi.

In those days, he hadn't been able to understand the protests. How could anyone be unhappy? Sure, life could be tough outside the city. But without Troi, the world would return to being a desolate wasteland. The ravages left over from the War of the Ancients would spread like a disease. If that happened, even the outer provinces as they were now would seem like paradise. To Drake, Troi had been a beacon of hope, a light to foretell what one day the future would bring. Sure, some people suffered. But it wouldn't always be like that. How they couldn't see it as he did had baffled him.

"Well, I sure as hell get it now," he muttered, staring at the flickering candle.

There was a knock at the door. Drake groaned. *Not now!* The door opened and a thin waif of a girl danced in, twirling and humming as she crossed into the kitchen. Her blonde curls and freckled face made her look barely ten years old, when in reality she was actually fifteen. She plopped down in the chair opposite him and rested her chin in her palms. Sadie lived upstairs with her father and stepmother. Like most of the other tenants in the block, her father was a hawker, and her stepmother would often go with him to help out, leaving Sadie to fend for herself.

"Why are you always sitting in the dark?" she asked. "It's creepy, you know?"

"I'm hiding from you. Besides, everyone is in the dark right now. Or didn't you notice the lights are out?"

"Of course I noticed. But you still sit in the dark a lot. My dad says it's because you're depressed."

"Your dad should know."

"Why do you say that?"

"He has to put up with *you*, doesn't he?"

Sadie frowned. "Don't be mean."

Drake shoved the water across the table, which she

accepted with a smile. "Shouldn't you be somewhere else, playing with your friends?" he asked.

"What friends? The only other kids around here are Hurley's boys, and they're too young."

Drake had always felt a bit bad for Sadie. She was a bright girl. Had she been born in Troi, she would be close to graduating by now. But here, the only education she received was from the few tattered books her father occasionally brought home. Poul wasn't a bad father, and he did his best to keep Sadie out of trouble. But the life of a hawker was unpredictable, and one thing Drake had learned was that children needed stability. The sad fact was that Sadie would likely end up working as a hawker herself, just like her old man.

"I need you to do me a favor," he told her. "I'm leaving for a while, and I want you to clean out my apartment."

Sadie crinkled her brow. "Leaving? Why?"

"You can sell whatever you find worth selling," he told her, ignoring the question.

"You're not coming back, are you?" She pushed the water across the table. "Don't bother lying. I know you're not. Everyone leaves eventually. Even Dad will leave one day."

"Your father loves you. Whatever happens, I know he won't leave you."

"Why can't you just stay here?" she persisted. "There's plenty of work. Only a few hours ago, someone showed up here wanting to hire you."

Drake sat up sharply. "Who was that?"

"Some guy. I don't know. Said he needed to find you. I told him you'd be back later."

"What did he look like?" His tone had become hard, clearly making Sadie nervous.

"I…he was in a black suit. Drove a green truck."

"What *exactly* did he say?"

"I told you. He pulled up when I was taking out the trash and asked if you were home. I told him you'd gone to meet a client."

"Nothing else?"

"No. He just looked up at your window and then drove off."

"Are you sure that's all?"

Sadie looked frightened. "I'm sure. Look, I'm sorry. I just thought…I mean, it had to be a client, right?"

Drake forced a smile. "I'm sure it was. Don't worry about it."

Only a very few people knew where he lived – and he would never share such personal information with a client. They might do something stupid like try to steal their money back. Whoever it had been, it sure as hell wasn't good news.

Drake stood and retrieved a small silver box from the counter. "Here. Take this."

Sadie's eyes lit up. "You mean it?" She reached out and cradled the box in her hands as if it were crafted from the most delicate of glass. Smiling, she lifted the lid. After a brief moment, a soft melody began playing. Sadie's smile developed into a wide beam of delight. She had coveted the music box since the first time she'd seen it.

Realization then dawned. She looked up at Drake and her smile faded. "You really are leaving for good."

"Probably." He wanted to be honest with her. The last thing she needed was the people she cared about filling her head with lies. "I might be back one day, though. You never know."

With the greatest of care, she placed the box on the table. The tune was still playing. If the man who had sold it to him years ago was to be believed, it was a love song from the ancient world...a time long before Vale. She crossed over and gave him a tight hug.

"I'll miss you."

Drake returned the embrace. "I'll miss you too."

With fresh tears forming, Sadie wiped at her eyes and then picked up the box again. "Just promise not to sit in the dark too much," she told him. "It's bad for you."

Drake smiled. "I promise."

Once she was gone, he began packing what few things he needed for the road. Everything else he would leave behind for her to sell. Better that Sadie profit from it than the landlord. Not that there was very much of any great value. His thoughts drifted to the man she had told him about. It was probably someone sent by his most recent client to finish off what the mage assassin had failed to do. All the more reason to leave quickly. He didn't have time to deal with any of this now.

It took him less than an hour to get ready. The wound on his leg and the burns on his back were already starting to heal. Only a red spot where the spell had actually struck him remained. But it was a different story with his clothes. They were ruined. He stared at the burn holes in his favorite coat and spat a curse. Finding another one of this quality that fit his broad frame would be hard, if not impossible.

He had originally planned to get a good night's sleep and head out at dawn, but now he didn't want to hang around in case the man in the green truck returned. He'd already had more than enough trouble for one day. Tossing his packed duffle bag over in the direction of the door, he pulled down a picture from the living room wall that had been left behind by a previous tenant. He then drew in a small portion of mana and touched the cracking plaster with the tip of his finger. The surface shimmered for a brief moment before allowing a long yet narrow recess to appear. Inside this was the only thing he valued as much as his P37.

Lifting the black scabbard from its hiding place, he ran his hand over the flawless surface, briefly allowing himself time to appreciate the perfection of the craftsmanship. He slid the sword's blade out a few inches. The mana infused into the steel glowed faintly, casting a blue aura. Royal guards were not the only people whose flesh was protected by magic. Where bullets failed, this weapon would not. And if he was to go after people dangerous enough to abduct the prince, he would more than likely be needing the power it provided.

Dousing the candle, he slung the duffle over his shoulder. Just as he reached for the door handle, the lights flickered back on. *That figures*, he thought dryly. After pausing for one final ironic glance at what had been his most recent home, he headed downstairs to the garage.

Only a few cars were down there. Most of the hawkers were out on jobs, and everyone else worked too far away to be home every night. He tossed his bag and sword into the trunk and walked over to press the door release button next to the garage entrance. With much clanking of gears, the door gradually lifted.

The sound of the shot came at the very same instant he felt a sharp stab of pain in his shoulder. The force of the impact threw him off balance and spun him almost completely around. Sliding down the wall, he dropped to one knee and reached for his weapon, his eyes scanning the garage for any sign of his attacker. Despite the pain, there was no penetration; the caliber being used was too small for that. Movement behind a red car on the other side of the 100-foot-long garage warned him just before another shot was fired. The bullet pinged off the wall above his head. This was no pro; that much was obvious.

Drake fired a series of shots, forcing his attacker to duck down out of sight, and grinned at the man's ignorance. This guy had no clue whatsoever who he was dealing with. The heat in his chest was pulsing as he let loose another round, this one aimed just above and beyond the red car. A green ball of light hovered for a second before splitting into three long strands of mana that fell directly on top of his would-be killer. His yelps of pain as the bindings wrapped themselves around him carried clearly to Drake. Leaping to his feet, he burst into a dead run. The grunts of his opponent struggling to free himself ceased just as he rounded the car.

Lying on the ground was a thin man wearing a pair of brown work pants and a blue plaid button-down shirt. Drake kicked a chrome revolver out of his reach and holstered his own weapon. Instantly, the bindings blinked out of existence.

"Who sent you?" he demanded.

The man simply glared back up at him. Drake was on the point of repeating the question when the assassin's eyes suddenly rolled back into his skull and dark foam began oozing from his mouth. A death charm, Drake realized. *Damn it!*

He had no skill with healing magic, though even if he did, from the speed with which the poison had taken effect, he doubted that it would have helped anyway. Even in the brief time it had taken for him to kneel down, the man had stopped breathing and his body had gone limp. Drake checked for a pulse, just to be certain. He was dead, sure enough.

Drake scanned the entire garage, just to be sure he was now alone. Satisfied that he was, he searched the assassin's pockets. Nothing. Not even a scrap of paper.

This made no sense. If the client was willing to spend money on a mage, why would he send someone with virtually no chance of succeeding?

The rush of wind from a car passing by on the road outside snapped him back into the moment. Time to go. He had no intention of dealing with Barnaby again, and a dead body would definitely bring the sheriff running. Until he could get a handle on whatever his double-crossing client was planning, he had better get moving.

He jumped inside Cal and pulled out of the garage, pausing just long enough to make sure he wasn't being watched by anyone on the street. One thing was certain: his client had a lot to answer for. One way or another, Drake swore to collect what he was owed... with interest.

Slamming Cal into gear, he peeled away from the lot. Three days to Troi. He pressed down on the accelerator. Better make that two.

CHAPTER FOUR

The gradually intensifying glow of the mana streams brought memories flooding back, memories he had not thought about in years. Here in the inner provinces like Jericho, people were far more civilized than those found in areas like Aurora. The closer one came to Troi, the better life was. Better…but a whole lot more expensive. So much so, the odds were that unless you were born here, you had little or no hope of aspiring to it. The buildings were far cleaner, power outages were rare, and food was a lot easier to come by. Some people here lived almost as well as those dwelling in lower Troi itself.

Most commonly used goods were manufactured in the inner provinces, a surprising number of them even finding their way into the homes of the high mages and the nobility within the upper city. It was also here in Jericho that Drake had trained during his first year as a royal guard – time spent mostly patrolling the streets and arresting protesters.

For all that, life in Jericho wasn't exactly easy. Most people worked twelve or more hours a day, often without so much as a short break. And if you couldn't keep up with the pace, you would quickly find yourself replaced by someone who could. Many people died far too young from sheer exhaustion. Even so, it was better than starving to death. Your job was literally your life. Losing it meant being forced to the outer provinces. And once you ended up there, you would never get back again.

Drake continued driving until he reached the northern checkpoint. Beyond this was the main highway into Troi. Vehicles were lined up for more than a mile, but he had no intention of waiting amongst them. Pulling into the emergency lane, he drove up to the gatehouse, where two men armed with heavy rifles waved for him to stop. Their grim expressions and aggressive postures were well rehearsed, designed entirely to intimidate anyone who might try to enter the city without authorization. Border sentries had a well-earned reputation for brutality; someone was shot at least once every week while trying to sneak in. The guards were also infamous for the casual beatings they delivered to anyone they considered not servile enough to their demands.

Drake rolled down his window and placed his hands on the dash.

"What the hell do you think you're doing?" demanded the lead sentry, a hulking figure with a square jaw and crooked nose. "This lane is for emergency and government vehicles only. And this damn sure doesn't look like either one of those to me."

"I'm here to see the magistrate," Drake explained.

"So? Get your ass back in line or you'll be seeing her without your teeth."

"I was summoned by the royal court. King Nedar himself sent the message. I don't think he'd want me to be delayed."

The sentry snorted. "Is that right?" He looked over his

shoulder to his companion. "Hey! This idiot says the king sent for him."

The other sentry huffed a laugh. "Well, then, I reckon we had better wave him right on through."

"That would be the best idea," said Drake.

The sentry reached in to grab Drake by the collar. "Watch your mouth, smartass."

Drake held up his hands. "Hey, take it easy. Call it in if you don't believe me. The name's Drake…Drake Sharazi."

The mere sound of his name had an electrifying effect. The sentry's eyes popped wide and he immediately took several paces back, at the same time training his rifle directly at Drake's head. It seemed like Xavier had thought to have a bit of fun and not leave word of his arrival.

"Don't move, exile!" the sentry shouted.

"It's good to see I'm remembered," remarked Drake. "But there's really no need for this. If you check it out, you'll see that I'm telling the truth."

The man waved his partner over. "If he moves, shoot him," he instructed, and took off at a dead run toward the gatehouse. By now, the commotion had attracted the attention of nearly all the nearby motorists, not to mention several other border sentries.

A minute later the first sentry returned, his face contorted into a furious scowl. "He's cleared to pass," he growled, almost choking on the words.

Drake could not resist giving the man an elaborate wink as he pulled away. *I guess I'm still famous*, he thought, grinning. *Even if it is for something I didn't do.*

The city of Troi towered before him. Thousands of spires climbed well above the clouds, each one a work of sheer genius and beauty. It was breathtaking, even though most of the more intricate features were blurred by the glow of mana.

Countless streams of magical energy flowed everywhere, carrying transport cars along their lines and conveying the rich and powerful to almost anywhere in the upper city they wanted to go. He could see the dots of moving light from the windows, provoking the memory of the first time he had ridden in one. It had been with Prince Salazar, when they'd both been only ten years old.

He had stared out through the window in utter amazement for the entire ride, completely ignoring the plush interior and beautiful décor. The other passengers knew he was a lower city dweller. His being with the prince kept their tongues behind their teeth, but he was perfectly aware of what they were thinking. He could see it in their eyes when they were disembarking as well. Not that this troubled him in the least. That was also the first day he had met the king. In fact, it had been the first day for a lot of things.

He tore his eyes from the city and concentrated on the road.

Security was intense around Troi. He would need to pass through six more checkpoints before actually entering; six more times of dealing with morons like the sentry at the border. He reminded himself he would need to find a suitable way to repay Xavier for his consideration.

The later it became, the more the sight of the approaching city teased out unwanted memories, as if the lights were digging deep into his soul and finding all of his pain simply for the sake of cruel amusement. He was now close enough to clearly make out the details. The outer buildings swirled up, intertwining with their neighbors in impossibly intricate patterns until the very tips of their spires exploded with mana streams of every color imaginable. Often it was difficult to distinguish one building from another as they wove together like vines guided by a celestial gardener. Those of the inner city shot up like great crystal formations of green and blue, escaping the darkness of the underground in order to favor the world with a glimpse of their magnificence. Light from their mana streams spilled from the upper levels and faded just beyond the tops of the outer buildings. It was like looking at a waterfall of magical energy feeding life into the whole of Vale. And climbing even higher than any of these was the royal palace itself, a gleaming white tower formed into a perfect cylinder that dominated everything else around it. To Drake, the simplicity of its design had always been the secret of its special allure: a solid core to hold together a fragile beauty. The highest point of this, completely obscured by cloud cover, was where the city's power station was located. Not that he had ever been up there to see it for himself; only the high mages and the king himself were ever permitted to enter.

It was well past midnight by the time he made it through the final checkpoint and into the lower city. The massive tunnel sloped sharply downwards and the road was packed with traffic as he dropped to the first level. He was now directly below the upper city's lush gardens, where the schools and most of the administrative facilities were located. But though there was plenty of brightness and daylight overhead, down here the sun never shone. The entire level was covered completely from end to end, as if to protect the top dwellers from possibly spoiling their day by looking down upon those who served them. Even so, there was no shortage of artificial light. There was never an outage, and despite the fact that those who lived here would never be allowed to move into the upper city, life was still pretty good; certainly when compared to the provinces.

People usually worked normal shifts and were paid enough to provide for their families, though never enough to advance their status. Most of the six levels were dedicated either to housing or some kind of important manufacturing. Almost all mana-powered devices were made down here.

Although the vast majority of top dwellers despised the lower levels, Drake had always taken the opposite view. Down here he'd found it much easier to imagine what the rest of the world would one day become. Top dwellers invariably lived in a stiff and proper way, but here people were free with their humor and wit, which meant there was always fun to be had. When he was still a rookie guard, he used to love going to the dance clubs with his co-workers. But one lesson he'd learned quickly was to make sure to change into his street clothes first. The royal guard was feared. Even hated by some. Most people would simply avoid them altogether, though inevitably someone would get drunk enough to voice their opinion and end up getting themselves arrested. That was the one thing you never did if you wanted to remain living in Troi − you always kept your opinion to yourself. Dissent was not tolerated. And it wasn't as if he could simply ignore the matter if someone mouthed off, not if he wanted to get promoted. There was always someone watching.

The directions given to him at the last checkpoint were unnecessary; he knew Troi like the back of his hand. He had spent two years of his life patrolling these streets before moving up top. And he'd been good at it, too. He seemed to have a gift for sensing trouble before it actually kicked off. His partner had said it was due to his talent for magic, that this had given him an intuition most people didn't possess. Though Drake had never been sure about the truth of this statement, he was grateful for the ability nonetheless. A perceived talent for magic meant that he would soon be considered for promotion to the upper city. There was only a handful of ways you could get there if you were not born to it, and that was most surely one of them.

He wound his way to the east side until he reached the office of the magistrate. By then, the ghosts of his past were close to overwhelming. One in particular was especially haunting him.

Don't think about her, he scolded himself. But he couldn't help it. The picture of her face in his mind, soaked in tears and looking at him with immeasurable sorrow, would not be denied.

He pulled into the parking garage and showed the attendant his identification. It was expired, but still good enough to get him through without a problem. At least Xavier had known when enough was enough.

After parking Cal, he entered the office through the garage-level entrance. The lift was available, but he always preferred using the stairs. A hawker never took the easy way if he could help it; such habits made you soft. At least, that was what he was telling himself. The real truth was, he didn't want to get too accustomed to the conveniences of Troi. This whole affair might well end up being one huge disappointment. Given even a small amount of encouragement, the tiny shred of hope that he couldn't quite shake off was likely to grow completely out of control. He'd already suffered enough the first time he'd been forced to leave. There was no way he wanted to feel any part of that pain again.

Upon reaching the lobby, he stopped for a moment to simply stare at the room. The floor was made from brilliant blue tiles, with the seal of the magistrate displayed proudly in the very center. As for the chairs provided for those waiting for their appointments, they were unrecognizable from the rickety and hard-to-sit-on offerings you found in the provinces. These were as plush and comfortable as anything you would see in a good class home. Holopics of the line of kings covered the walls – and in their proper order. His eyes lingered for a moment on the aspect of King Nedar, and then he continued to gauge his surroundings. The glass doors leading out into the street were etched with the Lion of Troi and noticeably clean of any dirt or fingerprints. An attractive young woman with honey-blonde hair and soft features was sitting behind the reception desk. Her bright yellow dress was neatly pressed and made from new material. Drake hadn't seen a woman looking like this in….

He shook away the thought.

"Is the lift out of order?" she asked, as she noticed him standing by the stairwell.

Drake shook his head. "I needed the exercise."

Her disapproving expression made him feel oddly uncomfortable. It was obvious from his worn jeans and threadbare t-shirt that he was not a city dweller.

"Can I help you?"

Drake pulled the slip of paper given to him at the final checkpoint from his pocket and placed it on the desk. The woman picked it up with the very tips of her fingers, as if implying that she might otherwise catch something from it.

"I see." She nodded in the direction of the chairs. "If you care to take a seat."

Without a word, Drake did as he was instructed. Part of him wanted to shout out that there was once a time she would have fallen all over herself to make him comfortable when he walked into the room. She might have even flirted a little, if she was bold enough. With a small sigh, he suppressed the impulse. Right now, he was exactly what she took him for: a vagabond from the outer provinces. *Even so, she could at least show some manners.*

After more than an hour had passed, a tall man in a deep crimson jacket with the lion of Troi stitched in gold on the lapel entered the lobby and approached Drake. He was holding a set of keys and a piece of paper.

"You are Drake Sharazi?" he asked.

This was definitely a top dweller; Drake could tell by the accent. "Yes. I'm Drake Sharazi."

"The magistrate told me to give you these." He handed over both items. "You are to wait at this address until you are contacted by Captain Mortimer. Do you understand?"

Drake looked at the paper. The only thing written on it was an address. "Did he say when I would be contacted?" he asked.

"A car will be waiting for you in the garage."

"I have my own car."

"I am aware of this. Arrangements have been made for its retrieval. You may take whatever you need from the vehicle, but you are to leave it with us."

Drake gritted his teeth. He should have expected this. Xavier wasn't about to let him run around without knowing where he was. Especially if he was being sent after the prince.

"I'll need to disengage the security," he said, trying to mask his irritation.

"Please do so. Now, if you will excuse me…"

Drake watched as the man spun on his heels and strode from the lobby. *Damn it!* He should have parked somewhere else. Oh, well. Nothing to do about it now.

He returned to the garage and saw that a truck was already backing up to his vehicle. Another car was waiting nearby. After grabbing his duffle bag and sword from the trunk, he turned off the security. Had they tried to take Cal with it on… He grinned at the thought.

Once alongside the waiting car, he presented his piece of paper to the driver. In return, the man handed him a sealed envelope bearing the stamp of the royal guard. Inside was a new identification card, though still bearing his old holopic.

After settling into the back seat, he stared at the ID. The image on his old one had been barely visible – faded away, just like everything else in his life. This one, however…

"Look at you," he muttered. "Smiling like an idiot."

The picture had been taken on the very day he became Captain of the royal guard. Prince Salazar had insisted he take a new one. To capture the joy of the moment forever, he had said. That was fine then. All it did now was mock him. He shoved the card into his wallet and looked out the window.

The broad walkways were already filling up with people. The deep gray metal of the buildings was a stark contrast to the splendor of what was to be seen just one level higher. Nonetheless, to Drake, these buildings held a measure of their own beauty. Each one reflected the street lighting in its own unique way, capturing colors and images that would otherwise have gone unnoticed. The distorted images of passers-by, like otherworldly spirits haunting the city, made him smile for a moment. This faded as his eyes rose higher. Only six stories were allowed on this level, the top one serving as a support for the upper city. In fact, all six levels had been designed primarily to keep the upper city standing. It was a perfect metaphor for the reality of life.

Brightly lit signs told him that they were now entering the market district. Each level had a market of its own, but here at this one you could buy some of the best food and drink in Troi. He briefly considered asking the driver to stop when he spotted a manga juice shop. The thought of a frosty mug of manga juice pouring down his throat was almost too much. A silly thing to long for, really. But he couldn't help it.

They still had to go down two more levels before reaching their destination. Before long, the spiraling road leading down in this direction became ever more jammed with vehicles, prompting the driver to pull over into the emergency lane. Drake couldn't help but notice the looks of envy and contempt from some of the occupants of other vehicles as they passed easily by. Being late for work even one time could be enough to get you fired. To reduce this risk, people usually did their best to live on the same level where they worked. Of course, there was always the possibility of a compulsory transfer, which could end up badly, especially if you couldn't find someone in the reverse predicament. This made apartment swapping quite a common occurrence. Even now, Drake could spot cars loaded down with bags and furniture.

He tore his eyes away and leaned back in the seat. "Mind if I smoke?"

The driver shrugged.

Drake took the cigar he had snatched from Barnaby, lit it up, and waited a minute to savor the aroma before rolling down the window.

"Are you really Drake Sharazi?" the up-until-now silent driver suddenly asked.

Drake closed his eyes, thoroughly enjoying the taste of the tobacco. "Yes."

"You know, not everyone thought you were guilty."

Drake cracked open one eye and furrowed his brow. "Is that right?"

"Folks in the lower city, anyway. They think you were framed."

"Why's that?"

"It just didn't add up. I mean, why would you do such a crazy thing?"

"I think everyone knows why."

"Yeah. But that's just it. That sort of thing goes on all the time. No one talks about it, but we all know it happens."

"You do realize they had a holovid of the incident, right?"

"Yeah. I remember. But those things can be faked easily enough."

Drake was finding it odd that this man would dare to speak so openly. "It doesn't matter anymore," he said. "What happened, happened."

"I suppose. I just thought you should know that not everyone here believes you're guilty."

"Thanks. But I really think you should keep that kind of thing to yourself."

The driver glanced over his shoulder, smiling. "You're not going to turn me in, are you?"

Drake returned the smile and clamped the cigar between his teeth. "Nope."

Having broken his silence, the driver now seemed keen to talk. For the rest of the ride he chatted almost non-stop about current events in Troi. Nothing was of particular interest to Drake. In fact, so little had changed, the man could easily have been recounting the days before his exile. Life in Troi had always been a series of routines. The only thing that was unusual was a mention of the rise in protests. Most people were afraid to speak out. But lately, it seemed, more and more were finding the courage.

"To be honest, I don't know what they have to complain about," the driver continued. "I mean, it could be a whole lot worse. At least here you don't starve. And I hear tell they might start allowing people to spend some time in the gardens."

"So what's it all about?" Drake asked. "What are they saying they want?"

"Hard to say. The guards chase them off before they can do much. The ones they do catch aren't heard from again. Exiled, I imagine."

Or killed, Drake thought. "What do *you* think about it?"

"Hey, I just drive a car. Whatever their problem is, it's none of my business."

Drake could understand why the man would not want to become involved. Being a government driver was a great job. You would have to be a fool to risk losing it.

They had now reached the level they wanted, and with no lanes on the streets this far down set aside for emergency and government vehicles, the conversation stopped as the driver was forced to concentrate on navigating his way through the dense traffic. Under such circumstances, it could have taken them hours to get from one side to the other. Fortunately, their destination was not too far ahead after exiting the main highway.

They pulled up, and Drake immediately slid out from the back.

"Are they letting you stay?" the driver asked, as Drake shoved his sword inside the duffle.

"We'll see."

"Well, I for one hope they do."

"Thanks."

Drake waited for the car to move off before approaching the front of the building. Above the glass double doors was a number; that was all. No markings of any kind, nor were there any distinguishing features to indicate what purpose the building might serve. Just inside was a desk, behind which a young man in a blue jumpsuit was seated, thumbing through a stack of papers. He glanced up at Drake and let out an exasperated sigh.

"How many more of you are coming today?" he said under his breath.

Drake pulled out his identification and handed it over. "I was sent by –"

"The magistrate's office," he cut in. "Yes. I know. Why else would you be here?" After looking at the ID, he opened his desk drawer and pulled out a sheet of paper. "Says here you're to be accommodated on the top floor." He chuckled. "Not too many of you from the outer provinces get to stay there. You should feel privileged."

"Should I?"

The man raised an eyebrow. "Of course. How many of you lot do you imagine are given a real apartment to stay in?" After tossing the ID card back across the desk, he sneered: "I must remember to call maintenance. It's going to need a good scrubbing down after you're gone."

Drake tried to ignore the insult, but his anger got the better of him. He leaned in closer. "You're from level six. Right?"

The man stiffened.

Drake grinned. "I thought so. I can tell by the way you slur your S's. Being a reception clerk is a hell of a promotion for anyone from that far down. Your parents must be so proud." He folded his arms and held his chin between his forefinger and thumb in an exaggerated pose of deep thought. "Let me see, now…your mom and dad both work in the sewage plant, right?"

The young man's face tightened, and he shot a quick look around to see if anyone was listening. "How did you know that?" he hissed.

"It doesn't matter. I bet it must have cost them a lot to get you this job. Do your co-workers know where you come from? They don't, do they? I wonder what they would say if they found out."

The door behind him opened and a young woman in an identical jumpsuit entered.

"Are you Drake Sharazi?"

Drake allowed his gaze to linger on the man for a moment longer before turning. "Yes. That's me."

"Captain Mortimer has asked me to see to your needs while you are staying here."

At the mere mention of the captain of the royal guard, the reception clerk's eyes shot wide and beads of sweat formed on his brow.

"Please tell Xavier thank you, when you see him," Drake said to the woman.

She nodded and then gestured for him to follow. Before doing so, Drake leaned down to whisper in the young man's ear. "Perhaps you should be careful of how you treat people in the future. You never know who you're talking to. Or who they might have connections to."

The young man nodded, but made no attempt at a reply.

Drake followed the woman through the door into a long hallway. Doors lined both walls at regular intervals, each one bearing a number. Offices, most likely, he thought. He was familiar with this sort of facility. They were used to house those with entry passes from the provinces, as well as lower level officials from the upper city who had extended business.

They entered the elevator at the end of the hall and rode it up to the top floor. His apartment was just a short walk away.

"Do you know how to use a mana lock?" the woman asked, upon reaching the door.

Drake nodded confirmation and then placed his hand fully over the knob. It responded by glowing brightly, at the same time sending a mild shock running up his arm. A sharp clack after a few seconds indicated that the lock had made the connection.

"Everything you will need should already be here for

you," his escort said. "I'll return later to check if there's anything further you require."

Drake watched as she walked briskly back to the lift. A true bureaucrat, he told himself. The kind who moves up quickly. Efficient and cold. If she did in reality look down on him for being from the provinces, she would never display even the smallest hint of this. In fact, he doubted that she ever let any feelings whatsoever show through.

The apartment was very nice by provincial standards: two bedrooms, a small kitchen, and a comfortable living room. The furnishings were all new and of good quality; there was even a holoviewer hanging on the wall opposite the sofa for his entertainment.

After tossing his duffle bag into the bedroom, an exploration of the various closets and cabinets turned up a good supply of both food and fresh clothing. The pants and shirts were of common style – t-shirts mostly, together with simple denim trousers – but they were a damn sight better than the rags he was currently wearing. It was really a bit surprising that Xavier would think to provide him with such amenities. But of course, Xavier always had his own motives. Drake seriously doubted that any of it was done from kindness.

He stripped off his clothes and jumped in the shower, letting out a long moan of pleasure as the steaming hot water poured over his body. This was yet another of those apparently simple pleasures that he had missed so much. He hadn't felt this clean in nine years and could have stayed there luxuriating in the feeling for hours. Eventually, though, the rumbling in his stomach urged him to finish and get dressed. Even the fresh clothes he selected felt good – clean in a way that he had almost completely forgotten.

He turned on the holoviewer, bringing an image of the

upper city garden to the screen. Carefully, he eased a slider at the bottom of the viewer to the left, continuing like this until he heard a familiar tune coming from the speakers. The screen was now filled with swirls of light and color, dancing to the beat of the song while creating random patterns and shapes. Before he even realized it, he was smiling.

"Don't get too used to this life," he scolded himself, settling down into an armchair. All the same, he couldn't help but enjoy it. Even if it was only temporary.

As it turned out, his pleasure was destined to be even more short-lived than he'd anticipated. Shattering the moment, the apartment door was suddenly thrown back noisily on its hinges.

Instinctively, Drake leaped to his feet and started to run toward the bedroom, where his P37 and sword were lying on the bed. But a sight of the black uniforms of the royal guard halted him mid-stride. Six men filed inside, one of them instantly recognizable. Gerard Vernon, a corporal when Drake had been exiled, now bore the insignia of a sergeant. An ill-tempered man even on his best days, Vernon barked out an order. In response, his men spread out and began searching the apartment.

"Good to see you again, Gerard," Drake said, smiling.

Vernon sneered. "Face the wall and place your hands on your head."

"I only just got here. What's this all about?"

Drake's tormentor stepped in close until their noses were almost touching. "Give me a reason, exile. I'm begging you."

"Take it easy, sergeant," he told him, still maintaining his friendly smile. "I'm going." He turned and did as instructed.

Vernon frisked him thoroughly – and roughly – and

then shoved him flat up against the wall. "Don't move from there until I tell you."

"Weapons in the bedroom," called a voice.

"Secure them in the hall," Vernon responded.

After a few minutes, Drake heard the men leaving. Then a different voice spoke.

"You can go too, sergeant. I'll speak to him privately."

Drake felt as if a cold spear had been shoved through his gullet. Though he knew very well to whom the voice belonged, he could still scarcely believe he was hearing it. When the door closed following Vernon's exit, he found himself unable to move.

The voice spoke again. "Please. Turn around and let me see your face."

Very slowly, Drake did as requested, eyes downcast and head bowed. "Yes, Your Majesty."

"Look at me."

Waves of conflicting emotions tore through him until he was no longer able to distinguish anger from love nor hate from sorrow. He raised his head. The king looked just as he had the last time he'd seen him. Silver hair with streaks of jet black flowed down to his broad shoulders, held back from his brow by a gold circlet. His careworn eyes and fatherly smile brought tears pouring down Drake's cheeks. In the monarch's right hand was a crystal staff crowned with a golden lion. A walking stick, he often called it. But it was far more than that – it was a mana weapon of such enormous power that it made Drake's P37 look like a child's toy. With this in his possession, the king hardly needed the protection of the royal guard. He wore a purple satin robe with silver trim and stitching over a silver shirt and black pants. His hands were adorned with rings beset with diamonds and emeralds, and a medallion of pure gold with the Lion of Troi in blood rubies hung from a gold chain around his neck. He was a tiny bit more bent than Drake remembered – though otherwise he seemed not to have aged a day.

"I never dreamed I would see you again," the king said.

Drake wanted to speak, but feared his tears would turn into open sobs.

Nedar sighed and placed his hand on Drake's shoulder. "I know you must hate me for what happened. I wish things could have been different. I hope you believe that."

Drake took a moment to compose himself before finally speaking. "I don't blame you, Your Majesty. You did the only thing you could do."

"I wanted to do more. But the evidence…"

"I understand, Your Majesty."

"Do you? Because I don't. Scarcely a day goes by when I don't think about it, asking myself how it was done…and who would do it."

"You shouldn't trouble yourself, Your Majesty. That you believe me to be innocent is all I ever wanted."

"Well, *I* wanted more for you. And I know I have no right to ask anything of you." Now it was the king's turn to shed tears. "They have taken my son, Drake. You have to get him back for me."

"I will try, Your Majesty. I will do my very best. You have my word."

The king gave him a fragile smile. "That is what I always admired about you. Most men would say without hesitation that they would get him back. They would say so as if their success were assured. But not you. You always tell me the truth. That is why I never doubted your innocence. And why it was so hard for me to send you away."

"I would never lie to you, Your Majesty. Just as you have

50

never lied to me. And there is one thing you can be certain of: whoever has done this, I will make them pay for it. Even if it takes me the rest of my life to find them."

The king nodded. "Yes. I know you will. And you will be amply rewarded for my son's safe return." He gave a small sigh. "I'm afraid I cannot bring you into the upper city. That would cause an outright feud, and the last thing I want is for the high mages to become involved. However, I will ensure that you are given a place here. You will also be provided with everything you could ever need to make your life as comfortable as possible. That is *my* word."

It was all Drake could do to remain standing. He had fantasized about this moment for nine long years. Even after all hope had deserted him, it still managed to plague his dreams. And now it was happening. It was actually happening. "Thank...thank you, Your Majesty."

"I dearly wish I could stay longer," the king told him. "I do miss our talks very much."

"As do I, Your Majesty." Drake bowed low. "Thank you for coming to see me."

"My boy. You never need to thank me for anything." He gave Drake's arm a fond squeeze before turning to the door, and then paused before opening it. "One more thing. When you see Salazar, please tell him that I understand why he did what he did. Also, that he is forgiven."

"Your Majesty?"

"He will know what I mean."

After the king had left the apartment, Vernon tossed Drake's weapons carelessly back inside. He could only stand there staring at the floor for the next fifteen minutes. Though he would not have said so to the king, he *would* succeed in his mission. That was the solemn promise he now made to himself.

For the rest of the evening he sat in the dark, listening to music from the holoviewer. He did his best to clear his mind, but the memories of his past would not be denied, forcing their way in like unwelcome guests: thoughts of his carefree days wandering the halls of upper Troi with the prince; the stern face of the king when they'd been caught causing mischief that always concealed a forgiving smile; but mostly his time with Lenora. As much as he tried to put her out of his mind, he couldn't. Just being in Troi again was enough, knowing that she was somewhere above him. So very close, and yet unreachable. It was maddening.

The young woman who had shown him to the apartment returned briefly, but Drake politely dismissed her. There was nothing more he needed. When he had first arrived, he'd considered taking a long walk around the city. Now, though, since speaking with King Nedar, all he wanted to do was to leave Troi and his memories and get on with his quest of searching for Prince Salazar.

He eventually went to bed. Sleep, however, proved elusive. Several times he got up and just wandered about the apartment looking in the various drawers and cabinets, even though he already knew perfectly well what was in them.

One question was constantly on his mind: how long would he have to wait before setting off? Not long, was his guess. He doubted Xavier was very happy that they had sought him out for the task; he was sure to have his own people out searching for the prince as well. But if the kidnappers were from the provinces, they would see Troians coming a mile away.

He was on yet another of his nocturnal wanderings when a soft, almost inaudible tap sounded at the front door. Hurrying back to the bedroom, Drake snatched up his P37 just as the door eased open. He leveled the weapon. Whoever this was, they were able to bypass a mana lock. That made them dangerous. From the moment he had touched the doorknob, the mechanism had linked itself uniquely to him. Only someone with magical ability could now bypass that security measure. A sinking thought then occurred as the door swung completely open – if this was a royal guard, they sure as hell were not going to like having a weapon shoved in their face. *Well, then they shouldn't sneak in like this.*

The instantly recognizable silhouette in the doorway and the scent of perfume had him quickly lowering his gun and stepping back several paces. He had been prepared for just about anything. Anything but this.

"Hello, Drake." Her voice was soft and musical. Stepping inside, she closed the door behind her.

He was utterly stunned. Seeing the king had been difficult enough. This…was unbearable.

"Lenora," he whispered.

"I wasn't sure if I should come. I didn't know if you would want to see me."

Drake's mind was reeling. Seeing her a little more clearly as she moved into the light coming through the window, he felt a violent ache strike his heart. She was every bit as beautiful as he remembered. Even more so, in fact. Her delicate features had not aged a day, and her slender frame still glided effortlessly as if she were walking upon a cushion of pure mana. Raven hair cascaded in loose glossy curls over her shoulders and halfway down her back. Then there was her most memorable feature of all – even in the dim light, he could still clearly see the ice blue eyes that had once so powerfully captured his heart.

"Of course I wanted to see you. I just thought…" He felt dizzy and could hardly get the words out. "I thought you would hate me."

"I did. For a long time. But then I came to realize that you were right. If I had come with you, they would never have stopped hunting us. They would have killed you. Instead, here you are now, standing right in front of me."

The image of her face, the sorrow in her eyes, and the harshness of her words had never left him. She had desperately wanted to go with him into exile – to abandon her life in Troi. In a weak moment he had almost agreed to this. But he'd quickly come to realize that it could never be. She was the daughter of the king. Their love had been forbidden. Should she have run away, the whole of Vale would have been relentlessly upended. There would have been absolutely nowhere for them to hide.

"I'm sorry I hurt you," he said.

Her smile was sweet yet somehow distant. "No. It was *I* who hurt *you*. I was angry when I last saw you. I've since spent nine years regretting every word."

He offered her a seat on the sofa, but she shook her head.

"I cannot stay. I just had to see you at least one time before you left."

Drake suddenly realized that he was standing there in nothing but a pair of cotton pants. He reached for a shirt he had thrown over the arm of a chair. "I...I'm glad you came."

While pulling the shirt over his head, he felt her soft touch on his shoulder.

"You're injured."

He'd forgotten about the bullet that had struck him in the garage. "It's nothing," he told her. "Just a bruise." He pulled his shirt down and stepped away.

"Don't be silly." She moved closer and placed her hand on the wound.

Drake closed his eyes, her touch instantly reminding him of the times he had held her in his arms and the gentle warmth of her breath on his neck as they'd lain together in the garden gazing up at the splendor of Troi.

The memory faded as the cold tingle of healing magic penetrated his flesh, sending waves of energy pouring into every inch of his body. Only a very few people had a true gift for healing; Lenora was one of them. He had seen her bring people back from the very brink of death with nothing more than a simple touch.

When she removed her hand, a soft sigh of relief escaped his lips. He heard her laughing, like silver chimes playing a sweet melody.

"Better?

He opened his eyes and saw her smiling at him. "Much better. Thank you."

"I have to go now. If my father finds out I came here…" She hesitated, clearly embarrassed to elaborate on this. "Well, you know how things are."

"It's fine. I understand. I don't want you to get into trouble."

She leaned in and kissed his cheek. "I think I'm already in trouble. And if I don't leave now, I'll be in even more."

She started toward the door. "You know, I was so happy when I found out it was you they had called upon to rescue my brother."

"I won't stop until I find him," he assured her.

"I know that. But the shame of it is, the thought of his rescue was not why I was happy. Not really. It was that it meant you would be returning to Troi."

Without another word, she turned and left. Drake wanted to chase after her. He wanted to tell her of all the things that had built up in his heart for nine long years. Most of all, he wanted to hold her in his arms again and tell her how much he loved her. But that wasn't possible. So, instead, he just plopped down on the couch and gazed blankly out of the window until the scent of her perfume had finally faded away. The apartment now felt like a prison, and the morning could not arrive soon enough.

He was coming, and whoever had taken Prince Salazar had better damn well pray with all their heart that he still lived.

CHAPTER FIVE

"Wake up."

Drake felt a firm hand shaking his shoulder. He groaned. What time was it? Peeling open one eye, he saw Xavier standing over him with a glass of ice water in his hand. He was grinning impishly.

"I don't care who you think you are," Drake warned. "Pour that over me and I'll smash your teeth out."

Xavier merely laughed. "A mighty threat from a tiny man. Now come on – get up. You have much to do today before you leave." He held out the glass. "I thought I remembered you being an early riser."

Drake sat up and accepted the water, as much to prevent Xavier from being tempted as from any great desire to drink it. He looked over to the window. Normally, he *did* wake early, at least an hour before the sun was up. But he hadn't slept in a soft bed in a very long time, and the temperature was just the way he liked it. Not too cold; not too warm. He had heard how some people found it difficult to sleep in a comfortable bed after enduring years of hardship, instead choosing a hard floor to rest on. Drake had encountered no such problem.

"I assume you are here for a reason?" he said.

"Get dressed." Xavier told him, turning to the door. "And don't take long about it. Your car is in the front. I'll be waiting."

Drake remained motionless until he heard him leave the apartment, and then took a moment to yawn and stretch. Yes, this kind of life could definitely make a man soft. And that would suit him just fine. Nine years of living in filth was more than enough, especially now after having seen Lenora once again. It was the thought of his promise to her that eventually spurred him out of bed. Delaying only long enough to enjoy another rapid hot shower, he was ready to leave in just a few minutes.

Though he'd chosen to wear one of his old V-neck t-shirts and a pair of well-worn jeans from his duffle, he took the much newer clothes from the closet with him anyway. They might well be a useful way of obtaining information later on; out in the provinces, good quality clothes were even better than money in some cases. The leather jacket was the only item amongst them that he actually put on. This was sturdier than the one destroyed by the assassin's magic, and quite surprisingly, an even better fit. But he had never liked its short style very much, far preferring a trench coat. Now, though, he would be carrying a sword, and the jacket's broad collar enabled him to wear this across his back without it being awkward.

As Drake entered the lift, he recalled the first time he'd been sent to the outer provinces. His partner, Sal, had warned him that things were different out there. But back then, Drake had been a young man filled with confidence, and the words of warning were shrugged off.

"I'm telling you," Sal persisted. "They'll kill you in the blink of an eye if you relax."

"With what?" he'd replied, certain that the protection his magic provided was impenetrable.

"People outside of Troi carry more than just pea-shooters, you know."

Later that day, the blood pouring from the huge wound in Sal's chest was something he would never forget. It was the first time he had seen a man die. And the first time he had taken a life.

It would be far from the last.

The few people he passed on his way out of the building shot him sour looks, most of them suspiciously eyeing the sword on his back and the P37 hanging at his side. To them, he knew he must look like a complete barbarian – a genuine low-life from the provinces. No one here normally walked around so dangerously armed. A few citizens might be permitted to own a weapon, but never anything more lethal than a small-caliber handgun – nothing that could possibly be a serious threat to the royal guard. Not that violence was common; people were far more afraid of being exiled than they were of being assaulted. Crime happened, but mostly petty theft and swindles. And if you were caught, you could always try to make restitution before the authorities became involved.

Upon exiting the building, he saw Xavier casually leaning against Cal's hood while fiddling with a small knife. He glanced up at Drake and let out a disapproving sigh.

"Why do you insist on dressing like a provincial dirt dweller?" he mocked. "I had plenty of good clothing provided for you."

"Yes, and if you want me to find Prince Salazar, I can't go around looking like I just stepped out of the lower city," Drake retorted quickly. "That's probably why your people haven't had any luck finding him. They can see your men coming a mile away."

Xavier flicked his wrist. "I suppose it is a challenge for us to blend in easily with the uncultured and the uneducated. But thankfully, we have *you* now. And you certainly seem to have mastered it well enough."

More than ever, Drake wanted to throttle him. He gave a short, humorless laugh. "Why don't you stop pretending to be something that you're not?"

"What do you mean by that?"

"Your accent. Do you really think people don't know where you're originally from? At least I was never ashamed of who I am." Drake could see Xavier's jaw tighten: even as a recruit he had hated the fact that his father was a lower city dweller. "I can tell you one thing," he continued. "Should by some amazing piece of luck your men do manage to find the prince before me, those at the top will still never accept you as one of them."

"You don't know a thing about me, exile."

"I wish I didn't. Now, if you don't mind, I'm sure the king wouldn't want me hanging around here doing nothing."

Gripping the knife handle with far more force than was necessary, Xavier's eyes briefly burned with hatred. He then composed himself. "Quite right. However, before we go, I need to show you the alterations we've made to your vehicle."

It was Drake's turn to feel a flash of anger. "What did you do to her?"

Xavier chuckled, his good humor now fully restored. "Nothing of which I am sure you wouldn't approve." Walking over to the trunk, he gestured for Drake to open it.

Inside, near the rear, was a small button that had not previously been there. At a touch of Drake's index finger, a section around the button eased open to reveal an added compartment. Inside this were two metal boxes. One contained spare parts for his P37 – something that had been always exceedingly difficult to come by. In the other was an envelope with a thousand gold notes and a square piece of foam. A variety of glass phials had been placed inside small holes within the foam to keep them from shattering.

"I thought this might come in useful," Xavier said. "Each of the phials is clearly marked, so I suggest you take time to examine them all once you've left."

"What's in them?"

"Did I not just say to look once you have left?"

Drake slammed the trunk. "What else?"

Xavier entered on the passenger's side and waited for Drake to get behind the wheel. Set in the center console was a blue button and a small holoscreen.

"Touch the screen and it will give you your exact location," Xavier informed him.

Drake did as instructed, but nothing happened. "Good job," he mocked.

"It doesn't work within Troi, that's why. But it will work fine once you're outside the city. Use your fingers to expand the map if you need. Press it firmly and hold, and it will display inside your windshield."

Drake ran his finger over the blue button.

"Don't press that unless you have no choice," warned Xavier. "If you do, everything within twenty feet of the vehicle will get blasted with mana fire. However, this weapon uses a significant amount of fuel, so be careful."

"And the tracking device?"

"Unfortunately, we cannot afford to risk its discovery. For that reason it currently remains inactive." He opened the glove compartment and pointed to a tiny silver switch. "Once you have secured the prince, simply turn it on, and we will immediately be on our way to you. Do not activate it on for any other reason."

That the royal guard believed the perpetrators of this abduction were capable of detecting a tracking device meant they must know at least something about them. It also suggested that they were far better equipped than the vast majority of lawless elements living outside of Troi.

"Any other little extras I should know about?" he asked.

Xavier closed the glove compartment and leaned back in his seat. "I think that is quite good for only one night's work. Now, if you don't mind, we're expected at the magistrate's office."

Drake fired the engine and threw Cal into gear. She was sluggish at first, but he knew how to fix that. He had to admit that the additions were quite clever and could likely come in useful, particularly the mana fire. He assumed the phials were a variety of poisons, truth serums, and possibly corrosives.

After jumping back onto the main highway, he wove his way up to level one. They were only a few miles away from their destination when, quite suddenly, he pulled over and turned off the engine.

"What are you doing?" Xavier demanded.

Drake pointed to a nearby manga juice shop. "I'm not leaving without one."

He was literally drooling with expectation as the man behind the counter handed over the frost-covered container. Straight away he gulped in a large mouthful, savoring the sweet flavor on his tongue for several seconds before swallowing.

After returning to the car, he settled back in his seat and took several more leisurely drinks without showing any inclination to start the engine. Xavier was looking more than a little displeased.

"This is by far Troi's greatest accomplishment," Drake remarked.

"If you are done being childish…"

Drake laughed. "Not nearly."

This time he left Cal in front of the magistrate's office. Two men of the royal guard were waiting inside to escort them to the rear offices, and Drake followed them, humming merrily as he continued to enjoy regular sips of his juice.

The interior was austere and functional. Only holopics of the line of kings disturbed the light gray walls and white tiles. The men and women darting in and out of the offices were all dressed in similar black suits, and each wore a silver medallion on their right lapel bearing the seal of the magistrate.

The magistrate herself was one of the most powerful people in the lower city. Velma Chase had been assigned the office more than twenty years prior, and had since built a reputation for strict adherence to the law, not to mention a cruel and unforgiving disposition. Rumors were that she had issued a warrant for her own son simply because he had stolen a twenty note from her handbag. Drake hoped she would not be attending whatever meeting Xavier had in store. If he was to live in the lower city once this business was over, better that she did not grow accustomed to seeing his face.

He could clearly recall an evening out with his fellow guards during which they had encountered a trio of drunken men in a nightclub who worked in this very office. Rather unwisely, one of them had made a slightly off-color remark about the magistrate in a public place. Only minutes later, all three were escorted from the building, looks of sheer terror on their faces. There was very little that happened in the lower city that didn't reach Velma's ears, and her employees were under strict orders to always be on their best behavior. Of course, the royal guard had a standard for public behavior as well. And it was quite high. But at least they were permitted to enjoy themselves from time to time. Following this incident, he had never seen anyone else from this office out on the town again. Not ever.

They arrived at a small conference room, where seated at the table with a sour expression etched deeply into her face was Velma Chase. Drake heaved a silent sigh. So much for his hope of avoiding her. The woman's silver hair was tied into a neat bun, and her rimmed glasses sat low on the bridge of her wrinkled nose. In addition to the silver pendant everyone else wore, she also had another button bearing a Lion of Troi fixed to the left lapel. As her piercing green eyes fell on him, Drake imagined that he felt the temperature in the room drop by several degrees.

"Is it your custom to be tardy?" she asked, her voice deep for a woman. "I gave the royal guard more credit than that."

"My apologies," Drake replied. "I stopped to buy a manga juice along the way." He held up the nearly empty cup as evidence.

"I see."

Xavier nodded for the two men escorting them to wait outside. Even he, who vastly outranked a lowly magistrate, looked ill at ease around this woman; not that he was about to let her cow him.

"Should we have brought you one as well?" Drake asked her.

Her mouth twisted into an even deeper frown. "Shall we get this over with? I have many other matters to attend. As, I am sure, do you."

With a smile of acknowledgement, Xavier moved over to the switch and turned off the lights. For a moment, the room was plunged into total darkness. Then there was the hiss of a holoplayer powering up and its screen illuminated on the wall behind the table. Xavier and Drake both took seats while the magistrate retrieved a small silver box with a series of buttons from the briefcase beside her chair.

"I assume that the Captain has already informed you why you are here," she began. "In that case, I will get right to the point. Six weeks ago, Prince Salazar left Troi without an escort and was captured by a radical group known as Exodus."

"Exodus?" Drake frowned. "Never heard of them."

"I'm not surprised," she said. "They work very hard to hide their presence. But it is our belief that they have been behind almost every major act of dissent for the past twenty years."

Drake drew back. "Impossible. No one could avoid detection for that long. Certainly not a group of any size or significance."

His remark instantly drew a stern look from the magistrate. "You will please refrain from any further interruptions," she snapped, then allowed a moment of silence to develop in order to punctuate her severity.

Satisfied that she had made her point, she continued. "Now, then. It has taken my office a very long time to piece together what little we know about them. They are led by a woman named Zara — at least, that is the name she goes by. Who she really is, I couldn't say. All we know for certain is that she comes from the provinces and her followers are fanatical. It is our belief that they intend to use the prince as a hostage in order to force the king to shut down the power station."

"What?" Such was his surprise, Drake was unable to hold his tongue. "Who in their right mind would want that?"

"Someone wanting to take over Vale," Xavier told him.

"That is our assessment," Velma confirmed. "This, of course, we cannot allow. Unfortunately, the royal guard has so far been unsuccessful in locating where the prince is being held. Time is passing, and the king is becoming increasingly worried."

BRIAN D. ANDERSON

"So naturally, His Royal Majesty thought of you," Xavier added with just a tiny hint of distaste in his voice.

Drake shifted in his seat. "Before I do anything, I need to know why the prince was outside of the city without protection."

"Actually, you do not," Velma corrected. "Though rest assured, you *will* be given all the information considered necessary for your task." She pressed a button on the silver box, and an image of a large warehouse appeared on the screen. "This is the last place we were able to track the prince's whereabouts. It is a storage facility in Indra. We believe that this is the place where Exodus abducted him."

"What's kept in this facility?" Drake asked. Indra was an outer province to the north, very nearly as poor as Aurora.

"Nothing of particular interest. Medical supplies are occasionally sent there to be separated before distribution. That's about all."

Drake tried to think of what else might be in the area, but came up empty.

"From there, we have no idea what happened," Velma continued. "Needless to say, our efforts to uncover Exodus have been stepped up dramatically. So far, however–"

"Let me guess," Drake cut in. "They always seem to be one step ahead of you."

There was clear annoyance on her face. "Yes. We've captured a few of their operatives, but they always die the moment they're in custody. It's some sort of remote suicide that we're still trying to identify. They simply send out a signal, and a moment later they're dead."

Just like the man who had attacked him in the garage, Drake recalled.

"Does this sound familiar?" she asked, seeing the recognition on his face.

66

Drake nodded. "Yes. I heard something about it a while back, though I didn't pay much attention at the time." The lie slipped out easily enough. The last thing he needed was Xavier getting too close and mucking things up; hearing what had happened might spur his unwanted interest.

The magistrate clicked the button again, and an image of a young man appeared. His dark hair and copper skin gave his sharp features a striking, almost sinister look.

"This a Samuel Friedman, a former instructor at the College of Mages, but now what you call a hawker. Since being expelled, he goes by the name of Bane."

Bane. Drake had definitely heard the name. Many times, in fact. His reputation was sketchy at best. A real killer. And young. But very good at his job.

"Our information suggests that he may know how to make contact with Exodus," Xavier told him.

"Bane's hard to find," Drake responded. "Any idea where I should start?"

With another click, a new face appeared, one that Drake recognized instantly.

"I see that you are familiar with this one," the magistrate remarked.

"You're damn right I am. That's the son of a bitch who tried to kill me."

Staring at him from the screen with narrow eyes set in a round face, smirking with confidence and with what little hair he still had tied into a wispy ponytail, was his double-crossing client.

"Fortunately for us, he failed. But that should make your job much easier. Bane is in his direct employ. Start there, and you should be able to find Exodus."

She clicked another button and the screen went blank.

"That's it?" asked Drake.

67

"If there were more, I would have told you."

He knew she was definitely hiding something. He could see it in her expression and hear it in the tone of her voice. Something wasn't right about all of this. The client, a man named Bolton Fisk, was a known criminal who had managed widespread bribery of the authorities and had a fierce reputation for terrorizing anyone who might even consider bearing witness against him. Which most of the time simply meant that they died. Fisk practically owned the outer provinces in the west and had nearly as much influence in the south.

When Drake was still serving with the royal guard, word had reached him about Fisk stealing badly needed medical supplies and then charging desperate hospitals outrageous sums to supply them. He had pressured the magistrate's office to take action, but no one could ever link Fisk directly to any crime. He was too clever for that. In the end, Drake had decided the matter was not worth his time to keep pursuing – a typical attitude for someone living in the upper city. *Funny how things change*. He had not known at first that it was Fisk who'd hired him; not that it would have mattered. He had never seen him until three weeks prior, when he'd been hired to find a runner who had stolen a truck filled with bolts of cotton. Though if he had known it was Fisk, he would not have been surprised to find out the runner had been killed. Or that the sheriff was too afraid to do anything about it.

Xavier rose to his feet and turned on the lights. "If that is all, we should go," he said.

Drake regarded the magistrate for a long moment. Though her face betrayed nothing to the eyes of most people, Drake was highly adept at reading subtleties. She still had something to say. He was certain of that.

"Are you sure there isn't anything more you can tell me?"

he pressed. "If the life of Prince Salazar is at stake, even the smallest detail might end up saving him."

There was a lengthy pause before she replied. "Would you give us a moment, Captain?"

Xavier bristled. "If there is more, then I should know of it. I am the captain of the Royal Guard. You have no right to keep information from me."

"And you are within my jurisdiction, Captain. So unless you come with official orders in your hand, I am the authority here. You will do as I say, or I will have you shown out."

The threat was not genuine; Drake knew that. Xavier, together with his two men waiting directly outside, could easily overcome whatever security the magistrate might keep in the building. All the same, she was right. He might outrank her, but she was still the ultimate authority inside her own building; not to mention that Velma had been around long enough to know everyone's secrets. Even someone as careful as Xavier.

"Once I return, we shall have a talk, you and I," he promised.

"You know where to find me, Captain."

Drake was forced to cover his mouth in order to conceal an ever-widening grin. After letting out a loud snort of exasperation, Xavier then strode from the room, slamming the door hard.

The magistrate waited a few moments before pushing another button on the box. A soft hiss emanated from the ceiling. "That should ensure our privacy," she told Drake. "And though I cannot prevent you from telling Captain Mortimer what I am about to say, I sincerely hope you do not. I am only revealing this because you are correct. If you hope to save the prince, then you do need to be fully aware of anything that might help."

He nodded. "If Xavier doesn't need to know, he won't find it out from me."

A thin smile briefly appeared on her face. "Yes. If I'm not mistaken, the two of you do have a somewhat troubled history."

"We've had our differences."

She had clearly done her research well.

"From your earlier remark, I know you are wondering exactly how the prince was able to put himself into such a dangerous situation."

Drake nodded. "Of course I am. Just shaking off his escort would be a challenge. It couldn't have been an accident. I figure he lost them on purpose."

"That he did. The plain truth is, Prince Salazar ran away. Unfortunately, I do not know all of the details. But I do know that the king was furious with him. So much so that he issued a warrant for his son's arrest."

Drake cocked his head. "A warrant? Are you serious?"

"Very. It has since been rescinded, though there's no way for the prince to know that. As far as he is concerned, anyone coming for him has only one purpose – to bring him back to Troi for prosecution. So you see, even if you do find him, he might not be as cooperative as you anticipate."

"What was the charge?"

The magistrate hesitated for a lengthy moment. "Treason. We're not even sure how it was that the prince found out. King Nedar rescinded it the same day. But we think that was the reason he ran."

Drake did not bother to ask exactly what he had done. Even if the magistrate knew, she would never tell him. But this did complicate matters. Prince Salazar would think he was facing a death sentence. It wouldn't be so easy to convince him to return – assuming that he was still alive.

"Does Exodus know about this?" he asked.

"We're not sure. We hope not. If they believe his life is already forfeit, they may well decide it best to just kill him. Every effort has been made to erase all details of the charge from the records, though there's always a possibility of them knowing about it anyway."

"I see. Well, that certainly changes things."

Her face softened to such an extent that, for a moment, she almost looked affable. "I know very well that you and the prince were friends. Which is why I stood with the king when he wanted to send for you. But heed this warning: Captain Mortimer may well try to work against you. He knows nothing of this. Nor should he. I believe that a man of his character should not be in possession of such knowledge."

After leaning back in his chair, Drake steepled his hands beneath his chin. There was no doubt that she was right. If Xavier knew any of this, he would certainly find a way of using it to gain leverage over the prince. Never before had a charge of treason been leveled against a member of the royal family. It would cause a huge stir among the nobles. What could Salazar have possibly done to make his father take such a drastic measure?

"You must make sure the prince understands exactly what has happened before he speaks with the captain," Velma continued. "Otherwise he might say something he shouldn't." She stood and crossed to the door. "If you do your job and this matter is handled properly, life for you in the lower city will be quite rewarding. That much I can promise."

Drake waited for a moment before exiting. Events had just taken a leap into the realm of the surreal. It had been hard enough to imagine the prince being abducted. But this – this was almost unbelievable. King Nedar loved his son fiercely. As hard as Drake tried, not a single thing came to mind that could cause him to do this. Not treason.

Xavier was waiting impatiently just outside. "Are you finished wasting time?" he growled.

Drake smiled. "It was anything but a waste of time, Captain."

When they reached the car, he jumped in quickly, flicked the locks, and then rolled down the passenger side window just a crack. "I'll take it from here," he told Xavier.

"Open this damn door," he demanded, jerking furiously at the handle. "You had better tell me what she said to you. You hear me?"

Drake fired the engine. "Sorry. I know all I need to know, so I can't hang around. I'm sure you can get a ride with someone else back to the upper city."

"If she told you something that—"

He slammed Cal into gear and sped away while Xavier was still in mid-sentence. In the mirror he could see him shouting curses and shaking a fist. Drake couldn't help but laugh. He had never liked the man. His conversation with the magistrate had been shocking, to say the least – yet one aspect was very clear. Xavier must not learn this information. A man like him would certainly use it to further his own ends.

"You've only got yourself to blame," he muttered. "You're the one who recruited the smug bastard in the first place."

He reached to the console and pressed a yellow pad.

"Hello, Drake," came a soft, almost seductive voice. "Please state your command."

"Camouflage. Low profile."

At once Cal's paint began to dull, and patches of rust appeared on the hood.

He stroked the dash. "Don't worry, baby. You're still beautiful."

He was certain he was being watched. Though this slight change in his car would not be enough to throw off Xavier's people, it wasn't them he was worried about. It was no coincidence that Fisk had tried to have him killed. Someone knew that he would be coming here and wanted to stop him – which meant that someone either in the magistrate's office or close to the king was working for Exodus. He had thought to mention this to Velma during their private talk, but the magistrate was clever enough to piece it together for herself. So was Xavier, for that matter. Even though Drake couldn't stand the man, he was too clever to underestimate.

He peeled onto the ramp leading from Troi. Yes, Xavier was smart. But not nearly as much as he imagined. It was always good when your opponents believed themselves to be intellectually superior. It made it easier to outmaneuver them. He imagined it was this failing more than anything that had prevented Xavier from finding the prince. He was simply incapable of seeing the enemy as anything more than uneducated brutes. And though Drake's own attitude had admittedly been little better in the days before his exile, he had since learned his lesson well. One did not need wealth to be clever.

He eased Cal a little faster. There was a long road ahead. But not before he had made one more important stop.

CHAPTER SIX

I t was a few hours before dusk by the time he reached
Dorn's place. Directly across the street from this, Drake
noted that the parking lot in front of the neighborhood
bar was filled to capacity. That was a sure sign trouble was
brewing. Before the night was over, there would be blood.

Dorn's garage door lifted open and an old man shuffled
out. His gray hair was wrapped in an oily cloth, and his back
had a permanent bend from countless years of toil. Adding
to this picture of infirmity, the lines on his face were deeply
carved. Only a pair of twinkling brown eyes as sharp as those
of a man in his twenties told a different story. The moment
he spotted Drake, he threw up his hands and let out a loud
moan.

"What have you done to her this time?"

Dorn was the only person Drake truly trusted to work
on Cal. Partly because he was the best mechanic in or out of
the provinces, but mainly because he was the one who had
actually built her.

"It's nothing *I* did, this time," Drake replied, smiling.

"And I suppose you think you can just show up here and

I'll drop everything for you."

Drake shrugged. "I can always go to Markus Drimsley's place, if you like. He's been dying to take a look under Cal's hood."

"The hell you will," he snapped. "I'll see her in pieces before I'd let that hack touch her."

"If you're sure you have the time. I mean, I wouldn't want to inconvenience you."

Grumbling under his breath, Dorn ran his hands over the fender. "So what's wrong with her? You haven't been putting that cheap mana fuel in her again, have you?"

"It was one time. And I didn't have a choice."

Dorn raised an eyebrow. "You hear that, Cal? He says he didn't have a choice."

"Look, forget about the fuel. The royal guard have installed some modifications. It's making her run sluggish."

Dorn glared at him accusingly. "You let those butchers get their hands on her? What the hell did they do?"

Drake told him about the alterations, adding: "They've put a tracker in as well. I need you to remove it…if you think you can."

He gave a derisive snort. "There's nothing those morons in Troi can do that I can't undo. She'll be in shape right quick, I can promise you that." By now his attention was completely focused on Cal. "I'll get you running right again, girl. Don't you worry." He glanced up. "You can sleep in the shed out back."

Drake knew that it was useless for him to say anything more. Dorn would work his magic tirelessly. He was the very best at what he did, though where he had learned such skill was a total mystery. Several times Drake had asked him about his past – surely at some point in his life, he had once worked within Troi. But all his questions were brushed aside. He could never get the old man to say a damn thing. Not even where he was from originally.

Across the street, cheered on by a small group of onlookers, two men were involved in a violent fight. Mable's Haven was about as rough a place as you could find. But the food they served up was good, all things considered, and there was no way for Drake to know when the next opportunity to grab a hot meal might come along. Dorn was already rolling Cal into the empty garage bay. Once he had closed the door, nothing short of breaking it down would get it open again until he was finished with his work.

After skirting the perimeter of the lot to avoid the brawl, Drake approached the bar entrance. A few of the onlookers glanced in his direction, but the attraction of the ongoing violence ensured that it was only a passing interest. If history was any indicator, this would be the first of many fights tonight. In that case, his shorter jacket would come in handy. People would notice his P37 and be much less inclined to give him trouble.

The moment he opened the door, his ears were assaulted by the roar of virtually tuneless music blasting out from ancient speakers, the distorted sound competing against a cacophony of crude shouts and raucous laughter to produce a hellish symphony. Scarcely had he stepped inside when a security guard placed a massive hand firmly on his chest. He was a full head taller than Drake and bore the scars of countless brawls.

"No weapons," he stated.

Drake reached into his pocket and produced a twenty note. "And I need a place to sit."

The guard snatched the twenty in a well-practiced movement, then let out a sharp whistle. Within seconds, a young woman in a short skirt and bustier bounded up, her bright smile and pleasant demeanor a stark contrast to just about everything else in the place.

"Get this guy a table," the man ordered.

The girl regarded him with an exaggerated frown. "It wouldn't kill you to ask nicely, you know." Before he could reply, she spun on her heels and headed briskly away. Drake was forced to move quickly to catch up.

The interior of Mable's Haven was exactly as one might expect of such a place: just a vast open room with a few tables lined up along the left hand side near a concrete dance floor. Adjacent to this was a small stage and a booth from where a young man was playing the ear-splitting tunes. Away on the other side of the room was a round cage. This was what really brought in the crowd. Already more than a hundred people were gathered in this area, most of them busy placing their bets for the upcoming fights. A long bar ran down the middle, separating the cage side from the dance floor.

With the fights due to start very soon, the tables were mostly empty. The girl showed him to one in a corner and then moved quickly away. Another girl, this one a bit older and wearing a simple pair of jeans and a t-shirt, arrived a few seconds later.

"You hungry?" she asked.

"Is the food here still good?"

She shrugged. "About as good as you'll get in these parts."

"A roast beef sandwich, then," he replied. "And clean water…in a bottle." He slid a few notes over the table, making sure there was a bit extra included. No one was served here unless they paid in advance. And without a tip, you could be waiting a long time.

The girl snatched up the bills and hurried away, leaving Drake to take a long and careful look around. No one seemed to be paying any attention to him, though he knew that could change in a second once the fights were in full swing. The combination of violence and too much drink invariably brought out the worst in people.

He had spent quite a bit of time in this area. Set on the very edge of the border separating the provinces of Aurora and Jericho, there had been good work to be found during the first few years of his exile. Lots of black market goods had passed through here, which in turn meant lots of thieves and bandits. Catching that kind of scum was easy money. They never ran hard, and once you cornered them, they just gave up. They knew they could buy their way out of trouble. Whoever they had stolen from was more interested in recovering their goods than seeing justice done. Eventually, though, the magistrate had caught wind of it and decided to run all the hawkers off. From then on, bounties were paid directly to the royal treasuries, and runners were jailed...or worse. Drake wondered if Velma Chase had ever understood, or even cared about, how much more dangerous she had made things around here.

Just as his food arrived, frenzied cheers erupting from the direction of the cage told him that the fights were about to start. Cage fighting was a brutal sport, and someone died in one almost every night. It was illegal, of course. Not that the authorities really cared very much if a bunch of provincials beat one another to death. Once in a while there would be a raid, just to show the people who was in charge. But following that, nothing was ever taken any further.

The food wasn't as good as Drake remembered, and he shoved the sandwich away when it was still only half eaten. They used to have real beef here, not the processed garbage that most other places served. It looked like beef, even smelled like beef, but in reality tasted like dried up old leather. A memory of how delicious the recent manga juice had been drew a smile. Soon, now, all of this would be nothing but a bad dream.

He was still imagining a new life in the lower city when, just a few minutes later, a sudden sharp pain in his stomach made him gasp. This was quickly followed by a burning sensation in his chest. Placing a hand to his brow, he could feel large beads of sweat forming. This shouldn't be happening, not even if the food was badly spoiled. Something else was wrong – something that his mana was struggling hard to fight off. His hand moved to his weapon, and he forced himself to his feet. If this were a spell, he would have sensed it.

Drake spotted the waitress on the far side of the room with her back against the bar, waiting for an order. He started toward her, but after only a few steps his strength drained away and he fell to his knees. From behind, he heard laughter.

"Looks like he's had enough," said a man.

"Shut up," a female voice responded. "He's got a gun. See?"

Looking back, he saw two men in dark suits closing in on him. He tried to free his P37, but a fresh spasm of pain sent him the rest of the way to the floor. A moment later, two pairs of hands lifted him roughly to his feet and began dragging him along. Drake wanted to struggle, but his limbs would not obey his commands. The heat in his chest was increasing, and his eyesight was failing. Whatever poison they had used, it was incredibly strong.

He barely heard the feral shouts of the spectators as they passed near the cage. Not that any of them would interfere. They would allow him to be abducted and never give it another thought. By now, he could see virtually nothing.

It was as if his eyes had been shrouded by the densest fog imaginable. Only a crash of the bar door slamming behind them and the feel of the brisk night air on his face told him that they were now outside.

He then heard a screeching of tires and the sound of a sliding door being yanked open.

"Let's go," said a gruff voice just ahead.

The two men hurled him into the back of what he imagined to be a cargo van. The floor was bare metal, and the air inside smelled of oil and wood.

"Make sure he doesn't slide around. Boss says he's to get there in one piece."

The door slammed shut, and a strong pair of hands pressed down on his chest.

"He's in bad shape," said the man holding him. "You sure we didn't give him too much?"

The van lurched forward.

"How should I know?" The answer came from the front. "I just used what I had."

Drake tried to gauge his surroundings. Three men; two in the front and one with him in the back. They had taken his weapon. And if the poison wasn't meant to kill him, he would recover. But how long would that take? Whoever had planned this must have known about his resistance – which meant they would probably also know the proper dosage needed to keep him immobilized. Luckily, he was still conscious, though the pain in his chest was making him almost wish that he weren't.

He could feel that they were pulling onto the highway heading west. He went over in his mind what lay in that direction. They were on the border, so that meant just more taverns and black market warehouses. Nothing there to tell him where they might be going or who these men were working for. Though he did have a couple of good guesses.

He tried to speak, but his tongue was swollen and his throat almost closed, and after about five minutes he gave up trying. He should have been more cautious. If Troi had been infiltrated, they might possibly have known he would come here first. *Never be predictable* – that was hawker rule number one. Followed closely by *Never let your guard down*. He had broken both of them. A huge mistake. And if he didn't shake off the poison soon enough, it could easily be his last.

"What the hell is that?" shouted the driver.

Drake was sent sliding hard into the back of the seat in front as the van screeched to a halt. A second later, he felt the vehicle bounce up and down in reaction to all three men rapidly scrambling to get outside. This was followed by the click of weapons and the scraping of hard shoes on pavement.

"Where the hell did he go?" one of the men growled

Hellfire! The familiar scent reached Drake first, and then the lights dancing in his eyes from outside confirmed it: there was a mage out there. And one powerful enough to cast hellfire. He knew what was about to happen even before the first shot rang out. All firing at once, the men emptied their weapons in mere seconds.

He could hear them still scrambling to reload when a calm voice said, "Are you gentlemen quite done?"

A short, high-pitched hiss was rapidly overtaken by a great whoosh of flames. Instantly, the inside of the van became overpoweringly hot. Drake tried once again to move but was still immobilized by the poison. The screams of the dying men sent a chill down his spine. Hellfire was just about as painful a death as one could imagine. *Poor bastards*, he thought. He had only seen it used once, but the contorted scream seared into the victim's features was still clear in his memory. His P37 could create it in very small bursts, but anything more than that and his weapon would shatter to pieces. Hellfire was just too powerful.

The heat continued to intensify. The men were now silent. Dead, he assumed.

"I think maybe I went a bit too far," came the same calm voice. "And you are going to be quite a load to carry."

Drake was dragged from the van. His eyesight was starting to improve somewhat, allowing him to see a hazy image of the man tugging him along. His features, though, were still impossible to make out.

"I should have parked closer," the man complained, grunting heavily with each step.

After a couple of minutes, Drake was bundled into the seat of a car.

"I'm not sure what it was they gave you, but I do need you to be calm for a while," he said. "So please forgive me for this."

The moment the words had been spoken, Drake felt as if a large hammer had struck him right between the eyes.

Total blackness immediately followed.

CHAPTER SEVEN

The wind felt nice on Drake's face, raising memories of driving Cal with the top down. It was a simple pleasure, but one of the few experiences since his exile that was sure to bring about a rare moment of joy.

Such pleasant thoughts vanished in a flash as his eyes popped open. He could see clearly now. Sure enough, he was traveling along in Cal, but only as a passenger. Someone else was doing the driving. A man in a long blue coat and well-fitted black pants and shirt was leaning back in the seat, his hand resting lightly on the wheel. At once he recognized the face: Bane. Instinctively, Drake's hand flew to his weapon.

"Your gun is in the back seat," Bane remarked almost absently.

"What the hell is going on?" Drake demanded.

"I'm taking you to Fisk," he replied, smiling.

Drake looked to the back. Yes, his P37 was right there, and it was within fairly easy reach. "Is that right?" he said.

"Yes, and before you think about doing anything foolish, check your left leg."

Drake reached down and felt something that had been

wrapped around his thigh. His heart sank. He knew precisely what it was. "What's the range?" he asked.

Bane shrugged. "No more than twenty feet, I should think. Never really bothered finding out for sure. Oh, by the way, that one has a deadman's switch attached. You know... just in case you try to get clever."

Drake had used these before: mana tethers. If the runner moved too far away, the device automatically exploded. And if he was being told the truth about this one having a deadman's trigger, simply killing Bane and disabling it was not an option.

"What's Fisk paying you?" he demanded.

Bane chuckled, shaking his head. "You think you can offer more?"

"Yes."

"You know I can't do that. What good is a hawker if you can't trust them to complete their mission?"

"But I thought Fisk wanted me dead."

"He does. But I'm not an assassin, so he'll have to do that job himself." He gave Drake a sideways grin. "It is a genuine pleasure to meet you, by the way. You're a true legend. A pity it can't be under better circumstances."

Drake reached into the back and retrieved his weapon. "I hope you don't mind."

"By all means. It won't fire. I disabled the mana chamber."

A simple fix, he thought. And a mistake for Bane to be free with that information. Unless he was lying, of course. But the man was not known for being careless, even though he looked far too young to have fully earned his impressive reputation. Drake noted that the only weapon he appeared to be carrying was a large knife on his belt. Not that Bane needed anything else. His magic was all the weaponry he required.

"Is it true that the men of the royal guard have a vex crystal inserted into their chests?" Bane asked.

Drake cocked his head. Only a counted few people knew of this. It was how they channeled mana and what gave them certain types of resistance. Normally he would deny it. But right now, he wanted to keep Bane talking. "A small one, yes," he admitted. "Where did you hear that?"

"You hear things at the College of Mages. It must hurt like hell. How do you tolerate it?"

"You get used to it."

Bane looked skeptical. "I suppose. All the same, it seems like a lot of trouble just for tough skin and some extra stamina."

"It's more than that, I promise you."

"I guess so. It certainly saved you from that poison those guys put in your food." He pointed to the glove box. "I almost forgot – Dorn said to tell you that the tracking device wasn't a tracking device at all."

"Is he still alive?"

Bane laughed. "Of course he is. Why would I kill Dorn? Seeing as how you were with me, he was more than happy to let me take Cal. Good thing, too. I would have hated to steal her."

Drake breathed a sigh of relief and then opened the glove box. Inside was the switch, together with a bundle of wires wrapped around a small metal orb. A bomb.

"He said it was a damn good thing you got him to check it out," Bane continued. "Said it would have killed anyone sitting in the passenger's seat before they knew what had happened. Oh, yeah, and he also disabled anything else Troi could have used to track you. Not that it matters now."

A frown formed as Drake mulled over this news. Why would Xavier plant a bomb? Killing the prince would not help him in the slightest. Of course, it was always possible that Xavier knew nothing about it. One thing was certain: when he got out of this mess, he would definitely be looking to beat some answers out of the dear captain. His frown deepened. On the other hand, getting out of this mess might prove to be damn near impossible. Bane was unlikely to slip up. And Fisk was known to be both brutal and highly efficient when it came to killing.

"Where are you taking me?" he asked.

"Not far," Bane replied. "We'll get there in a few hours. So relax."

There was little else he could do at present but just sit there and allow himself to be delivered to a man who wanted him dead. His eyes ran carefully over the rival hawker, taking in every detail. Youthful looking or not, he was certain now that Bane's reputation was well deserved. Which would make killing him much more satisfying, if the opportunity came.

For a time, the drive was made in utter silence, aside from Bane occasionally humming to himself. After crossing the border, Drake had expected them to veer toward the outer province of Zanabar. Instead, they turned northeast into Arbor. This was the region where most of Vale's produce was grown, and Troi made sure it was very well guarded indeed. In fact, there were more royal guards stationed here than in the city itself. Added to this, the magistrate imposed direct control over all law enforcement measures in the area. If Fisk were conducting business here, he was either insane or even better connected than Drake could have guessed.

Mile after mile of fences charged with mana ran along both sides of the road. Behind these were the fields that nearly every soul living in Vale depended on for food. Above the fields, mana streams burned brightly as they delivered power to the hundreds of facilities responsible for the maintenance and harvesting of the crops. Working here was a good job, if you could get it. At least you never went hungry, even though the labor could be back-breaking at times. Smart agro-workers had small fields of their own, usually hidden away somewhere in the outer provinces. The seeds here were far better than those the poor could acquire, if indeed they could find any at all. Though the soil wasn't nearly as fertile outside of Arbor and the yield smaller, one could still make enough money to retire in relative comfort from the income of a single field. Unless, of course, you were caught. Selling black market produce was about as serious a crime as murder.

"I heard once that the ancients had fields like this larger than the whole of Vale itself," Bane remarked offhandedly, breaking the silence. "Ever wonder what it was like back then?"

"Not really. What good would that do?"

"I don't know. I just wonder sometimes how it would be if everyone had enough to eat. You know, like if you didn't have to be born in Troi just to get ahead in life."

"From what I've read, the ancients were warlike barbarians who destroyed their world. I don't think I'd want to go there."

Bane shot him a sideways look. "That's what we've all been told. But what if it's not true?"

Drake straightened. "Have *you* ever been to the barrier?"

"No."

"Well, *I* have. Believe me – it's true. Beyond Vale there is nothing but wasteland."

Why anyone would doubt this was impossible for Drake to understand. Even so, some still did. They imagined the world of the ancients to have been some kind of paradise, and that the lessons all children were taught were propaganda and lies. But he had seen the devastation with his own eyes.

Nothing lived outside the barrier; there was only sand and dust as far as the eye could see. The wars had ravaged the entire planet, and only Vale brought any hope of redemption – the hope that the high mages would eventually find a way to heal the land…one day in the indiscernible future.

After a time the road narrowed, taking them past a succession of large warehouses and open lots filled with farming equipment. The smell of chemicals was in the air, and even over the wind coming in through the window Drake could hear the buzz and whir of machinery.

They eventually pulled in behind a tall silver silo where three other vehicles were parked nearby. Bane got out of Cal and waited for Drake to do the same.

"Before we go in," he began, "I want you to know that I really am sorry about this. It's just a job, after all."

Disgusted with himself as much as with Bane, Drake did not bother replying. How many times had those very same words come out of his own mouth? How many times had a runner pleaded to be let go, and he had ignored them? Many deserved their fate. But some did not, and he knew the difference. He knew, and didn't care.

Bane led him around the silo to where a steel trapdoor was set in the ground. He stomped on this three times and waited. Drake scanned the area, spotting three cameras, one of which was trained directly on the trapdoor. The deep clunk of a mechanism turning sounded, and a rush of air exited from around its edges.

Bane stepped back and gestured to a recess in the steel. "I think I'll let you open it."

When Drake did not move, he took another threatening step back and raised an eyebrow. "Do you really want to find out the range of that tether?"

Drake's jaw tightened as he resisted the urge to make

what would almost certainly be a suicidal jump on his captor. There was always a trigger, and Bane was sure to have his at the ready. Reaching down, with a great effort he raised the heavy door up on its hinges, revealing a stone stairway.

Drake entered with Bane just a few feet behind him. The steps ended in a long passageway that split left and right. Bane pointed left, and they continued this way until reaching a gray metal door. Through this was a small room with three cages at the far end, each just large enough to hold one man. Bane nodded toward the cage in the middle.

"You'll need to wait in here," he said. "I have to collect my bounty first." He held out his hand. "Your weapon, if you don't mind."

With little option, Drake gave him his P37 and entered the cage. Once he was secured inside, he watched Bane place the gun on a small table in the corner and then walk over to the door. A wave of panic struck him.

"Where are you going?" he called out. "The collar!"

Bane gave him a sheepish grin. "Don't worry. It's not real."

Drake fumed. "You son of a bitch."

"Sorry," he replied. "I hope you don't hold it against me."

The moment the door closed, Drake ripped the tether away. He then set about examining the lock to the cage. It was a good one. Even so, with a few simple tools, he might have had a chance of picking it. As it was, though, he had nothing suitable on him. Not a damn thing! And the bars were way too thick to bend. He gave them a sharp kick before sliding to the floor. He would definitely be killing Bane the first chance he got. Though he had to admit, the anger raging inside was as much against himself. He should have seen through such a basic ruse. He was slipping. Now he needed to get sharp in a big hurry if he was going to make it out of here alive.

After about an hour, the door opened and Fisk entered the room. He was dressed in a tan shirt and black pants, with a black fedora covering his round head.

"I was surprised to hear you were caught so easily," he remarked, his voice deep and rumbling. "Bane was a bit disappointed, given your reputation."

"Did you come here to gloat?"

"Not at all," he replied, waving his hand. "I just wanted to check that Bane was not attempting some sort of deception. He is known for that…as I gather you discovered for yourself."

The taunt stung Drake, and although he tried to conceal this fact, he knew that it showed. "What's in this for you?" he asked. "Because if it's money you want…"

Fisk shook his head. "I'm afraid you've become involved in something way beyond your understanding. There is absolutely nothing you can offer that will change what is about to happen."

Drake could see the resolve in his eyes. "Will you at least tell me who hired you?"

"Why? It will only anger you. I was given specific instructions. So no. I will not be telling you anything." He turned to the door. "But don't worry. I will see that it is quick and painless."

Drake let out a roar of anger the moment the door closed.

No, stay calm, he told himself, after a few seconds of venting his rage. *You need to focus. There has to be a way out of this.*

He examined the lock again. If he had his P37, dealing with it would be a simple matter. A mage would be able to open it easily enough too. As it was, the vex crystal in his chest all but prevented him from using magic in a traditional way. He concentrated instead on drawing mana inside himself. The heat in his chest began to build, but even after trying four times to utilize this, the lock remained stubbornly secure.

Bracing his back against the rear of the cage, he used both feet to push against it with all his strength. And again, with no result. He was about to resign himself to the fact that there was no possible way out of his situation when the crackle of gunfire drifted in from outside the room. This quickly got louder, and was accompanied by the shouts of men barking orders.

Someone was attacking the facility.

Less than a minute later, the door flew open and a man in dark blue fatigues rushed in, his rifle sweeping across the room. On spotting Drake, he glanced over his shoulder and shouted: "I got one in here."

Moving closer, the man leveled his rifle and took aim.

He never got to pull the trigger. A blue streak of energy struck him in the very center of his back, sending him crashing into the front of Drake's cage and then sliding to the floor. He was still falling when Bane ran in, his hands glowing with mana.

"If you promise to behave, I'll let you out," he said.

"What's happening?" Drake demanded.

"Look, we can discuss that now and end up dead. Or we can run. Your choice."

Deeply suspicious, Drake wanted to press Bane into explaining why he was prepared to release him, but more gunfire told him that now was not the time.

"Just open the door," he snapped.

"Not until you promise."

Drake grumbled. "I promise. Now get on with it."

Bane flashed a grin and then simply touched the lock with his forefinger. The cage door instantly swung wide.

Drake dashed over to the table where his P37 still lay.

"I don't suppose you were lying about disabling the mana chamber?" he asked. He checked the clip where six normal rounds were housed. It was empty.

"No. That much was true."

With a sigh, Drake snatched up the rifle dropped by the dead man. "You know a way out of here?" he asked.

"Of course."

"Then lead on."

Bane wagged his finger. "Remember. You promised to behave."

"I'll behave," he confirmed, but added as a silent afterthought: *For now.* It was obvious he had a much better chance of getting out of here alive with a man like Bane at his side. So, as much as he wanted to put a bullet into the guy's brain, he had to restrain himself.

They left the room together, Bane crouching low, Drake standing more upright and with his rifle pointing down the passage. They passed three bodies along the way, one wearing the same uniform as the man Bane had killed, the other two in tailored suits – probably Fisk's men.

The steps leading up to the entrance looked clear, but Bane shook his head. "There's an army out there," he said. "We wouldn't get five yards."

They continued straight on until reaching another door, this one slightly ajar. Voices could be heard inside. Bane looked over his shoulder and winked.

The glow around his hands intensified. In a single fluid motion, he kicked the door fully open and let loose a streak of blue lightning. Drake could see three uniformed men kneeling behind a pile of crates, their focus down a hallway on the far side of the room. The spell struck two of them simultaneously, burning fist-sized holes in their backs. The third man swung his rifle around, but Drake put a bullet in his heart well before he could aim.

"Nice shot," Bane told him.

Bullets pinged off the wall from down the hall, forcing them to lie flat.

"Aren't those your people shooting at us?" Drake asked.

Bane raised an eyebrow. "*My* people? What in Vale would make you think that?"

"Don't play games," he warned.

"I wouldn't dream of it. Let me handle this."

After crawling away from the line of fire, Bane raised himself up and waved his arms in a circular motion. In response, the crates the men had been hiding behind levitated a foot in the air.

"Get ready to charge," he instructed.

Drake got to his knees just as the crates erupted into flames and flew like meteors straight down the corridor. As soon as the gunfire stopped, Bane leapt to his feet and ran full tilt behind the advancing inferno. Drake followed close behind.

At the end of the passage was a large room stacked high with boxes and crates, most of them clearly marked as containing perishable items. It looked like Fisk was bold enough – or foolish enough – to run a black market operation right here under the nose of the magistrate *and* the royal guard. Six men were scattered about the room, two rolling on the ground with their clothes on fire and the rest busy scrambling around trying to find cover.

From behind, Drake could hear more men shouting. In the far corner of the room he could see a ladder attached to the wall. This led up to a metal hatch. Barely had his eyes settled on it when pain shot through his arm as a bullet grazed him from his right. He turned and fired, hitting his assailant in the leg. An angry growl slipped out. The wound wasn't too bad, but it hurt like hell.

Bane released a short burst of light that exploded at the feet of two others standing near the ladder. Such was the brilliance of this that Drake had to look quickly away to avoid being blinded. More gunfire reverberated off the walls, coming from just inside the passage leading into the room. Bane took off toward the ladder, casting more bursts of vivid light behind him. Drake spat a curse while chasing after him, barely covering his eyes in time.

Glancing back after reaching the ladder and beginning to climb, he saw a long line of uniformed men now pouring into the room. At the same time, Fisk's men were stumbling about aimlessly, shouting with pain and rubbing frantically at their inflamed eyes. It was only about twenty feet to the top, but at this moment it seemed to Drake more like a hundred. Bane had already reached the hatch and was crawling out. Then, just as Drake was preparing to do the same, he heard a voice ordering him to stop.

"Like hell I will," he muttered, his fingers closing around the top rung for a final pull up.

A violent burning sensation, like being stung by a giant man-sized hornet, struck him in the thigh even before he heard the shot fired. The pain of the impact raced up through his body, attacking his muscles with such force that he immediately felt his grip on the ladder slipping away. He was on the very point of falling when Bane reached down and seized hold of his wrist.

"You need to pull yourself up," Bane told him, grunting loudly. "I'm not strong enough to lift you on my own."

It was all the reprieve Drake needed. The pain was still there, but the sudden shock to his system had already passed. Regaining his hold, he scrambled through the opening just as a second shot bounced off the wall below the top rung, missing his trailing foot by inches.

Once out in the open, he looked around. They were close to the back of a wide wooden building about one hundred feet away from the silo. Voices carried, telling him that several more men were gathered on the other side quite near to the entrance – too many of them to confront head on without his P37. In the near distance, a line of cars was speeding away, with red magistrate vehicles in close pursuit. There was no sign of Cal.

"Can you walk?" Bane asked, shutting the hatch and then melting the hinge with a short burst of mana. That would hold their attackers, but only for a short time. And without Cal, Drake knew they were still trapped.

"I'll be fine," he said. Though the rifle had been powerful enough to penetrate the protection his vex crystal provided, he was relieved to see that the wound was shallow.

"Good. Then you drive."

As he spoke, Bane opened a small back door to the building. Inside was Cal. A wave of relief washed over Drake. Rapidly, he stripped off his shirt and tied it around his leg. The pain was still bad, but becoming increasingly manageable. The scratch on his arm had already stopped bleeding. Another vex crystal benefit.

He eased into the driver's seat and fired the engine. The large double door at the front was closed and locked, but that was no obstacle. Not for Cal. Bane was already seated and strapping himself in. Good thing, too. Drake would have seriously considered leaving him behind. *On the other hand, the guy did save me*, he acknowledged. But why? That was a question for when they were well away from this place.

He tossed his P37 over to Bane. "Fix it." Without

waiting for a response, he slammed Cal into gear and pressed hard down on the accelerator.

The doors were ripped from their hinges as they flew out of the building. Although taken momentarily by surprise, the cluster of men gathered at the front quickly recovered, and assaulted them with a volley of fire. Drake grinned as the rounds pinged and whizzed off Cal's bodywork. It would take a lot more than anything they were armed with to get through. From the rear view he could see two men getting into one of the few remaining vehicles. He slid onto the main road, and within seconds Cal was racing at over one hundred and sixty. The magistrate officers had no chance of catching them, that much was certain. Even so, they would need to get the hell out of Arbor and into the outer provinces as soon as possible.

The sun was sinking low when Drake pulled off onto a narrow road that split two fields. He touched the yellow panel on the console and a map of the area popped up on the screen. "Find us a way out of here," he ordered Bane.

"Good thing my father removed all the tracking devices," he remarked. "If he hadn't, they would know exactly where we are."

"Your father?" Drake shook his head, hardly able to believe what he was hearing.

Bane looked amused at his confusion. "Yes. Do you think Dorn would have given Cal to just anyone?"

"When we get out of here, you have a lot of explaining to do," Drake told him.

"You know, I've heard that quite a few times today," he responded with a grin.

"Yeah. I bet you have."

CHAPTER EIGHT

I t was well past midnight before they crossed into Bolivar province. Avoiding the magistrate's officers and the royal guard had not been so easy at first, and only the fact that Drake was familiar with their methods allowed him to eventually outmaneuver them. Once safely out of Arbor, he was then able to use Cal's vastly superior speed to put them well beyond the range of any search.

He changed the camouflage setting to make Cal less recognizable, then started toward an old hawker complex he had lived in for a time a few years ago. Bane was quiet throughout, apparently perfectly at ease with what was happening. The revelation that he was Dorn's son was still troubling Drake. He rarely placed trust in people, but Dorn had been an exception.

They pulled into the parking lot of an outdoor market. It was too early yet for anyone to be about or to find anywhere to stay.

"You need to get that bullet out," Bane told him.

Drake untied the makeshift bandage. The bullet was resting in the folds of the cloth, and the wound was already

97

starting to close. "No need," he said, tossing the round out of the window.

Bane shook his head in wonder. "I'm starting to understand why the royal guard is so feared." He handed Drake his P37. "I think you'll find it's working just fine now."

Drake checked the weapon to be sure this was true, and then pointed it straight at Bane's head. "Now tell me why I shouldn't just blow your damn head off."

Bane seemed unmoved by the threat. "Well, let's see. I did save your life. *That's* a reason."

"I wouldn't have needed saving if you hadn't brought me there in the first place." He noticed the mana building up in Bane. "If you think you're fast enough, go right ahead."

"It was just a job," he explained, though not making any attempt to release the mana. "Are you telling me you would have done it differently? Be honest. You aren't angry with *me*. You're angry with yourself for being careless."

He was right, of course. But that only made Drake want to pull the trigger even more. "Then why save me after going through all the trouble of capturing me in the first place?" he demanded.

"Because I need you to help me complete another job I've taken on."

"What kind of job?"

"Same as yours: finding Prince Salazar."

Drake stiffened. "Who hired you?"

Bane chuckled. "You know the rules. A good hawker never reveals the identity of his employer. But who hired me isn't what should be important to you right now. What should be of more interest is that I already know where the prince is being held."

"Bullshit. If you know where he is, why not go get him yourself?"

"Because he knows you...you're old friends. He's more likely to run away from me. And the last thing I want is to accidentally harm him."

There was sound logic behind this reasoning. But not enough. Drake shook his head. "Sorry, but I'm doing this alone. Now get out."

Bane's smile never faded for an instant. "That's fine...if you think you can find him. Why do you think I brought you to Fisk first? I needed a way back in. And you, my friend, provided this."

The thin hiss of the P37 charging cut through the air. "Don't insult my intelligence," Drake snapped. "You work for Fisk."

"Sure. Fisk hires me from time to time, but I am *not* one of his lackeys. He had the information I required, and so I traded it for you." There was a long pause before he added: "Who do you think informed the magistrate about Fisk's little operation?"

"You?"

"How else was I going to get you back out? Granted, the magistrate's men were a bit more enthusiastic than I'd anticipated. But it worked, all the same."

"Then who hired Fisk to kill me?"

Bane shrugged. "How should I know? I told you before, he only hires me from time to time."

Xavier and the magistrate had both claimed that Bane was in Fisk's employ. But then, Xavier possibly wanted him dead. For sure *someone* had planted the bomb in Cal.

"If you think you can find the prince first, then by all means go ahead," Bane continued. "But seeing as how I know where he is – or at least, where he *was* – and you do not..."

Drake gritted his teeth, his finger still itching to pull the trigger. At this close range, even the powerful protection that Bane was getting from his mana would not save him. "Okay," he finally conceded. "We'll work together. For now. But I promise you, get in my way and it will be the last thing you ever do."

"Fair enough." Bane glanced outside to where a truck was pulling into the lot. "Now, if you wouldn't mind lowering your weapon, maybe we should find a place where we can discuss a plan of action."

Drake holstered his P37 and fired Cal's engine. He knew of a lodging house a short distance away that would be open soon. Which was just as well. Fatigue was creeping into his joints and muscles; he badly needed to rest awhile. That Bane still looked fresh and full of energy made him dislike the man even more.

As he pulled onto the road, the world seemed as it did on that first day of exile: dark and sinister. The life of a hawker was dangerous, but at least it was comprehensible. They ran, you chased. You were in charge of your own destiny. Trust was something you never needed, not when you worked alone. This was fortunate, because he had quickly learned you couldn't trust anyone.

"Tell me one thing," Drake said. "Did your father know about any of this?"

Bane was clearly surprised at the question. "Hell, no! And if you ever want revenge, telling him would be the easiest way to get it. He thinks the world of you. *The only decent man in Vale*, I think were his exact words. If he knew what I did, he'd never speak to me again. It's bad enough I became a hawker."

This made Drake feel somewhat better. After a short pause, he asked, "Why did you leave the College of Mages?"

"A kind way of saying it might be that I was asked to go. The truth? I was expelled."

"Why?"

He gave a lopsided grin. "They said I couldn't be trusted."

"*That* I can believe."

The lodge opened a few minutes after they arrived, allowing Drake to quickly book a room. He then checked Cal's trunk. If Bane knew anything about the panel containing the case and the money, he certainly hadn't touched it. His sword was still where he had put it as well. Satisfied, he headed for the room.

Once inside, he immediately collapsed on the bed. Through weary eyes he watched Bane cast a protection ward over the door and then settle into a tattered chair on the other side of the room. Wards were complex, and most mages didn't possess the power or the knowledge to create them. There was definitely more to Dorn's son than met the eye. But for now, questions would have to wait. His body was near its limit, and the road ahead would be long and dangerous.

His dreams were filled with painful visions of his trial. The condemnation in the eyes of his fellow guards and the deep sorrow on the face of King Nedar were all too vivid. But most of all it was the voice of Lenora that threatened to break his heart – the way she had pleaded to go with him, and the fury she'd unleashed when he refused.

He woke in a cold sweat. Bane was standing at the window with a look of deep concern on his face.

"What is it?" Drake asked.

"Trouble."

Drake shot up from the bed. From outside, he could already hear screams of terror. At first he couldn't see what was causing the commotion. Then, after a moment, it became horribly clear as a hulking figure lumbered out from behind a building on the other side of the street.

Its pale green flesh was covered with what appeared from a distance to be scales, though in reality Drake knew them to be simply deep ridges. Just above a pair of black soulless eyes, two sharply pointed horns protruded from a narrow brow. The eyes shifted menacingly around as though searching for prey. Then, flailing its taloned arms about wildly and with thick globules of saliva dripping from its fanged maw, the creature let out an ear-rending roar.

"Hellspawn," spat Drake.

"I thought they'd all been killed," said Bane, a hint of fear in his voice.

"So did I."

"What do we do?"

Drake could not look away. "Nothing. The royal guard will be here soon enough to deal with it. We need to stay out of sight."

The hellspawn had stopped directly front of the lodge and was sniffing the air. Slowly, it turned its head to face the building.

"Your ward!" Drake shouted. "Get rid of it." When Bane did not move, he shoved him roughly over to the door. "Do it now!"

Snapping back into the moment, Bane waved his arms in a wide circle. The hellspawn was moving toward their room, still sniffing and with ever-increasing drool pouring from its mouth. A second later the ward was gone. Even so, the creature continued to move closer. It was only then that Drake realized why.

"Stop!"

Bane looked at him with confusion, his hands glowing with mana. But before Drake could say anything further, the hellspawn let out a feral cry and charged. In an instinctive reaction, he threw himself forward hard and low, wrapping his arms around Bane's waist and pulling him down. They hit the floor together in an untidy heap. An instant later, the creature smashed its way through the door, its massive body tearing the frame completely away from the building.

Both men scrambled to their feet just a couple of yards away from where the beast was standing. Bane let loose a spear of fire, but it had no effect whatsoever, dissipating the instant it made contact. The hellspawn swiped a huge claw at him in response, forcing Bane to jump awkwardly back. Drake seized on this distraction. Ducking low, he made a dive straight between the creature's legs and clear through to the other side. He was on his feet in a flash. As he ran, he could hear Bane continuing with what he knew to be a useless assault.

Cal was parked a short distance away from what had once been their door. Drake lengthened his stride. He had to hurry; otherwise Bane would be torn apart. He reached the car just as he heard the mage let out a terrible scream. Glancing back, he saw that the hellspawn had him by the leg and was holding him upside down like a rag doll. His arms flailed wildly as he bucked and jerked futilely against the beast's enormous strength.

Hissing a curse, he drew the P37 and fired three short bursts into the beast's back. The creature turned, flinging Bane into the wall like a child angrily discarding an unwanted toy. Its black eyes, glittering with malevolence, were now focused on Drake. Holstering his gun, he opened the trunk and quickly retrieved his sword. Once free from its scabbard, the soft glow emanating from the blade radiated power. But on this occasion it was cold steel he needed, not the mana with which it was infused.

The ground shook under the weight of the creature's rapid strides. Drake hadn't fought with a sword for quite some time, though he practiced often. Still, fighting an actual opponent was different, particularly one as dangerous as this.

The hellspawn struck out, its long talons threatening to rip him apart. Drake ducked low and countered. His blade sliced into the creature's left thigh, and it let out a howl as green blood spilled from the wound. The strike would have completely removed a human's leg, but hellspawn hide was as tough and resilient as the thickest leather.

It lunged in again, forcing Drake to roll away. But this time he wasn't quite fast enough. Caught by the shoulder, he was thrown violently into Cal's rear door. The impact forced every bit of breath from his lungs and sent pain shooting through his entire body. Gasping for air, he thrust the blade up, and the tip penetrated to the left of the beast's gullet as it moved in to finish him. Though this drew a fresh dribble of green blood and caused the hellspawn to step a pace back, the injury was still minor; not nearly serious enough to give Drake sufficient time to recover.

He tried to spin away, but a pair of massive hands hefted him up and over the beast's head. Drake slashed at its arms, but this only served to infuriate it to an even greater pitch. With another mighty roar of anger, it hurled him more than twenty feet into the lot. After thudding to the ground, as he slid along a few feet from the sheer force of the throw, he felt the unforgiving concrete tearing great strips away from his jacket. A thought flashed through his mind that at least this was sparing his flesh. But then he came to an abrupt stop and he struck his head. Immediately, he felt blood trickling from his scalp.

He tried to look up to see where the hellspawn was, but everything around was temporarily a blur. Only the thud of heavy steps advancing told him that his attacker was almost upon him. He struggled to his knees just as a dark shadow loomed. This was it, he thought. The beast would smash him to pulp before he had time to move any further.

Just as Drake was resigning himself to his fate, a sizzle cut through the air, and he caught the familiar smell of hellfire. Renewed hope surged. Bane must have recovered, though he still obviously had no idea that his magical attacks would not harm the beast. Nonetheless, the hellfire had distracted it, allowing Drake precious seconds to scramble away and get to his feet. His sight was now clearing as well, and he could see that the hellspawn had turned fully around to once more advance on Bane. For the moment, its attention was focused entirely on the mage.

Drake flipped his sword around and picked the spot where he thought the creature's heart should be. Bane was still peppering it with fire, though with no more success than before. But at least it was keeping the hellspawn's attention. Drake charged on unsteady legs, very nearly toppling over twice in the process. He spanned the distance between them, and with his eyes still fixed firmly, mustering up every last ounce of strength, he sank the blade in.

The roar that the hellspawn let out this time seemed to engulf the entire street. It spun sharply, using the back of its hand to strike Drake on both the head and shoulder. The force of the second blow sent him crashing onto the hood of a small truck nearby, once again leaving him dazed and barely conscious. Sliding from the hood onto the ground, he lay there not knowing what would happen next. Either he or the beast was about to die. But which one?

And then he heard it: a beastly wail of agony followed by a single heavy thump. He *had* hit the mark.

A few moments later, he felt a hand on his shoulder. "Are you all right?" Bane asked.

It took a moment to reply. "I will be. Is it dead?"

"Yes. It's dead."

Drake knew they needed to leave the scene as fast as possible. The royal guard would arrive soon, and the last thing he wanted was for Xavier to know where he was. "Help me up," he said. "Quickly now."

"You need to stay put. Medics will be here soon. You need healing."

"I'll heal on my own. We need to get the hell out of here."

Catching on to his sense of urgency, Bane pulled him to his feet as gently as possible. Drake's right arm was hanging limply at his side, and his hair felt sticky with blood. Gritting his teeth, he staggered over to a nearby car and leaned his dislocated shoulder heavily against it. The shock as it popped back into place caused a grunt to slip out. But at least he could now move his arm again.

As his vision cleared more, he saw the hellspawn lying face down on the ground a few yards away, the sword still buried in its back. Bane helped him over to Cal, pausing to retrieve the sword and then to gather their belongings from the room. People were emerging from the surrounding buildings. Drake groaned. *So much for incognito.* They were pulling away just as a line of black vehicles approached from the west. Thankfully, they took no notice of Cal, instead heading straight into the lot where the hellspawn lay.

"Where the hell did that thing come from?" Bane asked, still clearly shaken from the experience.

"Beyond the barrier."

"That's ridiculous. Nothing can get through the barrier."

"Then where do *you* think it came from?"

Bane had no answer to that.

"They first appeared when I was a rookie in the royal guard," Drake told him.

Bane nodded. "I heard about them. But I thought they were all killed."

"They were. It took us weeks to hunt them all down. They killed twenty-four guards in the process before we figured out their weaknesses."

"What weaknesses?"

"You can't use mana," he explained. "They feed on it. Unfortunately for us, the P37 is a mana weapon. That's why your spells didn't work, and why it was attracted to your ward. I found out later that there had been other attacks. But those were a long time ago, before even my grandfather's day. We never found out why they came back...or how they got inside the barrier. All we know is that they come from the wasteland."

"How do you know that?"

"The high mages," he replied. "Said they could sense that they were not from Vale. So if they aren't from Vale, where else could they be from?" He reached down and turned on the vibraplayer.

Bane frowned. "You really want to listen to music?"

"No, I want to see if there was more than just the one. If so, the royal guard will broadcast an alert."

Drake could well remember how the hellspawn had wreaked havoc throughout the provinces. The royal guard searched for months trying to find out how they'd managed to enter Vale. In the end they'd assumed the creatures must have somehow tunneled a way beneath the barrier, though there was never any real proof of this. Nonetheless, that was the story they had told the public when wild rumors began to fly around that the creatures were actually the dead brought back to life by corrupted mana.

Bane would have been no more than a child at the time, so it was no wonder he knew little about them. The high mages had assured the public that the problem had been solved, and in time it had become nothing more than a story told among the veteran guards.

After an hour of listening, there were still no reports coming over the air, not even one mentioning the hellspawn he had killed. *They probably don't want people to panic*, Drake surmised. But something also told him this was a sign. A sign of what, he had no idea. All the same, too much was happening for it not to be connected somehow.

"You said you know where they're holding Prince Salazar?" he suddenly asked Bane.

"I know where they *were* keeping him," he replied. "Of course, they might have moved him since then."

"That's good enough."

As long as he knew from where they had started, Drake had ways of tracking someone. No doubt so did Bane. A good hawker didn't need much to go on. Between the two of them, they should have no problem at all.

The trouble would come when they found the prince. Once he was safe, Drake would be looking to settle accounts with whoever was trying to kill him. He glanced over at Bane. His demeanor had relaxed and he was settled into the seat, eyes fixed on the road ahead.

For the time being, he needed the younger man.

But the moment that was no longer the case...

CHAPTER NINE

Drake had considered starting at the warehouse he'd been shown at the magistrate's office. But naturally, Xavier would be expecting him to go there. And even if the captain were not the one trying to kill him, whoever else it might be could also know about it.

Aside from saying that it was somewhere in Antwerp province, Bane refused to reveal any further details regarding their destination. Not that Drake really blamed him. As far as he was concerned, the only value the guy had was this information. The second he was no longer useful, he would get rid of him. He sure as hell wasn't going to risk Bane claiming credit for returning the prince to Troi.

Wherever in Antwerp they were heading for, it would take them several days to get there. That being so, Drake thought it best they skirt the inner provinces to avoid detection. This route took them through the hills of Lancaster. Only a few years ago, this area had been prime grazing land for sheep and cattle. But even here, as with the rest of the outer regions of Vale, the sickness that plagued the lands was growing worse. Small patches of green only made the brown now covering most of Lancaster's gentle slopes even more pronounced. The houses they passed in the area were mostly abandoned, their occupants herding closer to the border of Pasdonia where food was easier to come by. It was the same in many other dying regions, particularly those in the north where the winters were harsher and fresh water scarcer. Naturally, this was leading to severe overcrowding in the places least affected by the sickness – which in turn led to resentment and violence.

"You think the high mages will ever find a way to heal Vale?" Bane asked, as they made camp near a patch of sickly looking trees just off the road.

"Sure they will," Drake replied. "One day."

"It doesn't look like it to me."

"Look, if it wasn't for the high mages, nothing would grow at all."

"That may be so, but you'd think they could have healed it by now."

Drake leaned back with his hands behind his head. The stars, unhindered by the light of mana streams, were clearly visible in this part of Vale. "You're a mage," he said. "You should know better than anyone how hard they try."

"We don't all learn restorative magic," he replied. "Only those born to it."

Drake knew this already. Being a high mage was definitely genetic, and the knowledge was passed from parent to child. All children with magical ability were tested to see if they could use restorative magic, but as far as he knew, only the children of high mages had ever been known to possess the gift. Even so, he had always assumed that all mages from the college would at least be familiar with it.

"So, you have no idea how it works?"

"I know the same thing we all know. High mages infuse

it into the mana strings. But how it's done, or where the power comes from…" He spread his hands. "Beats me."

"But you can heal, can't you?"

He gave a puckish grin. "Not really my thing. I was more a fire and lightning kind of guy."

"No surprise there."

"What about you? How'd you end up in the royal guard? You don't seem the type."

"What type is that?"

"You know…stuffy and proper."

Drake snorted. "If that's what you think, then you don't know the first thing about us."

"Then tell me."

Drake was becoming irritated. He didn't like talking about the guard. Even after so long, he felt as if he were betraying the brotherhood if he spoke about their inner workings.

"I was recruited," was all he chose to say.

"I thought you had to have a parent in the guard to even have a chance."

"Not always."

Bane waited nearly a minute for Drake to say something else. But he had no desire to carry on a conversation with this man.

Bane eventually lay down and let out a long breath. "Fine. Be that way."

He was right, Drake conceded. To his knowledge, he was the only person ever to be inducted who did not have a parent or some other relative already in either the guard or the magistrate's office. Like everything else in Vale, it was the circumstances of your birth that determined your life. Once your path was set, very seldom could you alter it. This restriction was the cause of most protests. But what could be done? There was only so much food to go around. And the high mages certainly earned the extra comforts they were afforded.

"Anyway, I'm not a royal guard anymore," he said after a lengthy pause. "So what does it matter?"

Bane sat up again. "You know, I really imagined you'd be a little more skeptical than you are. I mean, you've been on the inside. You know everything that goes on."

"Exactly! I've been there. And believe me, there is *nothing going on*. Nothing at all. There are no secret fields of crops hidden beneath Troi. Certainly no sinister plan to starve the people to death. You can forget those lies, and any of the other crazy theories that people are always coming up with. Now, if you're finished being annoying, I'd like to get some sleep."

"I've only just begun to be annoying," he said. "But I'll let you sleep for now."

Bane continued to pepper him with questions over the next two days, most of which Drake refused to answer. But it was more out of spite than the questions being too personal. He was still wary of the man. His youthful appearance and jovial nature did not discount the fact that he was a trained killer. He might claim not to be an assassin, but the many stories Drake had heard of his exploits couldn't all be exaggerations. One in particular he knew for a fact to be true.

Bane had tracked a group of bandits from the inner provinces to just shy of the barrier. Six men ran, and he delivered six bags of ashes back to his client. The magistrate even brought him in for questioning over that one. Not that she could really do anything. The law was clear in these matters. Make a run for it and you voluntarily gave up all your rights. A hawker could use any means he or she saw fit to capture you. And if you resisted, lethal force was permitted.

Hawkers might not be highly regarded by the magistrate, but their word was taken over a runner's every time.

When they reached Antwerp, it was as if they had stepped into a completely different world. Here, you needed a special permit if you wanted to take up residence. Parks had been built for travelers and for those from the city who wanted to enjoy the outdoors, and a subterranean railway ran from the center of the province all the way through to the outskirts of Troi. From one end to the other took only five hours, faster even than Cal could go.

Drake used to come here with his father from time to time to camp and hike. This was the one activity they'd enjoyed together, and the only time they ever spoke more than a few words to one another. Drake knew his father loved him, but he was a man of science – an engineer. People simply didn't make sense to him. He was far more at home among the various gadgets he invented than with his own family.

By mid-afternoon, they had reached the town of Narsil. As with most of the northern towns, it was quite a bit larger than those found in the southern regions. Its streets were decently maintained and the houses not nearly as dilapidated as dwellings usually found in the outer provinces. But then, most of the provincial industry was in this part of the north, whereas agriculture was centered in the south where the growing season was considerably longer.

Bane directed him to drive to the west side of town and park in front of a tavern called the Trail and Stone. There wasn't anything much of note in this area, just a few shops and a fueling station. Most of the industry was on the east side, where a tire plant was the main employer.

Bane sat quietly for a time, just staring at the tavern's front door. A few patrons left, one of whom was barely able to walk from too much drink.

"Is this the place?" Drake asked.

"The prince came here to escape," Bane replied. "Needless to say, he didn't make it."

"Then what are we waiting for?"

Two large men emerged and positioned themselves on either side of the entrance. "That," Bane said. "The club owner is in the back, locked in his office. We'll need a key to get in."

"I don't want a trail of bodies," Drake warned him.

"Whatever you might have heard, I don't kill indiscriminately."

"What about the men who captured me in the tavern? You could have taken them out without killing them."

Bane shrugged. "They might have identified me. And I wasn't entirely sure who they were working for. Anyway, it's not like *you're* so innocent. How many men have you killed?"

"That doesn't matter. I just don't want to be explaining a whole bunch of dead bodies when this is over."

Bane climbed out of the car. "I'll do my best."

Drake grumbled. This would not go well. The magistrate would not be at all happy if he killed his way through the provinces – even if it was to rescue the prince. He got out and followed just behind Bane.

The two men saw them approaching and both crossed their thick arms, glowering.

"What's with the sour faces, boys?" Bane called.

"Five notes each," said the man on their left. "And your pal will have to check in his weapon."

Drake cursed himself for not putting on his shoulder harness. He wasn't about to give anyone his P37. However, it quickly became apparent that he wouldn't need to.

Bane's hands glowed blue. Before either man could move, two streams of mana sprang forth, each one coiling itself completely around its target. Both men struggled and twisted violently, to no avail. Muscles, no matter how strong, were never going to be enough to break the spell.

Bane looked back at Drake. "You see? I didn't kill them."

"Do you know who owns this place?" grunted one of the entrapped men.

"Of course I do," he replied, smiling. "Drake, if you wouldn't mind terribly... One of them will be carrying the key we need."

Drake stepped forward and quickly found a ring of keys on the second one's front pocket.

"Now, I can't have you two charging in and disturbing us," Bane continued. "So..."

The mana became brighter for a second; then there was a flash. Both guards immediately crumbled to the ground, their arms and legs twitching and jerking.

"Not exactly discreet," remarked Drake.

Bane flashed a smile. "Never mind. We won't be here long."

The thrumming beat of dance music could be heard when they opened the door, though at this point it was muffled by the carpet covered walls of the small lobby. The booth just ahead of the entrance to the main part of the club was empty. At least they wouldn't have to pay a cover charge.

Still taking the lead, Bane pushed open the steel door. At once the volume of the music tripled. To their right was a multi-tiered dance floor surrounded by a dozen or more cushioned booths. A spiral staircase, currently blocked off by a velvet rope, led to a balcony area directly above, where the more affluent guests could talk and drink without being bothered by the common rabble. Directly ahead was a long bar, illuminated by green mana bulbs. A few patrons were sitting and talking there, early arrivals eager to avoid the cover charge and take advantage of cheap drinks. Some of these glanced in their direction, but didn't register any more than a passing notice. Off to their right were the restrooms and more booths.

Bane strode straight up to the bar and pressed himself between two men, who glared at him angrily. "I need to see Remy," he told the bartender.

The young man was leaning casually against the cooler at his back, fidgeting idly with a bottle opener. "Who?" he asked.

Bane grinned. "I think you know who."

One of the men who he had pushed aside then grabbed his arm. "Why don't you get the hell out of here before you get hurt?" he snarled.

The man's tightly fitting t-shirt displayed a well-muscled frame. Together with his aggressive demeanor, most people would have been quite intimidated. But not Bane.

"That's some grip you have there," he remarked.

In the blink of an eye, his hand shot out and struck the man in the center of his chest with the heel of his palm. This sent him sprawling from his stool and crashing to the floor, flat on his back. The faint glow around Bane's hand was barely visible. Even so, the bartender had obviously seen it.

He straightened up, pressing himself hard against the cooler as if this might offer him some sort of protection. At the same time, the man on Bane's other side sprang from his seat and backed away, in his haste nearly dislodging another customer from his seat. Bane knelt down and hovered over the man he had hit.

"I really think you should stay down until I leave," he advised. Not that it looked as if the man could move anyway as he clutched at his chest, moaning from the magic-enhanced blow.

The remaining patrons were all now out of their seats and moving away. Drake groaned. Attracting attention like this was the last thing he wanted. His hand moved to the handle of his P37.

Bane rose and leveled his gaze at the bartender. "Where were we? Ah, yes, I remember. You were about to tell me where I can find Remy."

"He…he's in the back," the young man blurted out, jabbing a shaky finger over to a door on the left end of the bar.

"That wasn't so hard, was it?"

Drake saw that the door was slightly ajar. Instinctively, he drew his weapon. The shot pinged off the bar a moment later. Bane spun, hands glowing bright red. Drake felt like throttling him. Rather than taking Remy by surprise, they would now have to fight their way in.

Drake squeezed the trigger, sending a force shot into the door. It swung open, smashing against the wall. But whoever had attacked them was no longer there. This time, Drake took the lead. Shoving aside those who had yet to start running toward the front entrance, he ran up and pressed his back to the wall. Another shot ricocheted off the door frame as he peered inside, barely missing his head. Beyond was a dimly lit hall, at the end of which was the silhouette of the gunman. Before Drake could return fire, the shape ducked around a corner.

Adjusting the P37, Drake this time sent a blinding light streaking to the end of the hallway. Averting his eyes from the glare, he raced along behind. On reaching the next corner, he could see several doors lining the wall opposite. He crouched low and looked to the end of the corridor. At the end was another door, this one made from much sturdier metal and with a narrow slot at eye level. The banging of metal followed by the high-pitched whine served as a warning. Remy was ready for them. Or at least, he thought he was.

The crystal in his chest burned as he prepared the next shot.

"Don't bother," Bane told him. "That door is mana-shielded."

Drake furrowed his brow. "Are you sure?"

"Why do you think I bothered with the key?"

Drake fired at the door anyway. The shot struck dead center, but nothing happened.

"Damn it," he muttered. "This is not good."

"Yeah. Maybe I shouldn't have knocked that guy down." Bane's tone was unapologetic.

Drake ignored the flippant remark. A mana shield on the door meant that this Remy fellow was no run-of-the-mill nightclub owner. Such things were highly expensive and almost impossible to find. His P37 could probably overcome it; it was powerful enough. But it could take quite a long time. And if Remy had a means of escape, they needed to hurry.

He reached in his pocket and tossed Bane the keys. "Okay. You can be the one to open it."

He chuckled. "Of course."

Drake followed close behind him, halted a few feet away, and got down on one knee. Bane fumbled through the keys until finding one that looked as if it would fit the lock. Then, with a quick twist and a sharp kick, the door flew open.

In virtually instant response, a stream of blue light shot out from somewhere inside, only just missing Bane before continuing on to strike the wall right beside Drake. Though a miss, the force of the blast still slammed into his body and sent him sliding several yards back down the hall.

When he came to a stop, his vision was blurred and he was powerless to move. Despite this, he was still able to hear the unmistakable sizzle of magic. This was quickly followed by several sharp cries of pain.

Both his head and right shoulder, which was nearest to the blast point, were throbbing intensely, and the rest of him felt totally limp. Mana shield *and* mana weapons. Who the hell was this guy?

A minute later, he felt a pair of hands heft him up into a seated position.

"Are you all right?" asked Bane.

"I'll be fine," he croaked. "Just give me a second."

"Take your time. Remy's not going anywhere."

Drake allowed his weight to press against the wall. The sensation in his limbs was returning and the pain subsiding. He could see Bane squatting across the hall, smiling.

"Did you kill him?" he asked.

"Not yet."

He began to struggle to his feet. Bane quickly took his arm and helped him up. Drake wanted to shake him off, but the truth was, he needed assistance. Nonetheless, once standing, he waved Bane away, choosing instead to make his way forward by leaning against the wall.

Through the door was a small office. The walls were covered with holoviewers showing nearly every area of the club. Remy would have seen them coming regardless. On the far side, lying next to the splintered remains of a desk, was a short, thin man in his early forties with straight blond hair and a pale complexion. He was bound at the wrists with a thin cord.

Bane crossed over to give him a swift kick in the ribs. Remy grunted and curled his knees to his chest.

"That's for hurting my friend," Bane told him in a mock

scolding tone.

Drake noticed a long rifle propped against the wall. He recognized it immediately as a Baluride Model H957. They were illegal for the general public to own and were issued only to military and law enforcement personnel; to be in possession of one could get you life in prison. In the right hands, this weapon could take on twenty men. Only his P37 was considered deadlier.

Drake examined the room. Aside from the overabundance of surveillance equipment, nothing else appeared unusual. All the same, he was certain there must be a hidden door in the office somewhere. Any man who would take the trouble to arm and protect himself to such a degree would not allow himself to be easily cornered. Remy had probably not been aware of the nature of the men who had come for him. Had he been, it was most unlikely he would have chosen to stay and fight.

"Is he able to speak?" he asked.

"Give the poor fellow a minute," Bane smirked. "He's had quite a shock to his system."

Drake focused his mana into the P37 and pushed a small button next to the trigger guard. After a few seconds, a thin line of light in the shape of a door appeared on the wall behind where Remy lay.

"I was just about to do the same thing," remarked Bane. He approached the area on the wall and ran his hands over the surface.

Remy moaned and squirmed against his bindings. "You two are dead men. You hear me? Dead!"

Bane returned his attention to their captive. "Oh, I don't know. I feel very much alive right now. Which is more than I will be able to say for you if you don't answer our questions."

"Do you know who I am?" he snapped, some of his strength returning.

"We wouldn't be here otherwise," Bane told him. He held out the tip of his finger and pressed it to Remy's cheek. A moment later there was the sizzle of burning flesh, followed closely by a wail of pain.

He broke contact after a few seconds and plopped down onto the floor. "You know, when I was a fledgling, I was told that pain was an unreliable way to acquire information. But in truth, I've always found it to be quite reliable." He glanced over to Drake. "Wouldn't you agree?"

"We don't have time for this," Drake said. "I don't want to have to fight my way out of here."

"Quite right." Bane looked down at Remy. "You heard him. We don't have time for courtesy. So you'll be needing to tell us right away where Prince Salazar is being held."

"Why would I know that?"

Bane clicked his tongue. "Now, now. Lying will only make me upset. Have you ever seen a mage when he's upset? It's not pretty, I can tell you."

"Go to hell," Remy spat back.

Drake almost felt sorry for the man. He had seen mages interrogate prisoners before. His own methods could be quite brutal when pressed. But mages... He particularly remembered seeing one burn the hide from a man's body, only to heal him and start all over again. By the third time, the victim was begging for death. Thinking about it still gave him a chill.

Reaching down, Bane pressed his right palm to Remy's brow, then shut his eyes. Remy instantly stiffened.

"That's it," Bane whispered. "Now you can tell me everything."

"What are you doing?" asked Drake.

But Bane ignored him. "Yes," he continued. "Very good. Just relax and let it all out."

Very quickly, tears began streaming down Remy's cheeks, even though his face remained a stone mask. After more than a minute Bane released his hold and stood. There was an odd look of fatigue in his eyes, as though he had not slept in days.

"The prince *was* here," he confirmed. "But they moved him further north, near the barrier. Exactly where, I can't say."

"What the hell did you do to him?" Drake demanded. Remy was still motionless, though drool was now spilling from the corner of his mouth and his tears continued to flow.

"Much tidier than torture, wouldn't you say?" Bane answered. "A trick I learned when I was a lad. The mind is far more fragile than people think. Just a little push, and most people will tell you anything you want to know."

"You read his mind?" Drake had never heard of such magic. He knew that healing spells could create a temporary bond between people, sometimes even allowing them to share their thoughts. But this…

"Not exactly. I convinced him to tell me his secrets. Well…in a manner of speaking. Terrified him into it would be a more accurate description, I suppose." He stood and flicked his wrist dismissively. "Either way, I learned what we need to know. Prince Salazar came here thinking he could find sanctuary. Apparently, he knew Remy. Or at least, he knew who Remy works for."

"How would Prince Salazar know Fisk?" Drake asked.

Bane shrugged. "Couldn't say. But Remy is the greedy sort. And not particularly loyal to the crown, as it turned out. Exodus had already been here and paid him quite handsomely to hand the prince over."

"So Fisk is in on this?"

"Perhaps. He certainly knows what happened. It seems poor Remy was waiting to die when we arrived. Fisk doesn't like it when his subordinates don't give him his cut. That's why he spotted us so quickly. Poor guy was just sitting here staring at the screens, waiting for Fisk's assassins to arrive." He glanced down at the man. "For all the good it will do them now."

"What do you mean?"

"I'm afraid there are certain side effects to this form of interrogation."

"Side effects?"

A wry grin crept up on his lips. "You could pull out his fingernails right now and he wouldn't twitch a muscle. As far as I know, it's a permanent condition."

Drake shuddered at the thought. It was one thing to torture a man. But this was gruesome and cruel in a way that turned his stomach. It made him despise Bane that much more.

"Don't look at me that way," Bane retorted. "He was dead anyway. And we haven't the time to do this the old-fashioned way."

Every time Bane was right, it served only to stoke Drake's hatred. He pushed this thought from his mind and turned to where the hidden door was located. "Can you open it?"

"Yes. But there's nothing in there we need."

Drake caught a flash of emotion in his eyes. Just a hint, but it was enough. "Open it," he snapped.

After an extended moment, Bane sighed. "As you wish. I'm warning you, though, you won't like what you find."

Grabbing hold of Remy, he dragged his body over to

the wall. He then took the man's palm and pressed it flat to where the door was hidden. With a hiss and a clunk, a thin line appeared and the door swung outward.

A stairwell led down to a lit hallway. As Drake descended, he noticed that Bane wasn't following.

"You're not coming?"

He shook his head. "I already know what's down there. I saw it in Remy's mind. And it's nothing I care to see first-hand." His tone was uncharacteristically dark. "I'll be here once you've seen your fill."

This gave Drake pause. What could be down there that was so terrible? As a hawker, he had seen all manner of atrocities, and he was certain that Bane had as well. After a while, there was very little that shocked you in their line of work.

At the bottom, the hallway continued for about fifty feet. Several doors were spaced evenly along the walls, and he checked every one. They were either empty or merely used for storing items of a common nature, mostly boxes of plates or metal containers. Certainly nothing of particular interest or even illegal. Then, at the end of the passage, he came to a set of double doors. Written across these in large red letters were the words KEEP OUT.

Drake unholstered his P37 and tested the door. It was unlocked. Cautiously, he cracked it open and a foul odor immediately rushed out, striking him as forcibly as any slap to the face. His features contorted. It was like an unholy combination of rotted flesh and the musky smell of livestock. After pausing briefly in an unsuccessful to spit away the stench, he very carefully stepped inside.

At once he saw what it was that Bane did not want to face. The room was roughly thirty feet square, with a long table set directly in the center. Atop this lay the mangled form of a hellspawn, though this one was not nearly as large or broad as the one they had encountered. Even so, the cracked, pale green flesh was unmistakable. It had been cut open from the chest to the stomach, much like an autopsy, its skin pulled to the side exposing its organs. But it was the face that was most troubling to Drake. Somehow, although it had the horns and fangs, it was still not quite the face of a hellspawn. In fact, there was more than a touch of human about its features.

Set along the walls of the room were glass tanks containing more of the creatures; all of them had been dissected and some completely stripped of their organs. A smaller table with a variety of surgical implements on top was near to the door.

"What the hell is this place?" muttered Drake.

He walked slowly around the room examining each tank. Some of the hellspawn were of typical size, while others were no larger than the one on the table.

"You need to hurry," Bane called down the stairs. "Remy's friends will be here soon. Or worse, the Sheriff."

Drake took a long look around before exiting the room. For sure, the magistrate would want to know what was happening here. Though he was not in the habit of being an informant, this was something quite different. This was something that needed to be stopped...whatever it was.

He was sorely tempted to simply incinerate the foul place and rid the world of an atrocity. But common sense told him it would be better for the proper authorities to sort it all out. Suddenly, he felt unclean and had an overpowering urge to wash away the stench of the room. A terrifying notion occurred to him as he ascended the stairs. What if somehow hellspawn were...?

He banished the thought from his mind even before completing it.

"Maybe next time you'll listen to me," Bane told him as soon as he arrived back.

"Do you know anything about this?"

"No. And I don't want to."

The two men exited the office and headed back to the main part of the club. Though the music still boomed from the speakers, the place was now completely empty. A wave of urgency washed over Drake. He should not have lingered. They needed to leave fast.

A crowd had gathered across the street, and all eyes fell on them as they crossed the lot toward Cal. Headlights could be seen coming from the north – too bright for most cars. Drake jumped into the driver's seat and fired the engine.

"North?" he asked.

Bane nodded but said nothing.

Slamming Cal into gear, he peeled out of the lot. Just as he thought, the lights were those of a sheriff's vehicle. He pulled up the map.

"Find us a quick way out of here," he told Bane.

This was a large enough city to have a sizable sheriff's department. And though Cal could certainly outrun most other cars, outrunning a communicator was something else. He switched his camouflage mode off, returning Cal to her normal appearance. That should be enough to give them a bit of breathing space.

As Bane pointed out directions, Drake couldn't shake a sinking feeling that he had bitten off more than he could chew. The almost human face of the hellspawn continued to haunt his thoughts well into the night.

It was just before dawn when he was confident they were far enough away to stop for some rest. Still, he wanted to avoid prying eyes, so he pulled behind an abandoned building that looked to have once been a general store. Bane had been noticeably subdued throughout.

Drake leaned his seat back in an effort to clear his mind and focus on the future. At least, the kind of future that he hoped fate held for him when this was all over.

The last thing he saw before sleep took him was the smiling face of Lenora.

CHAPTER TEN

The barrier was not a place Drake would have imagined Exodus might choose as a base of operations. Although it was undoubtedly secluded and largely uninhabited, it would be easy enough to detect activity there. They would need supplies, for instance. A single person might be able to stay reasonably well hidden, but not a large group, certainly not for any length of time.

Bane was still sleeping. He had woken briefly once, still looking thoroughly exhausted, only to promptly shut his eyes and settle down once again. Drake guessed that whatever magic he'd used on Remy had taken a lot out of him. Powerful magic could do that to a mage. Unlike the royal guard, who centered their power in the vex crystal, mages used their entire body to channel spells. This was bound to take its toll. A strong spell might be painful to Drake, but he was otherwise left physically unaffected. And where one could grow accustomed to pain, fatigue could never be ignored indefinitely.

The image of the hellspawn continued to plague him. With the need to focus on the job at hand, this was a distraction he definitely didn't need at the moment. He rolled down the window and let the cold air blast against his skin. Normally he despised the cold, but right at that moment it felt refreshing – cleansing.

"Where are we going?"

Drake looked over and saw that Bane was raising his seat upright. He looked better. "We won't make it to the barrier unless we get some fuel," he replied.

Bane rubbed the back of his neck. "We must have passed several fueling stations by now."

"I don't put that cheap crap in Cal," Drake told him firmly.

There was only one place in the vicinity that he could acquire good mana fuel. Though it meant going a bit out of their way, it couldn't be helped.

"Fuel is fuel," said Bane.

"Considering who your father is, I would think you'd know better than that. You don't want to be trying to outrun someone using cheap fuel. I learned that the hard way."

"So where are we going?"

"Grim Lake."

Bane groaned. "You can't be serious."

Drake gave him a lopsided smirk. "Of course I'm serious. What's wrong with Grim Lake?"

Bane blew out a hard breath. "Oh, nothing. It's lovely. That is, if you like the stench of fish and urine."

"That's too much for someone as refined as you, I suppose."

"It's too much for someone as refined as a hellspawn," he complained. "You can't think you'll find good mana fuel in a place like that."

"Just relax. We won't be there very long. You can stay in the car if it bothers you so much."

Bane frowned. "I don't like this. We're wasting time. The prince is in more danger with every minute that passes. You do realize that, don't you?"

"I am well aware of that. But unless you want Cal stalling on us in the middle of an escape, you'll shut your mouth and leave this to me."

Grim Lake was about as unsavory a place as ever existed in Vale. Drake had chased many a runner into its depths. Some had almost managed to get away. Almost. It was a place of contradictions. Food was abundant, and you could find many of the luxuries typically reserved for the people of Troi. The problem was staying alive long enough to take advantage of it.

"I don't suppose it would make any difference to you that Fisk might be there?" Bane said, still scowling. "In fact, I would almost be willing to bet that he is."

"Good. Maybe he can help us find Exodus."

"He'll help you find an early grave. It's one thing to mess around with him down south, but this is *his* territory. Especially Grim Lake."

"From your reputation, I wouldn't think you scared so easily."

"And from yours, I would have thought you less foolhardy."

Drake reached out and stroked the dash. "Cal has saved my skin more times than I can count. I'll take the risk to keep her running right."

"Well, I'd rather not."

"You could get out here if you want." Drake lifted his foot from the accelerator to punctuate his words.

"I guess I have no say in the matter," seethed Bane.

"An astute observation." He resumed their speed. "Don't worry. We won't be there long enough to attract attention. Just in and out."

Of course, that wasn't strictly true. He would also make

time to buy a manga juice. Grim Lake was the only place outside of Troi that made them. They weren't nearly as tasty, but still a lot better than nothing.

From a practical standpoint, having Bane with him was good. He hadn't been wrong about the level of risk involved. Someone as powerful in magic as Bane would be a big asset if they were spotted. Were he alone, Fisk might send men after him. But if they saw Bane as well, that could easily make them think twice.

The sun was touching the horizon when Drake caught the scent of moldy air. Grim Lake was more of a bog than an actual lake. The narrow channels and weed-covered marsh stretched out for miles. Flat boats crisscrossed it both day and night, most of them fishing for cruxfish and pinchbugs, the main staples of the locals. Quite tasty, actually. So much so that Drake had often considered that, should the people of upper Troi ever discover them, the residents of Grim Lake would very soon be without. Grim Lake was also a fine place to dispose of bodies, which was one of the reasons it had attracted Fisk and so many others like him. If ever there was a place created specifically for the criminal underworld, this was it.

Drake turned off the main road onto a narrow trail that split the marsh in two. The town was almost dead center, which was the only stretch of solid ground to be found in the area. Vehicles going the other way frequently forced him to the edge of the road, while a line of others following Cal could be seen in his rear view mirror. Dangerous or not, the pleasures found in Grim Lake attracted quite a few people after the sun went down.

The long wooden bridge spanning the marsh was guarded by what passed for the law hereabouts. Though they didn't work directly for the underworld, these men were nearly as corrupt. Not that Drake was worried about them. So long as there was no trouble, they wouldn't be stopped. Still, he was glad he'd remembered to return Cal to camouflage mode. There were people in Grim Lake who would definitely recognize her in her natural state; that was the price you paid for driving a one-of-a-kind vehicle.

Ahead, set beneath a delta of mana streams, the town lights twinkled like stars. Only a few areas were well lit; the remainder was kept in a dim twilight state with strings of tiny mana bulbs hanging from posts. This made it simple to pass unnoticed. Most visitors would rather remain anonymous anyway, and most of the residents were just as guarded. This was to be expected in a town where ninety percent of the wealth was acquired illegally.

At the end of the bridge, Drake turned right and entered the large lot where all non-commercial vehicles were required to park. A scraggly youth ran up the moment they stopped.

"That will be ten," he said.

Drake cocked his head. "Ten? Are you kidding me?"

The boy spread his hands. "What can I tell you? Price has gone up. Don't blame me. I just work the lot."

Drake grumbled and pulled a twenty from his wallet. "See that no one comes near her, got it?"

The boy's eyes lit up at the sight of the money. "You got it, mister. No problem at all." With a sharp nod, he shoved the money into his pocket and raced off to his next customer.

Bane was still looking displeased. "A soft spot for street urchins?"

"I bet that boy makes more money than half the people living here," Drake told him.

That was probably true. The lot attendants did quite well, and it was a highly coveted job. In the early days, when Drake had spent most of his time in this region, he'd had two lot attendants on his payroll. They knew better than anyone who came and went, and Grim Lake was a hot spot for runners. A good lot attendant could be raking in a thousand a week if they played their cards right and kept their eyes open.

Bane's frowned deepened. "Yeah. And if anyone is looking for us, you can bet that's where he's off to."

It was a possibility, but Drake doubted it. Even if Fisk were looking for them, he wouldn't have had the chance yet to put the word out. They had made good time. Anyway, who would ever think they might come to Grim Lake? Like Bane had relentlessly pointed out to him, it was too risky.

Drake retrieved his shoulder holster from the trunk and slipped it on. His P37 would be sure to attract unwanted attention. It was uncomfortable, but until he could buy himself another long coat, he would have to put up with it. For a moment he even considered looking for such a coat here, but dismissed the idea. This would soon be over, and he could get whatever he needed when back in Troi.

They passed through the lot and walked down a nearby street. The buildings were dilapidated wooden structures, covered in the slime and mold of the marsh and in constant need of repairs. Even the sturdier buildings looked worn and decaying. Only one or two were higher than two floors, mostly apartments for the merchants and crime bosses. The broad walkway was already filling with people ready for a night of debauchery, and the music was seeping into the street from the taverns.

One or two smaller vehicles passed through, transport for well-to-do visitors and the richer residents. Aside from these, the avenues were mostly occupied by people zigzagging their way from tavern to tavern or shop to shop.

They threaded their way to the west end of town. Here,

the crowds were thinner and the scent of fresh bread and spices partly overcame the moldy smell of the marsh. As Drake spotted the building where his first stop was to be, he frowned.

"What's wrong?" Bane immediately asked.

"It's gone," he replied. He stared at the empty storefront with no small measure of disappointment. "The one place outside of Troi that sold manga juice. How in the hell can it be gone?"

Anger sprang up on Bane's face. "Manga juice? Are you kidding me?" Spinning on his heels, he began striding rapidly back the way they had come.

"Where are you going?" Drake called out.

"Back to the car."

He was about to shout for him to stop, but could tell from the determined way Bane was walking that it would be a waste of breath. Maybe he *was* being too reckless, he admitted. The prospect of going home had certainly changed his behavior. He was no longer resigned to a life of filth and struggle. He now had hope, and hope could be a dangerous emotion if you allowed it to blind you to the present. After all, he wasn't home yet. And if he failed in his task, he never would be.

He wasn't about to apologize – not to Bane. But he would be more conscious of the man's warnings in the future. Up until now he'd been allowing his dislike to color his judgment. The fact was, Bane was an experienced hawker. More than that, he hadn't gained such a reputation by being stupid.

Forgetting his desire for manga juice, Drake continued on until reaching a small building with an open front. The large doors were swung wide to reveal three small blue vehicles – the taxis that he had seen earlier. An older man in red coveralls was working on the one nearest the entrance. Drake knew him well. Aside from Dorn, Vic was the only man he trusted to look at Cal.

"You busy?" he called. "I need some fuel."

Vic gave him a sideways look and heaved a breath. "Oh, it's you. Haven't seen you around in a while. You after a runner?"

"Not this time. Just passing through."

The old mechanic stretched his back and groaned as his joints cracked and popped in protest. "Just as well. Rumor is the magistrate is about to run all your kind out of here. Setting up their own office right in the middle of town, they are."

"You know better than to listen to rumors. They've been saying that for years."

"Yeah, but this time it's true. They've already bought a building right next to the sheriff's office."

Drake could see the concern on Vic's weathered face. He made his living serving the crime bosses and the hawkers. If the magistrate's office ran them out, he would lose his livelihood.

"Maybe you could get a contract to repair their vehicles," Drake suggested. But he knew it was a ridiculous idea. The magistrate sent their own people for maintenance. Men like Vic would be forced to service legitimate customers. This meant permits and fees, almost certainly more than he would be able to pay. If the magistrate moved in, he would be forced out.

Vic waved a dismissive hand. "It doesn't matter. I'm too old to let it bother me. When it happens, it happens. No use worrying about it until then. Where are you parked?"

Drake told him the lot number. "How long?"

"Give me an hour. I have to finish this up first."

Drake took out three hundred from his wallet and handed it over. It was a bit more than the fuel was worth, but Vic had been fair with him over the years. And he hated to think about what was likely to become of him. Not that anything could be done about it.

"I want you to go see Dorn if they kick you out of here," Drake told him. "I'm sure he could use someone as good as you."

Vic chuckled as he thumbed through the notes. "That old goat's still alive?"

"And still working. Just tell him I sent you."

"I appreciate that. You always had a kind heart...for a hawker, that is. All the same, I think I've worked long enough. It's time for me to retire." Turning back to the taxi, he snatched up a rag and wiped the back of his neck. "Now get going. If you want your fuel any time soon, you better stop pestering me."

Drake took a quick look around at the garage that had taken Vic a lifetime to build. So many people were cast aside once they were too old to work. The outer provinces were filled with those waiting to die because they could no longer provide for themselves. The few who were fortunate enough to have families willing to care for them only bought themselves a little time. Eventually, the strain of another mouth to feed would become too much; that, or they would suffer an illness. The elderly were not given priority when it came to medical treatment. Resources were spent on those who could be productive. If you could no longer work, you rarely received care. Unless, of course, you lived in Troi. Then it was a different story.

Drake wandered about for a time, keeping to the shadows just in case he ran into someone who might know him. Not much had changed since he was last here. Only the faces.

On every corner, peddlers and beggars jammed the walkway. Prostitutes of every gender and catering for all tastes tempted passers-by with their wares. Three times he was forced to shoo away groups of children attempting to steal his wallet. As a guard, he had come here once and thought it to be the most repulsive place in Vale. It was only later that he began to see the beauty in it. Through the dirt and grime there was a freedom here that existed nowhere else. Sure, you could get yourself killed. And if you got mixed up with the crime bosses, you probably would. But at least you could live – and die – on your own terms. But if what Vic had told him was true, all that would soon change. The magistrate would come and impose its will. They would bring order to this splendid chaos. And with it, even more hardship.

When it was time to return to Cal, Drake had resigned himself to the fact that these things were beyond his control. Life had always been hard in Vale. The only thing to look forward to was that one day, the land would be healed, and there would be plenty for all. One day.

Only the fact they he was intentionally keeping out of plain view prevented him from running straight into Bane. He was being led away by three men in dark blue suits. One was carrying a P37 and had it pointed straight at the mage.

Drake melted back out of sight. What was the royal guard doing here? And why were they interested in Bane? A chill shot through him. Xavier must have somehow tracked them here. That was the only explanation he could think of for the royal guard being involved. *Damn it.* Right now, it felt as if there were no one he could trust. At every turn, it seemed that people would rather see the prince dead than rescued. Only the magistrate herself had given him no reason to doubt, but he didn't really trust her either. For all he knew, Fisk could be working for her.

He knew where to start looking, so he should run. That was his initial instinct. However, a nagging doubt quickly started to plague him. It wouldn't go away. He owed Bane. He might not like him, but the guy had saved his life.

Keeping far enough behind, he followed the men until they reached precisely the place that Drake had been hoping they wouldn't be heading for: the sheriff's office. He knew the layout reasonably well – only one way in and one way out. And inside were roughly fifteen armed deputies, possibly more; not to mention members of the royal guard.

He waited until Bane had been shoved through the front door before turning and hurrying back to the lot where Cal was parked. Vic was already there, looking very displeased. Beside him stood a small pushcart, inside which was a cylinder about five feet tall and two feet in diameter. At the top of this was a metal tube attached to a square box that hung down the side.

"Where the hell have you been?" the old man demanded.

Ignoring his complaining, Drake grabbed the handles of the cart. It was not easy going. Vic was clearly stronger than his years suggested. The cart squeaked and cracked as they made their way over to Cal.

"Got her in camo mode, I see," remarked Vic. "What are you into?"

Drake positioned the cart so that the tube could reach the fuel receptacle just above the left rear tire. At a touch of his finger, the three-inch-square door that prevented others from stealing his fuel popped open. Drake hurriedly put the box end of the tube in place.

"I need to know if there's another way into the sheriff's office," he said.

Vic stiffened. "Have you lost your mind? You can't break in there. Why would you want to, anyhow?"

"Do you really want to know?"

Vic held out his hands and shook his head. "No. Not even a little."

The fuel cylinder hummed as it filled Cal's tank. Drake looked around. The fact that there had been no one waiting for him here in the lot meant they must have picked up Bane somewhere else. A lucky break for the mage. If Drake had been forced to fight his way to Cal, he would have had no choice but to leave Bane behind.

"I just need a way in," Drake pressed. Vic would know that building better than most. He not only worked on their vehicles, he also did a few minor building repairs as well.

"Look, lad. The whole building is a steel box from top to bottom. The only other door is on the roof. That locks from the inside, so you'd need a cutter to get through. And I'd sure like to see you get one of those up there without being spotted." His frown deepened. "Whatever you're after, give it up."

Drake opened the trunk and then the box containing the various phials. After selecting two of these, he shoved them into his pocket. "Just do yourself a favor and forget I was here," he said.

A sharp crack indicated that Cal was filled, and Vic detached the tube and chuckled as he lifted the cart handles. "Don't worry. There's not much they can do to an old man like me." He paused to meet Drake's eyes. "You're a fool. You know that, right?" He let out a sigh before adding: "But you've always been a lucky fool."

Drake watched Vic until he was out of sight. If anyone had seen them together, it could go hard on the old mechanic. And despite what he said, there was still quite a bit they could do to him if they chose to.

Returning to the heart of town, Drake went over in his

mind how he would set about freeing Bane. He would either be in a cell – the best possible scenario – or in an interrogation room. If the latter, the royal guard would be with him. Or very close by.

Like Vic had said, the two-story office was essentially a steel box. The outer frame had been covered in plates thick enough to repel most weapons. His P37 could get through, though not without destroying half the building in the process.

Deputies and other people with business at the office made for a steady stream of traffic passing through the front door. What had been a bakery stood to the left of this, though the windows were empty and the light shining through revealed that workers had recently been stripping it out – no doubt the building Vic had said the magistrate had bought. On the right-hand side was a tavern where one was sure to find off-duty officers and those trying to curry favor or just outright bribe them. Drake casually strode up to the bakery and, after waiting until he was sure that no one in the street was looking in his direction, slipped down a side alley to the back.

Scaling the sheriff's building was out of the question. Its smooth sides offered no hand or foot holds whatsoever. His eyes shifted over to the bakery's rear wall. Difficult, but not impossible. The bars on the windows would certainly make life simpler. After finding a wooden crate, he tested it for strength, and once satisfied that it was capable of supporting his weight, he placed it just beneath a second-floor window at the far corner.

Climbing up, he eyed the bars and steadied his breathing. The sinews of his legs tensed, then burst into life. His jump was just high enough to grab the bottom of the bars with the tips of his fingers. For a moment he dangled there, fervently wishing that he were a few years younger. Eventually, after a few anxious seconds of feeling around, his feet found a tenuous hold on a slightly protruding lintel over the window directly below. This, in turn, allowed him to gain a better grip above. Inch by inch, he then climbed until he was able to wedge his boot between the bars.

A storm drain overhead was now just about within his reach, though it was obviously too flimsy to support his weight. A little above this drain, the very top edge of the building was surrounded by a thin lip. This was what he would need to grab.

With a heavy grunt, he straightened his legs and threw out his hands. Panic struck as he felt his fingers slipping the moment they made contact. In desperation, he grabbed at the drain. As expected, a section of it ripped free from its fixings. But at least it slowed his fall slightly, giving him time to seize hold of the lip with his other hand. He cringed as the drain section smacked into the ground below. So much for being silent; not that there was anything he could do about the noise now. As quickly as he could, he pulled himself up and rolled over onto the flat roof.

After a minute, it was clear the commotion had not been enough to draw attention. One piece of luck, he told himself. Now he needed about fifty pieces more. Had he ever been that lucky? He couldn't recall a time.

Rising to a crouched position, he crept over to the other side of the building. From this vantage point he could see across to the door that Vic had mentioned, which was set into a slanted rise in the near corner. He gauged the distance between the two buildings and backed away, focusing his strength. It was a leap of at least six feet; not normally a long way, but at this height and with only a very short approach available, he would need to take care.

He sprang into a run, managing just four paces before launching himself.

His boot struck only a few inches inside the edge of the opposite roof, and he tumbled forward into a roll to stop his momentum. Though the metal plating dulled the sound of his landing, he still waited for a few minutes before approaching the door. This was made from the same metal as the external shell and gave every impression of being extremely thick.

After pulling out one of the phials from his pocket and removing the stopper, he carefully poured the clear liquid into and around the door's lock. Within seconds, there was a hiss as a cloud of acrid smoke rose up. He shuffled back a few paces so as not to breathe in the fumes. Slowly the liquid ate through the metal until he heard a low clunk. When the smoke cleared, there was a two-inch deep hole in the door, though no sign of it yet breaking through to the other side. He hoped this had been enough to disable the locking mechanism. He had a second phial, but he might well need this to free Bane.

Gripping the handle, he tugged. The hinges screeched, halting him at once. This door clearly hadn't been opened in a very long time. Bringing a bit of oil with him would have been smart, he told himself.

Careful not to touch the still-bubbling hole, he pulled again, only this time very slowly. The hinges persisted with their complaint, but now at a much lower volume. He continued this way for nearly a minute before the door was open far enough to pass through. Just inside was a flight of stairs leading down to another door – though as he drew close, he could see this one was made from wood and bore no lock at all.

He pressed his ear to the door. Nothing. He cracked it open and could see that this was a storage room – boxes and old furniture mostly. After entering, he paused for a few moments to take stock of his situation.

He had been here a few times several years ago. In fact, he had once paid the sheriff to house a runner he'd caught overnight. He knew that the cells were all on the top floor. The interrogation room was on the bottom level, along with most of the offices.

If they were just holding Bane, there would be maybe four men on duty. Possibly fewer, at this time of night. Drake considered the best approach. A smile crept up from the corners of his mouth as he settled on his course of action. It would either be bold and decisive, or the pinnacle of stupidity.

He brushed off his jacket and pants, ran his fingers through his hair, and strode from the room.

The hallway was empty, though he could hear voices coming from behind the closed doors of the rooms on either side. This was somewhat troubling. The last time he'd been here, the upstairs offices were used only to store files and to give privacy to officials from the magistrate's office when they had reason to visit. Still, there was nothing to do now but keep going. He rounded a corner, passing the stairs that led to the ground floor, and continued on to the end of the next hall.

Here, a man was sitting at a small desk station flipping through a stack of papers. He looked up at Drake as he approached and scowled.

"You're not supposed to be on this floor," he said. "Let me see your identification." His hand drifted below the desktop, where a gun was certainly kept in easy reach.

Drake plastered on a friendly smile and raised his hands. "Take it easy. I'm with the guard." He pulled back his jacket to reveal his P37.

"So?" he snapped back. "Your man is downstairs." He was angry, but no longer reaching for his weapon. The sight of the P37 had been enough to convince him of the lie.

"Yeah, I know. I was checking to be sure you guys had room up here."

"Of course we have room. What's wrong – you and your friends think you wouldn't get to have a night out?"

Drake spread his hands and shrugged. "We can't get away with it in Troi. They watch us too closely. Anyway, I was just –"

He was mid-sentence when the entire building suddenly shook violently, throwing Drake against the wall. The man at the desk was pitched from his chair and left clutching at the floor in wide-eyed shock.

Three more tremendous booms resonated from the walls. Shouts came from downstairs, quickly followed by the sound of gunfire.

"What the hell?" the man shouted, starting to crawl back toward his desk.

Drake could make a very good guess as to what had just happened. Recovering his balance, he took a few quick steps, unholstered his weapon, and struck the man on the back of his skull. He collapsed face down in an untidy heap.

As Drake reached the stairs, smoke was already filling the corridor. More gunshots pinged and whizzed, followed by the sizzle of mana lightning.

On reaching the bottom, he saw that the walls of what had once been a conference room were completely destroyed. Beyond this, and now clearly visible, were the interrogation rooms. Fire from the wooden tables and chairs nearest the stairs licked at the ceiling, the updraft pulling the smoke to the second floor. Several men and women were emerging from the offices, all of them covering their faces and coughing uncontrollably. In the chaos, they ignored Drake completely.

The crack of a P37 could be heard just beyond his line of sight. He crouched low and started toward it. As he stepped into the interrogation rooms, he immediately saw two bodies – two of the three royal guard who had been escorting Bane. They were sprawled out, their dark blue suits smoldering and their flesh horribly scorched. The third guard was several yards ahead, ducked behind a toppled steel table. Six more men nearby were busy firing their weapons at an open door, the surrounding walls riddled with burns and holes.

A flash of green light shot from the room, striking the table. The guard flinched and held his P37 to his chest. Drake knew what he was about to do. There was no way Bane would survive it.

Drake had a choice, one he'd never thought he would have to make. Either allow Bane, a man he despised, to die; or kill a member of the royal guard. He leveled his weapon and pushed the switch beside the trigger guard. The heat of the vex crystal surged in his chest.

"Sorry about this," he muttered.

The impact of a bullet smacking into his right shoulder spun him around just as he fired, sending his shot well wide. The pain was intense, even though the caliber was too small to penetrate his flesh. Ignoring his intended target, Drake rolled and turned. He saw a young woman kneeling behind a shattered table. She let loose three more shots, and one struck him in the left foot while the other two passed just above his head.

He responded with a small burst of mana that hit her on the forearm. Not a lethal shot, but enough to disarm her and send her screaming to the floor.

The remaining royal guard, now aware of Drake, was scrambling to the cover of a hallway off to his left. Drake knew there was nothing more he could do. In his present position he was badly exposed, and the remaining guard's weapon would be fully charged by now. One shot would end it.

Rising quickly, he headed at a full run back up the stairs. The flames were more intense by now, and the smoke stung at his eyes. The man he had hit was moaning and wheezing but still completely immobilized. Another thunderous boom shook the building; the guard had apparently decided to use his shot on Bane. And from the feel of the explosion, he had possibly killed a few deputies with it as well.

"Help! Don't leave me in here!"

The voice of what sounded like a young girl was barely audible through the door leading to the holding cells. His good sense told him to ignore it, but the repeated pleas to his conscience soon overruled his brain.

He fished a bunch of keys from the pocket of the injured deputy and unlocked the door. Inside was a passage with five cells on either side. All were empty save for one at the end right. A young girl, even younger than Drake had guessed – no more than sixteen – was gripping the bars and shaking them wildly.

"Please. Let me out!" she screamed.

She was a waif of a figure, with mouse-brown hair and a deep tan complexion. Her dark brown eyes were filled with fear as she gazed pleadingly at Drake. She was wearing the typical green coveralls of a prisoner, which meant she was likely to be transferred to a more permanent facility. Drake knew better than to get mixed up with a fugitive, but the smoke was increasing, and he sure as hell couldn't just leave her here to suffocate.

Finding the right key, he opened the door. "Follow me," he told her.

The girl simply nodded. Drake led her back out of the passage and toward the storage room through which he had entered. As they passed the stairs, the pop of gunfire was followed by a bullet striking the wall just ahead of him, sending bits of concrete digging into his face. He let loose a shot in return. Though not specifically aimed, he heard a cry of pain as it struck his attacker.

Just as they reached the storage room, Drake glanced back to see the head of the royal guard peering around the corner. He grabbed the girl's arm and flung her inside. A split second later, the door burst to splinters.

"Up there," he shouted, pointing to the stairs that led to the roof.

The girl obeyed without hesitation. Once outside, Drake pulled the girl behind him and used his P37 to blast away the steel door's hinges. In no time at all, the door fell completely free of its frame. He waited, and after a tense moment, the guard cautiously appeared on the bottom step, weapon at the ready. Grunting loudly and with his muscles taxed to their limit, Drake lifted the door and sent it crashing down onto the advancing man.

At once his P37 was back in his hand and pointed at the door. But after a few moments, it was clear that his gambit had worked. The guard was still alive, but totally incapacitated. *At least I didn't have to kill him*, Drake thought.

He turned to the girl and nodded toward the bakery. "You think you can make the jump?"

A cheeky grin appeared on her thin lips. "Can *you*, old man?" She spun on her heels and in a flash launched herself through the air, landing on the other side with barely a bend to her knee.

Drake suppressed a smile. *I bet catching her wasn't easy.* With no small effort, he jumped across the void, though unlike the girl, he was forced to roll to a halt. He was about to tell her to get ready to climb down, but she had already moved over to the edge of the roof.

"You have a car?" she asked.

"You're not coming with me," he told her firmly.

She smiled and winked. "Of course I am."

Before he could object, she was over the edge and already on the way down. Grumbling to himself, Drake followed. By the time he had a hold of the bars on the second-floor window, the girl was already down and checking around the corner. Dangling for a moment, he dropped heavily, stumbling back several paces.

"Where are you parked?" she asked.

"You are not coming with me," he repeated.

"Is that right?" She walked around the building a few steps. "Here we are!" she shouted at the top of her voice. "Come and get us! Yoo-hoo!"

He sprang forward and covered her mouth. "Are you crazy? You really want to get us caught?" Only when she stopped struggling and trying to call out did he remove his hand.

"Unless I have a way out of here, I'm as good as caught anyway," she told him. "What do I care if you get caught with me?"

"I saved your life," he pointed out.

"Not yet, you haven't," she retorted. "So you had better make up your mind. They'll shut the bridge down soon enough. Then we're stuck."

Drake's jaw tightened. He wanted to throttle the girl. But there was no time to argue. What she said was right – Grim Lake would be locked up tight within minutes, and then he would be forced to shoot his way out. With a stifled grunt, he pushed his way past her. "You had better keep up then," he said. "I'm not waiting for you."

The girl laughed. "You don't worry about me, old man."

Old man? Yeah, I guess I am, he thought. In more ways than one.

"Keep close behind me," he instructed. Her jail attire would bring the law down on them in a hurry.

Curious onlookers had gathered across the street, and deputies were stumbling from the front door. Drake skirted the edge until they were well into the thickest part of the crowd before picking up their pace. The flames were now leaping from the office windows, and smoke was rising from the roof, probably through the opening where the steel door had been. This was just the distraction they needed; no one so much as glanced at the girl.

Drake figured it would take some time for the officers to get their bearings and think to shut down the bridge. What was more, until the royal guard or the deputy guarding the cells regained consciousness and were able to tell their story, nobody would be looking for either of them.

The attendant was sitting atop the hood of an old truck when they reached the parking lot. On seeing Drake approaching, he hopped down and ran up to greet him.

"No one has so much as touched her since you left," he announced.

"Is that right?"

"Well, not since I got back from lunch," he admitted. "But I checked on her and she's fine. He paused before asking, "Did you see what's causing all the commotion? I thought I heard…"

His voice trailed off as his eyes fell on the girl, and he took a step back.

Drake hastily pulled a twenty note from his wallet. "Why don't you go buy yourself some supper?"

The boy hesitated for a long moment before snatching the note and shoving it into his pocket. "Yeah. I think I'll do that right now."

Drake watched him jog away toward the far side of the lot. As promised, Cal was still there. Once inside, he fired the engine and drove steadily off.

After a short period of silence, he asked, "You have a name?"

"Linx," she replied, admiring Cal's interior. "That's what they call me, anyhow."

Drake pulled onto the bridge. "What's your real name?"

"What do you care?"

"I don't," he told her. "Just know that mine is Drake. So you can stop calling me *old man*."

"Nice to meet you, Drake. Nice wheels."

"Don't get too comfortable. You won't be here long."

"You *say* that…"

They reached the end of the bridge and passed the guards without incident. The moment they were back on the road, Drake pressed down on the accelerator, pushing Cal to one hundred and twenty. He needed to find a place to shed his new-found passenger, though something was telling him it wouldn't be as easy as all that.

Linx pulled her knees into her chest and began humming softly.

"We need to find you some fresh clothes," Drake said.

"I have my own things," she replied. "I stashed them before they caught me."

"Where?"

"You're going the right way. I'll tell you when to turn off."

Drake heaved a sigh. "And then you're on your own. Understand?"

Linx pretended not to hear him and continued to hum.

He concentrated on the road ahead. Yeah. He had a kind heart, for a hawker – just like Vic had said. But that was what invariably caused him the most trouble. And he doubted this time would be any exception.

CHAPTER ELEVEN

They drove due west for a few hours before Linx told him to pull off onto a narrow dirt road. She had been rather quiet throughout, as if in deep contemplation. A small miracle, from Drake's point of view. The less he knew about her, the easier it would be to leave her behind.

Several abandoned houses whizzed by, their yards totally overgrown with thorns and weeds. A few lights from candles could be seen in some of the windows. Stragglers, most likely. People without a home, wandering from place to place while waiting to die.

"Is this where you lived?" asked Drake, instantly regretting the personal inquiry.

"No. Just a place to hide."

"What did you do to get locked up?"

He scolded himself the moment the words came out. *You don't want to know. Stop asking stupid questions.*

She smirked. "Why don't you guess?"

Drake regarded her for a moment. "To send someone your age to prison means it must have been something pretty bad."

"I'm eighteen," she informed him. "I just look like a child."

She didn't appear offended, as was often the case when a young person's maturity was called into question. Hell, she probably used her youthful appearance as an advantage. There was definitely more to Linx than met the eye.

"Then I'd say you must have stolen something."

Linx placed her hand over her chest and gave him a hurt look. "A thief? Me? I should say not." Her face then melted into a smile. "Okay. You figured it out. I'm a thief, sure enough. But only when I need to be."

"So that's why you were in jail?"

She shook her head. "Nope. But I'll give you a hint. My next stop was Barmouth."

Drake cocked an eyebrow. "Barmouth? So they were going to…"

"You got it. They were planning to strap me into a chair and send mana current straight through the top of my cute little head."

There were only a few crimes punishable by death. "Who did you murder?"

"No one. But that's not what they think. And you know how it is in Vale – no money means no defense."

"What will you do?"

She shrugged. "I don't know. Keep running until they finally catch up with me, I guess. What else can I do?"

"If you're innocent, you could try to find proof of that."

"I didn't say I was innocent. I said I didn't murder anyone. The guy's dead, for sure."

"If you're going to ride with me, I think you had better tell me what happened."

Linx spread her hands. "What's to tell? Some jerk thought he could have his way with me and I killed him. Plain and simple."

Drake looked at her incredulously. "You're allowed to protect yourself. There has to be more to it than that."

"Yeah. He was the son of a sheriff's deputy." She leaned back and stared out the window. "Funny thing is, it's all on holovid. He was kinky and liked to record his little escapades. But fat chance of me getting my hands on it. Can't have a nobody like me stirring up trouble."

Drake had heard just about every story there was. Runners were always trying to convince him that they were innocent. Somehow, though, he believed Linx. He had seen it all before too many times – people with power taking advantage of those without. But that was the way of the world, and there wasn't a damn thing he could do about it.

The mana streams were almost non-existent here. Not much need for power. The few people living in the ramshackle dwellings couldn't afford to pay, even if there was.

Linx pointed to a small barn at the end of a long dirt driveway. Once parked there, she hopped out and scurried around to the back. Drake considered driving away. The very last thing he needed was someone slated for execution tagging along with him. That could really complicate matters. All the same, he knew he couldn't live with himself if he simply deserted her in this dump. He would find somewhere safe for her to hide. Maybe even get her a new identity. He knew the right people who could make counterfeit papers and ID cards, and thanks to Xavier, he had plenty of money to pay for it all.

She returned a few minutes later wearing a pair of jeans, a t-shirt, and a blue jacket. A duffle bag was hanging over her shoulder, and he could see a long knife strapped to her waist. Once she was in the car, she tossed the duffle in the back seat and kicked her feet up on the dash.

"That's better," she sighed. "Now, tell me what it is

you're after. Maybe I can help. You know…pay you back for breaking me out."

Drake turned Cal toward the road. "I doubt it. Not unless you know where I can find Exodus."

"Exodus? Sure. Take you right to them if you want. But why do you want to find that bunch of weirdos?"

Drake slammed on the brakes. "You know where they are?"

Linx was nearly thrown from her seat. "Hey! Take it easy. I said I did, didn't I?"

Drake called up the map and had her point out the area. It would only take a few hours to get there if he hurried.

"How did you find them?" he asked.

"I followed one of them."

Drake eyed her incredulously. "Why would you do that?"

"To steal. Why else? Those Exodus guys come around from time to time. They always have the best stuff to trade. I figured they have to keep it somewhere, right? So I followed one of them back to the base. Didn't do me much good. Everything is underground. And there's no way to sneak in."

"I need you to tell me what you know about them and their facility. Everything."

"There's not much to tell. It's not like they go around advertising. I mean, folks in the black market know about them, and there are rumors that they have spies everywhere. But as far as I know, I'm the only one who knows where they are. No one else has ever had the guts to follow them."

"And no one turns them in?"

Linx burst into laughter. "To who? The sheriff? The magistrate? Believe me, anyone who knows a thing about Exodus isn't wanting that kind of attention. I mean, once in a while someone comes around asking questions. We know they're from Troi. They always offer a reward, but talking to them is more likely to get you locked away than anything else. People just keep their mouths shut. Especially when you're only one background check away from a prison cell."

Drake nodded. "I see."

This had always been the problem when searching for fugitives. Wherever you were, locals could sniff out people from Troi in a heartbeat. And even if the money was right, giving information to the magistrate or royal guard could get you killed. That's why hawkers existed in the first place. They could go where the authorities couldn't.

She went on to describe the facility. Apparently, it was well hidden among the barren hills near the barrier. Just a small shack, inside of which was a steel door that led down to Exodus's base of operations.

"You're not really planning on trying to get in there, are you?" Linx asked.

"I'm leaving now," he told her flatly. "If you don't want to come, you should get out. I'm not stopping."

Her face twisted into a scowl. "You're insane. I hope you know that."

Drake simply stared straight ahead.

"Fine," she pressed on. "It's your funeral. I'll show you the best way to get close without them seeing you. But after that, we're even."

He pressed down hard on the accelerator. "We're even now."

It was nearly dawn by the time they arrived. Linx warned him against getting too close. "They always have a couple of guys watching the shed," she explained.

The road ended five miles from where she had indicated on the map. The ground here was mostly hard packed clay and gravel, allowing Drake to continue driving until within a mile of his destination. After that, the dust Cal was kicking up and the hum of her engine prevented him from taking her any closer. This was not ideal. A mile was a long way to run when you were being chased. And if the prince were hurt or otherwise incapacitated, he would have to carry him. That was, assuming he was even still there. Or that his information was accurate.

He found a spot behind a low hill and parked. The sky was clear and covered in starlight. The mana streams didn't come this far, but there was nothing to power out here anyway. Which made him wonder how Exodus ran a base this far away from Troi. It was possible, he supposed, that they drew their power from the barrier somehow – it was only another thirty miles from here. Not that Drake had any idea how the barrier was powered. A friend from his guard days had once suggested that it might be vex crystals, but that sounded ridiculous. Any vex crystal larger than the tip of your finger was unstable. Mess around with those, and boom!

He shoved aside these thoughts. It was time to focus. All he cared about was rescuing the prince…and going home.

He retrieved his sword and strapped it across his back. After shoving a phial of corrosive in his pocket, he leaned in the window. "Keep an eye out. I may be returning in a big hurry."

"You mind leaving her running?"

Drake chuckled. "You must really think I'm stupid."

Linx grinned. "Well…yeah, I do. After all, you are going to break into Exodus."

"Can't argue with that logic."

Drake gave her a confident smile and then started up the embankment. The ground was dry, with only a few sickly shrubs and patches of gray grass scattered about. It was widely believed that coming this close to the barrier would make you ill. That wasn't exactly true, though with no moisture and mile after mile of scorched land, no one would want to be stuck here without food or water. North or south, the days brought miserable heat. This was due to the energy from the barrier. At least, that's what he had been told.

He kept low, even though the lack of mana streams overhead would have made it nearly impossible for anyone to spot him. The crunch of his boots was the only thing that might give him away.

He had just crested a low hill when he caught the sound of nearby voices. Instantly, he dropped to his stomach and listened. Two men. This was confirmed as he eased his way forward. Just as Linx had told him, they were guarding a small shack.

"I hear we might be expecting company," said one of the men. "Better keep alert."

The other man sniffed. "They tell us that every week. Have you ever seen anyone out this far?"

"I don't know. Having *him* here makes me nervous. If they find us…"

"If they find us, then we'll all be dead. And you'll know in plenty of time. They'll roll in here with a hundred men or more. And not just those magistrate morons; it'll be royal guards armed with P37s. Hell, they'd probably send the mages along too, just for good measure."

"Well, I don't know about you, but I ain't fighting. If they come, I'm running my ass off."

"Go ahead. It won't do you a bit of good. Where you going to go? The barrier? If you ask me, it would be better to die fighting. Maybe take one or two of those bastards with you."

Drake smiled at that. If the royal guard found this place and sent one hundred men, it would be a slaughter. From the look of the light rifles these two were carrying, they would have to be at point blank range to do any damage at all.

He drew his P37 and channeled a small amount of mana into the chamber. The shots needed to be powerful enough to kill yet weak enough to be silent. At the thirty-yard range separating them, it was difficult to be sure his aim was true. He took a series of deep breaths.

Two dim balls of light streaked down from the hilltop. The first found its home in the center of one guard's chest. The second was a bit less accurate, striking the target in his right shoulder.

The injured guard spun from the impact, landing on one knee. His comrade was dead before he hit the ground. Drake fired again just as the man was reaching up toward the door to the shack. This time the shot did its job, hitting him at the base of his spine.

Drake sprang up and ran headlong down the other side of the hill. Quickly, he searched the bodies. No keys or anything else useful. He regretted the need to kill these men, but he couldn't risk having them alive at his back. There was no telling how long it would take to find the prince, and should they wake up while he was still here, that could mean trouble. Of course, a bit of information from them would have been useful.

"I must be slipping," he muttered.

Inside the shack was a four-foot-square steel trapdoor set into the ground. A mana pad was placed on a raised panel just beside it. *Definitely slipping*. He could have used one of those men alive. Too late now. He didn't have enough corrosive to burn through, so this left him with only one option.

He aimed his P37 at the mana pad. This would open the door, sure. But it would also probably alert everyone inside that he was coming. The burning in his chest increased as the power flowed into him. He shut his eyes and concentrated. In truth, the P37 wasn't really made for this sort of magic. But you learned to improvise when you were a hawker.

An instant before Drake fired, there was a loud beep and then a rush of air as the door began to swing upward. He instinctively backed away. A moment later, a young lad of no more than fifteen years stepped out carrying a covered tray, preceded by the scent of steamed vegetables and cooked beef. With his attention focused firmly on his feet as he stepped cautiously over the lip of the door, the boy didn't notice Drake at first.

Drake leveled his weapon and waited until the youth's eyes raised. When they did, the tray immediately fell to the ground, scattering its contents. For a long moment the boy simply stood there, seemingly paralyzed with shock.

He wasn't about to kill a kid. But he sure would scare the hell out of him. "Don't move," Drake ordered in his toughest voice.

Ignoring this, the boy suddenly jerked into life. He reached for his belt, and Drake saw the glint of a handgun. Rushing in, he grabbed at the boy's wrist. To his surprise, he was struck twice on the cheek before he could wrestle him to the ground.

The boy was still determinedly trying to reach for the gun. "What the hell is wrong with you?" Drake shouted.

"Help! Intruder! Help!"

It was easy enough for Drake to overpower him. Wrenching the weapon away, he tossed it to one side, though letting go with one hand earned him a few more punches. Fortunately, the boy wasn't nearly strong enough to cause any real damage.

He quickly shifted his knees and sat heavily on the boy's stomach. This promptly took the wind out of him, yet still he struggled. Drake pressed the barrel of the P37 to his head.

"I would rather not kill you," he said. "But I will if you make me."

"Go ahead," the boy spat.

"Look, kid. All I want is to know where the prince is being held. Tell me and I'll let you walk out of here alive."

"Fuck you. Pull the trigger. You'll never get to him."

Drake groaned. "Listen to me. There's courage, and then there's just plain stupidity. Do you really want to die?"

The boy said nothing. He just kept glaring at him defiantly.

Drake shrugged. "Fine. Have it your way."

He squeezed the trigger and the boy went rigid for a second, then fell limp. After checking his pulse, Drake let out a sigh of relief. Still alive. Though this one would definitely need to be tied and gagged.

The sound of fast-approaching footsteps coming from below reached him. They must have heard the boy's shouts. He shot up and ran from the shack, taking up a position just outside. The echoes from the corridor masked the number of people coming.

The first figure emerged up to shoulder level with a large caliber revolver poised and ready in his hand. His eyes darted over to where the boy still lay.

"Tomis is down," he called back.

"Get inside and close the door!" shouted another voice.

Before the first man could respond to this order, Drake fired with eyes closed. The flare exploded with a deep thump immediately above the open trapdoor. Cries of panic erupted as the blinding flash and massive concussion ripped down into the hideout. Drake opened his eyes and rushed back inside the shack.

The first man, dressed in blue coveralls, was still half in

and half out of the opening. His mouth was hanging in utter shock, his red raw eyes shot wide, as he clung desperately to the trapdoor for support. Without hesitating, Drake fired a round into his chest. The man's grip on the door instantly fell away, and he tumbled down the flight of metal stairs he'd been standing on. Drake followed him below.

Three more men were at the bottom, roughly ten feet down, screaming and cursing, the nearest one bleeding profusely from both ears. Drake shot twice more, then hurried over to the remaining man who had been standing further back from where the flare had exploded.

Drake threw his shoulder into the man's gullet and slammed him into the wall. He then glanced over to his left to note that there was a long corridor with a number of metal doors evenly spaced on either side. It ended in a set of double doors about a hundred feet away.

He struck the survivor sharply in the temple with his elbow. This was more than enough to quell any resistance, and the weapon he had been holding dropped harmlessly to the floor. Drake then forced him down and onto his back.

"Tell me where the prince is," he demanded. For a moment, he thought perhaps he had hit him too hard. "Talk, if you want to live."

The man shook his head. His eyes were open, though from the way they moved about it was clear that he was still blind. "You'll never get there," he said.

"That's not your problem. Just tell me where he is."

"Two levels down. In a holding cell near the far end."

Just as he spoke, the double doors at the far end flew open to reveal an older woman wearing the same blue coveralls as the others. Drake spun his victim around just as a stream of green mana sprang from her hands in his direction. His human shield screamed in agony as the spell seared his flesh. Drake fired back, sending a coil of white light spinning toward the woman. The mage tried to counter the attack, but her reaction was too slow. The light wrapped itself around her body, pinning her arms to her side. At the same time, the stricken man was flailing about wildly. Drake ended his suffering with a shot between the eyes.

The mage was still chanting feverishly in a desperate attempt to dispel the magic binding her when Drake drew close. A grin formed as he clicked the switch above the handle on his P37 twice and then squeezed the trigger. In an instant, the mage froze completely motionless, her face still contorted into a mask of pure fury and hatred. She had likely never encountered a weapon like the P37 before. Mages were an arrogant lot, unable to fathom that a non-magic user could ever be their match. Too bad this one didn't know whom she was dealing with.

The mage was still trying to mumble her spell. "Don't bother," Drake told her. "If I fire once more, you're dead. Now tell me, how many are coming?" He placed his finger on the trigger and weakened the spell enough to allow her to speak. The pain in his chest doubled as the mana re-entered his body, causing a wave of nausea to wash over him. Drawing power back from a mage was always unpleasant, something for which he could never really prepare himself.

"You're royal guard?" she asked.

"I was." He peered through the double doors – another long corridor identical to the first one. "Now, quickly. Tell me who's coming and I'll only knock you out."

"No one," she replied. "There isn't anyone else on this level."

Drake chuckled. "You know, I never did care very much for mages. They lie when the truth would serve them better. And you are definitely not improving my opinion of them."

Raising his weapon to her eye level, he placed his finger ominously on the trigger. "Last chance to be straight with me." He jerked his head over his shoulder to where the man hit by her spell lay. "Believe me, what you did to him will be heaven compared to what this will do."

Fear showed in her eyes. "I have your word you won't kill me?"

"That all depends on what you tell me."

After an extended moment, she nodded her agreement. "Six more men are waiting in the last room at the end of the hall."

"And how do I get to the holding cell from here?"

Surprise registered. "You're here for the prince?"

"That matters?"

"Why would you want to save that pig? Do you realize what he's done? And what more he'll do if he ever gets free?"

"I don't care. Just tell me."

Her jaw tightened and she looked again at Drake's finger poised to deliver pain and death. "It's simple. End of the hall and take a left. You'll find the stairs. Two levels down, turn right."

"That's it? A bit vague, don't you think?"

"They're waiting for you. You'll never make it to the cell."

"I see. So I just follow where all the bullets are coming from."

Drake could see the last room positioned on the right-hand side of the corridor. Very deliberately so that the woman could see him doing it, he altered the spell, changing its light to a pale green. Just before he fired, a thought occurred.

"You didn't think I was here for the prince, did you?" he asked.

She shook her head.

"What then?"

"Vex crystals."

Drake furrowed his brow. "Why on Vale would I want those?"

When there was no answer forthcoming, he squeezed the trigger. The mage let out a muffled groan as the spell did its work. Very quickly she became limp and crumpled to the floor. After gasping twice, she then became perfectly still.

Drake lowered his head and sighed. "Sorry. But I can't risk having you at my back either."

He hated killing women. And even after living in the provinces for all these years, he was still uncomfortable about lying. But at least it had been more or less painless compared to what he could have done to her. He reminded himself that, given the chance, she would have roasted him alive.

Pushing these thoughts from his head, he crouched low and took aim at the six mana bulbs fixed into the ceiling. Each burst with a sharp pop, leaving the hall in complete darkness. As soon as the last one was extinguished, he edged forward with his back pressed against the right wall until reaching the door immediately before the one the mage had indicated. Once inside, he could see it was a sparsely furnished office containing just a desk, a few cabinets, and an outmoded holoplayer shoved into one corner. He pressed his ear to the wall. A muffled cough told him that they were indeed waiting for him in the next room. Likely they would have burst out as he passed by.

He crossed to the far wall and pointed his P37 low. After four quick shots, he exited the office and threw himself flat on the passage floor. The explosion that quickly followed sent the doors to both the office and the room where the men were waiting flying from their hinges and crashing into the opposite wall. Through the dust falling from the ceiling in great clouds, he could see flames spewing from the room.

The screams of dying men and the crackle of furnishings being consumed tore through the air, though the screams fell silent after less than a minute.

Drake waited until the flames had receded before continuing to the end of the hall, pausing only briefly to glance inside the last room where the wall had been blasted inward from the other side. Six bodies were strewn about, their coveralls burned away and their flesh scorched black.

Poor bastards.

Following the directions given to him by the mage, he came to the stairs. They were situated beside a lift, a light above indicating that it was currently on his level. He grinned inwardly. Perfect. He used this to descend just one level and then peered out. Off to his right several yards away was a heavy looking door with the word *station* written in bright yellow letters. Right next to this was another door, this one held open by a stop at the bottom.

The sinews in his legs erupted, propelling him in this direction. He raced up to the open door, glancing inside before spinning around and heading back toward the lift. As he'd suspected: another trap. A burst of gunfire reverberated down the corridor in response to his fleeting appearance. Dozens of bullets ricocheted off the stone wall, but such was the speed of his movement that he was already well away from the line of fire.

They obviously hadn't expected to encounter him here. Drake figured they had been waiting for him to reach the next level and then attack from behind. A good plan. Or it would have been if he were just some guy trying to steal vex crystals…for whatever reason.

From his brief look, he reckoned on about fifteen armed men, each wearing shaded goggles. Smart. But not smart enough. Once back at the lift, he stopped and turned. The heat rose in his chest as he prepared a powerful shot. He needed to be precise…and very careful. He could hear orders being barked. Within seconds, they would be coming out after him.

"Did you see how many?" shouted a voice.

"I only saw one," came a reply.

"Could be a trap," suggested another.

It made sense that they should wonder about the number of intruders. What kind of fool would attack this facility alone? They were probably thinking it was a large group of magistrate's men or the royal guard. The explosions from upstairs would have furthered that assumption. By the time they realized he was alone, it would be too late.

He fired at the floor halfway between himself and the open door. A fist-sized red ball of gelatinous fluid sprang out and landed on target, where it wobbled around for a second before splitting itself in two. Drake wished he could see the confused looks on their faces as the two balls then split into four, and then again to become eight, now forming a line right across the width of the corridor. This was one of his favorite spells, though one that he rarely had the opportunity to use.

Thick clouds of pink smoke began issuing from each ball until it formed a dense fog. At the same time, Drake heard the pounding of a lone pair of boots drawing near. One of the men had rushed blindly forward. *Fool.* There was a gasp of someone catching their breath, and then a thin man with short-cropped blond hair came stumbling into view through the smoke, screaming as it clung to his face and began eating away at his flesh. Barely had he appeared when he spun around and headed back in the direction of his comrades. His screaming reached a frenzied crescendo…then he went silent.

Drake focused another shot. This one need not be very powerful: a simple gust of air. The fog cloud slowly drifted toward the remaining men, settling to about waist high as it went. The shouts of fear and trampling of retreating boots told him that it had worked. The spell would only be lethal for about five minutes, but they wouldn't know that. The smoke would linger for at least an hour, the spell having been crafted to resist being sucked up by ventilation. The poor soul who had made himself an example came into view. Now motionless on the floor, there was nothing left of him but a few chunks of bloody meat clinging to bone. A painful way to die.

Drake did not waste time dwelling on this. Crossing to the lift, he drew his blade and used it to pry open the door. A service ladder was fixed to the shaft wall. Looking down, he frowned. The next level below was the last. He had been hoping to go down one further than that and then climb back up.

"I guess you'll be blasting your way through instead," he muttered. At least they wouldn't be expecting him to arrive that way. As the lift had not moved, most of them would be watching the stairs.

He climbed down until able to stand on the lip of the lift door at the bottom, the steady hum of machinery masking any slight sound he might have made in his descent. Using the ladder to steady himself, he found the release for the door and eased it open a few inches. Through this he could make out a massive chamber with a series of black cylinders placed in neat rows, each one five feet tall and roughly half that in diameter. The rear wall was about one hundred yards away, but he could not yet get a good look to either side.

He widened the opening. He needed to know exactly where they were, otherwise…

A bullet pinged off the door, answering his question. More rounds rapidly followed, forcing him back onto the ladder. The gunfire ceased, and he could hear muffled shouts. This was not good. It would take them only a few seconds to work out what they should do. Holstering his weapon, he began to climb. But it was already too late.

The whir of the motor came to life and the cables began to move. He had just a few seconds before being crushed by the lift above.

Drake spotted a small crawl space covered by a metal grate just below where he was. But the grate was bolted, and right at this moment his P37 wasn't charged enough to blast apart the lock securing it. He let loose half a dozen quick shots anyway, but as expected, they did only minor damage.

"Fuck!"

There was only one alternative. Reaching out, he jerked the lift door fully open and dived through, throwing himself flat as quickly as possible. Still not quickly enough. Pain shot through his stomach and shoulder as bullets found their mark. Large caliber...they were penetrating, though he couldn't be sure yet how deeply. He returned fire, blindly at first. Then he spotted a dozen men knelt behind a row of toppled tables.

The nearest line of cylinders was only a few feet away. As he scrambled toward these, another round struck his right thigh, very nearly sending him back to the floor. Somehow he made it all the way, though not before yet another bullet had grazed his neck.

More rounds pummeled the cylinder now shielding him. A thought flashed through his mind. If these things were filled with vex crystals, they wouldn't be shooting at them...would they?

A door flew open on the opposite side of the chamber and more men ran in. Blood was now soaking his arm and pouring down his stomach. The wounds burned like hell, but he had little choice other than to fight on. It was either that or simply give up and die. Channeling power into the P37, he loosed six shots at the newcomers. Blue light streaked across the room, erupting into a wall of flames only a few feet ahead of them and halting their advance.

Dropping to his knees, Drake continued firing into the flames until the P37 needed to be recharged. He had barely started to do this when a bullet pinged above, very nearly parting his hair. The first group were now maneuvering around on either side of him. He returned fire with what little mana he had so far managed to absorb, hitting his assailant in the throat. He then flipped on the manual switch just below the rear sites. Six shots...standard .45 rounds. He hadn't fired an actual bullet in some time. The first round he let off went wide, but the second one was deadly accurate, thudding into the forehead of a man who was lying on his belly.

Drake darted toward the next row of cylinders before they could completely outflank him, letting loose two more shots as he ran. One of these hit another foe in the chest, sending him down in an untidy heap. Violent stabs of pain accompanied each pace he took until he was at last back behind cover. From this position, he spent his remaining two rounds. Those attackers still uninjured were taking cover among other rows of cylinders and squeezing off random shots, keeping him pinned down.

I don't know what's in these things, he thought. *But I'm sure as hell about to find out.*

He placed a bloody hand on the surface of the one next to him. It felt solid enough. He increased the mana to the

P37 and took aim at a cylinder two rows away from the main group of attackers. A stream of green light streaked out, hitting the target dead center.

The explosion that followed was far beyond anything he had expected. At first, flames merely shot out from the point where the mana struck, but a second later the entire container erupted in a huge fiery ball of molten steel. Such was the power of the blast that it ripped through two more cylinders alongside in an instant, inducing the same devastating effect.

Drake was sent sprawling more than ten feet. His head slammed into the stone floor, leaving him momentarily dazed. With all the strength and speed he could muster, he scurried up and ran headlong toward the still burning wall of flames he had created to stop the newcomers. Another explosion from behind then lifted him completely off his feet and sent him literally flying through the barrier. Only the speed of his passing saved him from serious burns. As it was, he escaped with nothing more than some superficial scorching. Landing on his side, he saw that he had already taken out all but two of the men who had rushed the room, and these were slumped on their backsides holding their heads after being thrown against the wall by the latest blast. Drake let off two quick shots before they even realized he was there.

Large hunks of the ceiling were crashing down onto the floor as the chain reaction of blasts continued. Drake dashed through the door from where the reinforcements had entered and found himself in a small room filled with boxes and crates. Two more exits were on either side. With the ground rocking beneath his feet and no time to think about it, he raced over to the nearest door on his left. Just as he reached it, a woman staggered through. She was unarmed, and looked up at Drake with a terrified expression.

"Don't go in there," he told her. She turned to run, but he caught her arm. "Where is the holding cell?"

The woman stared back at him, for a moment speechless. "That way," she then said, pointing to the opposite door. "All the way down."

"Show me," he said.

Though hesitating at first, she quickly changed her mind when he pointed the P37.

She led him through a series of halls and small chambers. Drake was forced to shoot four people along the way; unlike his captive, they were all armed. He saw to it that the woman remained in front of him, so that anyone ahead wouldn't recognize him to be an intruder until it was too late. Each time he killed, she glared at him with hatred and disgust. Only a fierce warning look and a wave of the P37 prevented her from trying to escape.

The facility continued to tremble and the lights flickered repeatedly as yet more explosions erupted. The place was much larger than Drake would have thought possible. How Exodus had managed to build it without being noticed was beyond his understanding.

Well, it damn sure won't be here much longer, by the sound of it, he considered grimly.

When they reached a thick steel door, the woman stopped. "The cell is in there," she told him. "But I don't have the key."

"Is there anyone inside?"

"I don't know," she replied. "I'm just a researcher."

He locked eyes with her for a moment. She was telling the truth. "Go," he instructed with a wave of his weapon.

She did not need telling twice and started away at a dead run.

He considered using the corrosive, but thought he might

still need to use it on the way out. Instead, he channeled mana into his weapon and took several steps back. The shots to the hinges were precise, and the door landed in the corridor with a deep boom.

To Drake's relief, no one was waiting on the other side ready to shoot at him.

Pain stabbed through his stomach as he took a step forward, doubling him over for a moment. Being gut shot was extremely serious if it had gone in too deep. His shoulder was also throbbing wildly. And to top things off, the wound to his leg might be superficial, but it was still hurting like hell.

Fighting through the waves of pain, he staggered inside. Sitting on the floor in the far corner was a figure wrapped in a green blanket. His straight blond hair was covering his face and his knees were raised up to his chin. Even so, Drake knew him at once.

"Your Highness," he said.

The prince did not bother to look up. "What's happening out there?" he sneered. "Did your little hideout get discovered? I suppose you're here to kill me."

Drake crossed over and held out his hand. "It's me, Your Highness. It's Drake. I've come to rescue you."

The prince raised his head. Bruises covered his face, and his right eye was swollen so badly that it was almost completely shut. He squinted at his rescuer through the left one. "Drake? Is that really you?"

"Yes, it's me, Your Highness. We have to hurry. This entire place is falling down around us. Can you walk?"

The prince kicked away the blanket. His hands were shackled and his once-fine attire was covered in blood and grime. Even so, his voice was determined. "I'll damn sure walk out of here," he stated. Salazar's eyes then fell on the blood covering Drake's arm and stomach. "You've been shot."

"I'll be fine," he said. "Right now, we need to go."

The prince took Drake's hand and then held up the shackles. "Can you get these off me first? They're mana suppressors."

Drake was now glad he'd saved the corrosive. After producing the phial, he poured a small amount of its contents onto the chain. It only took a few seconds, and the two halves separated with a sharp pop and a spark.

Salazar swung his arms around twice, enjoying the freedom of movement once again. "Let me look at your wounds," he told Drake.

"I'll be fine until we get out of here," he insisted. "Let's get moving." Another explosion punctuated his words.

"How many men are with you?"

"Just me, Your Highness."

"Then what the hell is all that commotion?"

Drake allowed himself a smile. "It seems I was enough. Well, that…and apparently these fools have been messing around with vex crystals. Which brings me to a point. Is there another way out of here? I've a feeling that the way I came in might be blocked off."

"There's a ventilation shaft not far away. I used it when I tried to escape just after I was brought here."

They exited the cell and wound their way through another series of corridors. After a time they passed a small group of people scurrying around inside what looked to be a laboratory. The prince halted, his hands suddenly glowing bright red. With his jaw tightly set and eyes ablaze with vengeance, such was the intensity of the mana he held that the shackles melted from his wrists.

Drake was about to call out, but the prince unleashed his fury into the room before he was able to utter a sound. A wave of mana fire leapt from his fingers, instantly spreading itself wide and consuming everything it touched. It was all over in seconds, and the stench of charred flesh filled Drake's nostrils. The prince stared at his handiwork for a long moment, a satisfied grin on his lips. It wasn't until Drake touched his shoulder that he looked away.

"If you knew the terrible things they did to me..." His voice trailed off.

"You don't have to explain, Your Highness."

The prince smiled then nodded his appreciation. They soon reached a narrow passageway that twisted along for another hundred feet. At the end was a square ventilation shaft, its opening covered in razor sharp wire. Drake made quick work of this obstruction with a single shot. After looking up into the pitch-dark opening, he then fired a small bulb of illumination that struck the top grate nearly forty feet above. This clearly showed that the sides were smooth all the way up. There was nothing whatsoever to hold onto.

He felt a hand tug at his shoulder.

"Let me go first," said the prince.

Drake opened his mouth to object, but the prince raised a finger. "You're hurt. And I sure as hell don't want you falling on my head." His hands started to glow. "Don't worry. Last time it took me more than an hour. This time it will be much easier."

By now, Drake's bleeding had almost stopped, the burning in his chest telling him that the mana was hard at work healing him. Even so, he needed to get the bullets out quickly. Particularly the one in his stomach.

The prince thrust the top half of his body into the shaft. Drake could hear the hiss of mana as he watched Salazar's feet slowly rise and then vanish altogether. When he was sure the prince was well on his way, he entered the shaft himself. His eyes immediately stung from the lingering fumes. The prince was burning handholds into the side of the shaft in order to pull himself up. Prince Salazar had always possessed an extraordinary talent for magic. It was widely speculated that, had he not been heir to the crown, he would surely have become a high mage. It did run in his family. But it had long since been determined that the royal family, unlike other nobles, should not study that sort of magic. It was simply too much power for one person to command.

Slowly, painfully, Drake climbed, his injured shoulder feeling as if it were ablaze from the effort. By the time Salazar reached the top, the rumbling below had ceased and the last of the explosions faded away. It was a simple matter for the prince to blast away the grate. Once outside, he thrust an arm down to help Drake up the remaining distance.

Drake lay on his back for a moment with a hand covering his shoulder. Before he could rise, he felt hands being placed on his stomach. The prince was drawing out the bullet.

"I don't have much skill with healing," he said. "But I'll do what I can."

By now, Drake was in too much pain to argue. He had lost quite a bit of blood. Were it not for the vex crystal in his chest, he knew for sure that he would never have made it this far. He sucked his teeth as the first bullet exited the wound.

"You're a lucky man," the prince remarked. "Any deeper and I would have had to open you up."

Drake was about to thank him when a searing hot wave of agony shot through his body. The sickly-sweet scent of burning flesh surrounded him as the prince cauterized the wound. The shot to his leg hurt far less, and his shoulder was already in so much pain that he barely noticed the bullet exiting. The burning, however, was difficult to bear without yelping out in pain.

Just as he was finished, they heard voices off to the east.

The prince was on his feet in an instant, his face a mask of fury.

"Forget about them," Drake said, rolling to his knees and pushing himself up. "I need to get you away from here." He took the prince's arm. "Please, Your Highness."

Gradually, the prince turned to face Drake. "You are right, my friend. Let us leave this foul place. I assume you have a vehicle nearby?"

Drake smiled. "Of course. And I think you'll like her."

He led them down a path that avoided the main entrance to the compound. Though he doubted anyone would be able to escape that way, he didn't want to risk that Exodus would choose to rally there. There was no way of knowing how many of them had survived, and Prince Salazar seemed determined to kill every last one of them he saw. Right now, all Drake cared about was getting him safely out of the area and back to Troi. The end was almost in sight.

Though his wounds were still aching severely, they had now become manageable, and he was able to keep walking at a fairly quick pace. On cresting the hill where Cal was parked, he caught the sound of Linx humming softly to herself. She was stretched out on the car's hood staring up at the stars.

"You're back," she said, as if surprised he had made it. She squinted through the darkness. "Who's that with you?"

"A friend," Drake told her. "Now get in. We're in a hurry."

"You got it." Linx hopped up and jumped into the back seat. "I guess all that noise I heard was you."

He removed his sword and placed it in the trunk, ignoring Linx's question. A shadow moving in the corner of his eye then caught his attention. The prince was just reaching for the door handle.

"Prince Salazar!" a voice called out.

Drake's hand shot to his weapon, but he relaxed as the figure drew closer. It was Bane. "How the hell did you find us?" he asked.

"You know him?" asked the prince warily.

"Yes. He was hired to –"

The flicker of mana cut off Drake's words. He made a dive for the prince, pushing him aside just as a fiery spear sprang from Bane's outstretched hands. The spell missed, instead striking Cal's door in the exact spot the prince had been standing only an instant earlier. Bundling the prince toward the front of the vehicle, Drake pulled out his P37. As he did so, two more spears smashed into the hood. For now, Cal's tough body was able to withstand the punishment, but....

Drake returned fire, only to see the shots dissipate before reaching Bane. This was a strong counter-spell. One Bane would have needed time to cast. And one that would take an exceptionally powerful shot to overcome.

Bane waved his arms in an exaggerated circle, and the crackle of mana filled the air.

"Get in the car," Drake shouted.

The prince did not hesitate, rounding the hood and jumping head first through Cal's open window. Drake followed, firing the engine just as Bane let loose a devastating ball of mana energy. It hit Cal in the passenger's side door, lifting the entire vehicle up onto two wheels. The second it slammed back down, Drake dropped her into gear and stomped on the accelerator. Another attack hit their rear end, causing them to swerve erratically. But Drake knew Cal well. He knew how to keep her under control, and after only a few yards had straightened her out and was leaving Bane behind in a cloud of dust.

A small car was parked a few yards up ahead. Drake

slowed just enough to fire a shot into its engine before speeding away.

"Who the hell was that?" shouted Linx.

"His name is Bane," Drake told her.

CHAPTER TWELVE

They drove in silence for a half an hour, Drake constantly checking behind them for any sign of pursuit. Linx leaned in several times, scrutinizing the prince.

"How did you find me?" Salazar asked Drake.

"Bane," he replied. "He told me he'd been hired to rescue you."

"You were working with that maniac?" cried Linx. "You're even crazier than I thought."

"You've heard of him?"

"Bane? Who hasn't? He's Fisk's top killer. The guy's killed more people than I can count."

Drake did not respond. Linx leaned back in her seat, and the prince spent the next minute or so staring silently out of the window.

"Are you all right, Your Highness?" Drake eventually asked.

Salazar smiled over at him. "Yes. I'm fine. Just a bit shaken."

"Your Highness?" Linx repeated, leaning forward once again. "I thought I recognized you. So that's why you broke in?" She gave a loud sigh. "I knew I should have stayed behind."

Drake frowned. "You can get out now if you want."

"I'm not going anywhere until I'm far away from this mess. And you had better not try to dump me off somewhere."

The prince turned to face her. "You are quite…spirited, aren't you? But please, do not be alarmed. You have my word that no harm will come to you. If you travel with Drake, I will consider you a friend and under my protection. Is that acceptable?"

She regarded him closely for a long moment. "Just remember you said that if the magistrate finds us."

The prince smiled. "I see. A fugitive from justice no doubt. And what is your name?"

"Linx."

"Well, Linx, as you already know, I am Prince Salazar. And seeing as how I am also a fugitive, I think you can count on my discretion."

"I should have already mentioned that," Drake cut in quickly. "Your father has rescinded the warrant."

Salazar looked at him incredulously. "Are you certain of this?"

"Absolutely."

A smile of relief slowly formed. "Excellent. So you see, Linx, staying with Drake was the right thing to do after all."

"And why is that?" she asked.

"Because once we're back in Troi, I can have you pardoned."

"About going back," said Drake. "That might not be quite as easy as you think."

He went on to tell Salazar of the events leading up to his rescue. The prince listened with keen interest as the entire web of lies and deceit was laid bare, especially the bit about a bomb being hidden in the car.

"I see," he mused once Drake had finished. "So you think whoever is behind this might try to prevent me from returning?"

"I don't think I want to find out," Drake replied. "If it's Xavier, he'll be able to watch every way into the city. Of course, I have no idea what other enemies you might have made over the years. Can you think of anyone who would want you dead?"

Salazar laughed. "Only about half of all the noble families. You know how they are. But perhaps I can narrow it down to just a few." He glanced over to Drake, and his laughter ceased. "I'm sorry. I forget sometimes what a difficult life you must have led during your exile. I always believed in your innocence. So did Father."

Drake shrugged. "Don't worry about it. What happened, happened. Nothing can change that now."

"Perhaps. It was insensitive of me, all the same." He paused. "But there is one thing you will be pleased to know. Lenora never stopped talking about you. Particularly to Xavier. I think she delights in how insecure it makes him to hear your name."

Drake could not prevent a smile from forming. "It will be good to be home again."

"You lived in Troi?" Linx chipped in.

"Young lady," said Salazar. "You are looking at a man who was quite possibly the best royal guard ever to wear the uniform."

"Royal guard? Are you serious? One step away from execution, and I'm riding with a member of the royal guard?"

"I was exiled," explained Drake. "Years ago."

"Well, at least that explains how you were able to get out of Exodus alive."

The prince cast Linx a curious look. "You were to be

executed? That is hard to believe. I didn't think they put people so young to death."

"I'm older than I look," she told him, then went on to explain what had happened and why she was to be executed.

Salazar shook his head. "That's terrible. Once I am back in the palace, you have my word that justice will be served appropriately. Young women should not have to fear such men."

"A lot worse than that happens out in the provinces," she said.

"Such as?"

Linx shrugged. "It doesn't matter. It's not like anything will change. People living in Troi don't care what happens outside the city."

"Linx!" Drake snapped. "That's enough."

"No," said Salazar. "She's right. People don't care. And I am as guilty as any other. We've lived cut off from the tragedy that is Vale for far too long. We refuse to admit that while we live in luxury and safety, the rest of our people are dying by the hundreds. Our bellies are full while others starve. But I swear to you that I will ignore it no longer. This suffering must end."

"I wish I could believe you," Linx told him. "I want to. But the truth is…"

"I know. The truth is that you've heard this before. Vague promises of how Troi is working to cure the sickness that plagues our world. But I say we are not doing enough. Not even close." He looked over to Drake. "That's why I left. And how I ended up in the clutches of those Exodus monsters."

"I shouldn't be hearing this," Drake said. "The reasons you and your father fought are between the two of you."

Salazar slapped him on the shoulder. "Always the cautious

one. And I understand that well enough. If I had lived the life you have been forced to, I wouldn't want anything to jeopardize my chance to go home again. But know this: I genuinely do intend to honor my promise. Life in Vale *will* get better for all those who live within the barrier."

They drove until dawn before finding a small town where they could purchase fresh clothing for the prince and some decent food. After they had eaten, Drake sent Linx off to find them a room where they could rest and figure out their next move. Once she was gone, he and the prince sat down on a bench in front of the eatery.

"Not the best fare," Salazar remarked. "But better than the bile Exodus fed me."

"You'll be home soon. Then you can leave all this behind."

"No," he retorted. "I can't. I meant what I said. Things must change. I see that now more clearly than ever." He cast his eyes over the broken buildings and ragged people walking about. "Look at this. People should not be forced to endure such conditions."

"Begging your pardon, Your Highness, but you've always known what it's like out here. What's changed?"

"*I* have. After you were exiled, I spent most of my time lost in drink. I was miserable without you." He lowered his head and chuckled softly. "What a selfish child I was. Here you were, living in misery, and I was the one feeling sorry for myself." His eyes were welling with tears. "You were like a brother to me. I hope you know that. It tore me apart to know what had become of you."

Drake placed his hand on Salazar's shoulder. "I thought of you in the same way. But none of it was your fault."

"Wasn't it? I knew the evidence was false. So did my father. And yet we did nothing."

"Your father spared my life," said Drake. "And because of that, I get to go home."

"Say what you like, the fact remains that we were both cowards unwilling to stand up to the other noble houses." The prince wiped his eyes and leaned back in the bench. "I sent men out to look for you so I would know how you were faring. They reported back that you had become a hawker. I could hardly believe it. You, of all people – a hunter of men and a paid killer. It was then that true realization dawned. If this world could cause a man of your strength and quality to sink so low, what must it be doing to the rest of the people in Vale?" He paused to look Drake in the eye. "Please forgive the insult. I know you only did what you had to in order to survive."

Drake was not insulted. "I appreciate what you are saying, Your Highness. But what can you do? There is only so much food to go around. The land is still sick. Nothing can change that."

Salazar's face hardened. "You are wrong. There *is* something I can do. I have found a way to help the people."

"Really? How?"

"You will see. I'll explain in full once we're safely back in Troi." He smiled warmly. "And with you to aid me, I know we can do it."

Linx bounded up a few minutes later and led them to a small boarding house where they were able to bathe and get some rest. The prince fell asleep on the bed almost the moment his head struck the pillow. Linx decided to lie down on the floor, while Drake kicked his feet over the arm of the only chair in the room and slumped down. Though his wounds still ached terribly, they were healing and no longer a major concern.

The final thought before sleep took him was: How the

hell were they going to get into Troi without being seen?

∂◌

When he woke, his neck was stiff from sleeping in an awkward position. Though it was still dark, he could see could Linx curled up in her blanket nearby. She was mumbling softly in her sleep. His eyes then shifted over to the bed. It was empty. He scrambled up to his feet.

"I'm here," said the prince.

Only then did Drake see his silhouette in the window. "Are you all right, Your Highness?" he asked.

"When we were children, you called me Salazar."

"As I recall, your mother did not approve."

The prince laughed quietly. "She was always a bit too proper for my taste."

"Maybe. But if not for her, you would have been running around the streets of Troi with me instead of learning your lessons."

"I think I might have been better off with you," he said, his tone distant and filled with regret. "What has it all achieved?"

"I'm not sure what you mean."

He sighed. "I've spent my life learning about the politics of Troi. Yet I know nothing of Vale. If I am to be king one day, I must look to the good of all. My father…" His shoulders sagged.

"Your father is a good man, and a wise ruler. If you see what needs to be done, speak with him. I'm sure he'll listen to you."

"I have tried. I know you love him, Drake. But my father is too weak to do what is needed. And I fear that when my time comes to rule, it will already be too late."

Drake creased his brow. "What are you saying?"

Salazar looked over his shoulder and smiled. "Nothing, my friend. Take no notice of me. You should go back to sleep. I am just unsettled right now. So much has happened, and I am not as strong as you. Tomorrow is a new day. I'm sure I will be myself again by then."

He turned and crossed over to the bed, pausing to place a hand on Drake's shoulder.

Drake returned to his chair and settled back down. But sleep was now elusive. There had been a time when he could practically read the prince's thoughts. Something was disturbing him...deeply. And it went well beyond his captivity. It was as if a shroud had been placed over Salazar's heart and he was struggling to find a way to remove it.

Drake watched his childhood friend until his breathing was steady. Dawn would come soon, and they needed a plan. The key was the magistrate's office in lower Troi, he felt. If the prince could make it that far, then there would be no hiding his presence from the king. Even if somehow the magistrate were in on the scheming, there would be no way for her to keep the prince's arrival a secret. One thing was certain: should it be Xavier who was behind all of this, he would do everything possible to stop them from reaching it.

Then, of course, there was Bane. How could he have not seen through the man's lies? Drake swore to settle with him in due course. Fisk too. And whoever else was involved.

As the first light began filtering through the window, he still had no idea how to get Salazar into Troi unseen. But one thing *was* clear: they could not stay here for much longer. Even battered and bruised, someone was bound to recognize the prince sooner or later.

He heard Linx stir.

"Didn't you sleep?" She yawned, her eyes peeling open. She smacked her lips and crinkled her nose, blowing a breath into her palm.

"I've only been up for a short while," he told her.

She stretched and rubbed the back of her neck. "You figure out what to do yet?"

Drake shrugged. "I'm working on it."

Pushing herself up, she retrieved a toothbrush and paste from her pack. "Well, I know how *I'd* do it."

"And how is that?"

"The train from Antwerp, of course. There are only a few guards there. They don't even check you getting on, and it takes you right inside Troi." She paused before entering the restroom. "Much easier than storming the gates, don't you think?"

Drake thought about it. It was actually a good idea. Very few people rode the subterranean rails. And she was right – you were only security-checked as you got off. They could board the train without being challenged at all. If they could somehow then get through the checkpoint after arriving, they would be home free. It certainly wouldn't be possible to make it to upper Troi from there, but that wasn't the objective. Nothing after that was in place to prevent them from entering lower Troi.

Even so, getting through the checkpoint would not be as simple as all that. The fact that only a few guards manned it was mainly due to the lack of traffic coming in from Antwerp. Everyone arriving still had no choice but to show their identification. Drake had one, although Xavier would likely be notified the moment he used it. And that didn't get either the prince or Linx safely in.

Salazar awoke a short time later, and Drake informed him of Linx's idea.

"How many men guard the entrance?" was the first thing he asked.

"No more than three."

"And will they be magistrate officers or royal guard?"

"Magistrate," Drake told him. "Usually new recruits. Though occasionally the royal guard does send someone there for a short spell as a punishment. It's hot, and there's nowhere to sit. Just a booth for checking identifications. There's a parking garage just beyond that, which should be helpful. I'm afraid we'll need to steal a vehicle." He hated the thought of leaving Cal in Antwerp, but he would come back for her as soon as possible.

"And you're sure we couldn't make it through the main highway into Troi?"

Drake spread his hands. "If I knew who to trust, it would be possible. But remember, doing it that way would let them know very early on that I'd found you."

Linx, who had been listening silently to the pair of them, suddenly spoke. "I think I can get us through the checkpoint." She rummaged through her pack and pulled out a small cloth. Inside were three blank ID cards.

"Those won't get us in," said Drake. "They'll know they're fake the second they're scanned."

"They're not fake," she insisted. "They're blank. All I need is a minute at the station console in Antwerp, and ta-da!"

Drake raised an eyebrow. "You've done this before?"

"Once."

"Did it work?" asked Salazar, looking equally skeptical.

Linx shifted on her feet. "Well...not exactly. But I know what went wrong, so it'll definitely work this time."

"The problem would be getting access to a terminal."

"Oh, that'll be easy," she countered. "Just knock the

guard out. It only has to last long enough for us to get into Troi, right?"

"It's a five-hour ride," Drake informed her. "We'd have to kill them."

"Is that a problem?" asked Salazar.

"No, Your Highness, I suppose not. But you should be aware that the guards minding the Antwerp end of the rail are usually very young. Not to mention, the magistrate might not be involved at all. Killing one of their officers is probably not the best way to enlist their help."

He couldn't help but be bothered that the prince was so willing to take a life. The bastards at Exodus were one thing, but killing like this was something else completely. The person minding the platform was there simply to help people. They didn't even check identifications. The mana terminal was mostly used to help visitors find the best spots to camp or fish.

"I suppose I could stay behind," offered Linx. "I'll keep the guard prisoner. But you have to promise to send for me once everything is sorted out."

Drake looked at Salazar, who nodded his approval.

"You haven't promised yet," Linx told him in a stern tone.

The prince smiled and bowed. "You have my word, dear lady. Moreover, once I send for you, you can remain in Troi for as long as you wish as reward for your assistance."

"Will I get my own apartment and everything?"

The prince laughed. "Of course. I think that would be a most fitting reward for your service to me."

A tiny smile crept up from the corners of her mouth. "What about Cal?"

"If something happens to me, she's yours," said Drake.

"Then what are we waiting for? It's a long way to

Antwerp." She handed the prince one of the blank ID cards.

Salazar watched as Linx began shoving her things into her pack. "I value loyalty above all else, young lady," he told her, flicking the card with his thumb. "Do well, and your future is assured."

Drake was unsure if he could count on Linx being able to pull it off. Falsifying identification was extremely difficult. Each card was infused with a tiny piece of mana linked to a specific person. The records were stored in an immense chamber within the power station itself. To add a name to the records, one needed to be a level six officer of the magistrate. The person watching the train platform would be level one – two at best. But Linx seemed confident. And without a better alternative, her plan was worth a try.

After a quick breakfast, they started out. Seeing Cal in daylight brought a heavy frown to Drake's face. The damage to her door was bad, and on starting her up, he thought he could hear a slight tick in the engine. A pity he couldn't take her to Dorn.

He wondered if the old man knew just what a bastard his son was. He liked to think that Dorn was completely unaware of what had happened. But even if that were true, Bane was still his son. And it would be wrong to do business with the father of a man whom you intended to kill. That said, he would likely have to get to him before the prince did. Salazar was indeed a man who prized loyalty; he always had been. But he was also a man who held a grudge like no other.

Bane's days were definitely numbered.

CHAPTER THIRTEEN

S alazar and Linx spent hours talking along the way. Mostly the prince asked about her life in the provinces and seemed highly impressed with how she had managed to survive. Drake could tell that something was going on in his old friend's mind, and whatever that was, it was weighing heavily on him. Each time Linx told him about some atrocity or injustice, his eyes would close for a moment as if having some heated debate with himself.

Salazar mostly told stories about his childhood with Drake.

"Drake always says that we met by accident," he told her. "But I say it was fate. His father was demonstrating some new gadget he had invented. For the life of me, I can't remember what it was. Something to do with uniforms, I think."

"It was a projectile resistant cloth," Drake told him. "They still use it for magistrate officer uniforms."

Salazar rolled his eyes. "Well, of course, *you* would remember." He gave Linx a playful grin. "He was always so proud of his father's work. You should have seen him as a child, constantly boasting, as if his parent had created mana itself."

"He was a brilliant man. Besides, *your* father was the king. I had to brag about something."

Salazar blew out a long breath. "Don't let him lie, Linx. He was genuinely proud of his father's accomplishments. And to be honest, the man was indeed brilliant. The best researcher in Vale, according to my father....*and* Drake."

"The king allowed the two of you to be friends?"

"Allowed? He insisted upon it. Drake was with his father at the demonstration. Did I mention it was in the magistrate's training facility? Well, that's where it was. I was playing with some other children – nobles, and spoiled rotten, the lot of them. We were up on the balcony while the adults were below on the training floor. When I heard gunfire, I went to see what was happening."

"Gunfire?" said Linx.

"Yes, my father was demonstrating the cloth's resistance to bullets," explained Drake.

Salazar feigned irritation at his interruption. "Would *you* like to tell the story?"

Drake raised his hand for the prince to continue.

"Anyway, when I went to look, one of the other children decided to try and frighten me. Well, he succeeded. He frightened me right over the edge of the railing. Drake was looking up just at the right time and ran over to catch me."

"He caught you?" She eyed the prince dubiously.

"He did indeed. I fell fifteen feet straight into his arms...both of which were broken, along with several of his ribs."

Drake tapped the side of his head. "And a fractured skull."

"Ah, yes. I always forget the skull," He reached over

and flicked Drake's forehead. "I, on the other hand, was uninjured. They rushed him to the hospital. My father insisted that they take him to the very best one in upper Troi. Along the way, he was asking only one thing: 'Is the little boy who fell all right?'"

"You didn't know it was the prince?" asked Linx.

"I didn't know he was even there. It wasn't as big a deal as they made it out to be. But for about a week, I suddenly became quite famous."

"My father insisted that Drake come to the palace and play with me," Salazar continued. "He said being around Drake would give me character."

"A feeling your mother didn't share," Drake added.

"No. She thought a reward and a royal letter of appreciation were more than enough. Fortunately, my father did not agree and saw to it that, from then on, Drake spent at least three days every week at the palace."

"So is that how you ended up as a royal guard?"

Drake nodded. "I didn't have my father's brains, but I did have a certain talent for magic. So it was either the mages' college or the royal guard."

"Let me guess," said Linx. "You couldn't bear to leave your best friend."

"Oh, no, my dear," Salazar told her. "It wasn't me he was unwilling to leave."

Drake felt a cold chill in the pit of his stomach. "I wanted to stay near my father," he lied. "He was starting to get sick by then."

Salazar gave him an understanding look and smiled. "Yes. That's exactly right. He was a very dedicated son."

Drake was grateful that he didn't mention his love for Lenora. Salazar had heartily approved of their romance, and had even offered to speak to the king about it. But they all knew it would have been useless. Certain rules not even the king could break, and marriage of a noble to a commoner was expressly forbidden.

Clearly sensing Drake's unease, the prince steered the conversation onto other topics.

They skirted the border of the inner provinces, staying in the most out-of-the-way places they could find. Drake kept a careful eye on their fuel. They would make it to Antwerp, but not much further if it turned out they could not travel by train.

The prince continued to pass the time talking to Linx. Drake noticed her to be exceptionally bright. She had learned to infiltrate a mana console simply by reading an old instruction manual she found in an abandoned building.

"I relate to machines much better than people," she told him.

"You would have gotten along great with my father," Drake responded.

By the time they reached Antwerp, Drake could sense that Salazar's nerves were on edge. By contrast, Linx seemed to be in high spirits, though this was hardly surprising. The prospect of leaving behind a life of hardship – not to mention receiving a pardon for her death sentence – was enough to make anyone excited.

They stopped at a local store to buy some hiking gear and a fold-out tent. At the very least, they would look the part of holidaymakers returning home to Troi. The station was situated almost dead center of the province and just south of a stretch of low hills. With a large lake nestling between these, the area was a magnet for campers and fishermen.

"Why can't all of Vale look like this?" mused Linx.

"Maybe one day it will," said the prince.

"Are you kidding? Too many people. Where would they all live? In the trees?"

"Yes," agreed the prince in a half whisper. "Far too many people."

The road twisted and dipped erratically as they neared their destination, prompting Linx to complain several times that she might be sick, though fortunately she was able to contain the impulse. The massive parking lot was virtually empty when they pulled in. This did not surprise Drake at all. The vast majority of visitors came from Troi, and very few of those chose to bring their own vehicles. Almost no one visited here from the provinces. This was where one came to relax, and who had time for relaxation when you were busy working yourself into an early grave?

A large staircase led up from the lot to the rail platform. Just at the top of this was a small shop, where people could purchase last minute supplies and maps of the park. It was also where the guard would be positioned.

The train ran only once a day in each direction, and unless its schedule had been recently changed – which was unlikely – there was still more than an hour to pass before it arrived and then headed back to Troi. The three of them got out of the car and donned their camping gear. Drake did his best to hide his sword, but it still poked out just above his shoulder. Not that it mattered much. By the time whoever was in there noticed, it would all be over. Still, he thought it best to leave it in Cal's trunk.

He handed Linx a scrap of paper. "This is the code for Cal. Just touch the mana pad and say it out loud."

She shoved the paper into her pocket. "Thanks. But I'm hoping I won't be needing it."

"Me too," Drake said. "Make sure you stay where you can see her. If guards show up for you, they'll be holding their weapons above their heads. If they're not, then we didn't send them and something bad has happened. You should run."

"And what if no one comes?"

"Someone will, one way or another. But if for some reason you don't see anyone by this time tomorrow, take Cal and get as far away as you can."

They climbed the stairs and approached the shop. Drake peered inside the glass door. A young woman in a magistrate's uniform was reading behind a small counter. She gave them a welcoming smile as they entered.

"Just returning?" she asked. "Or just heading out?"

Her smile instantly turned to fear as Drake drew his P37 and pointed it at her head.

"You'll be fine so long as you do as you're told," he said in a level tone.

"There's nothing here to steal," she said. "I swear that's true. Only about twenty in notes. That's all."

The prince stepped forward. "Young lady, do you recognize me?" Drake caught his shoulder, but he held up his hand. "It's fine."

The girl ran her eyes over Salazar's face. The swelling had gone down considerably, though many of his bruises still remained. Nonetheless, after a few seconds her jaw went slack and she covered her mouth.

"Are you really him?" she gasped.

The prince smiled. "I am. And I need you to do exactly as you are told."

"Did *they* do this to you?" she asked, nodding her head at his injuries.

"No. These are my friends."

"But how –?"

"I want you to listen to me very carefully," he said, cutting her short. "This young lady to my left is going to tie your hands. After that, you will go with her and do exactly as she says. You have my word that she will not harm you. Understand?"

"But, Your Highness, if you need help…"

"I need you to obey me; that is all. Do so without incident, and you will be well rewarded."

Her eyes shifted over the group. "Of course, Your Highness."

Linx immediately bound the young guard's hands with rope from her pack and moved her from behind the counter.

"How long until the train arrives?" asked Drake.

"Half an hour," the girl answered.

Linx set to work on the console. "Press your thumbs down on the center of the card," she told Drake and the prince. After they had done as instructed, she took the cards back and continued pushing buttons at a furious rate.

"Last time I wasn't fast enough," she said through gritted teeth, while still working away feverishly. "But…not…this…time."

"Got it!" She handed them back their cards, grinning from ear to ear. "Good for one trip only."

"What happens then?"

"After one time, it gets run through the system for a check. Any new card does. They'll know which terminal it was entered from, and that I didn't have authorization to issue it. But that won't happen until you try to use it twice."

Salazar took Linx by the hands. "You have done very well. I see a most promising future ahead for you."

"Thank you, Your Highness." For a moment or two she blushed. Then she glanced over to the girl. "Come on. We should get going."

Drake and the prince waited until they were well away before exiting the shop and heading along the platform.

"I'm glad the girl cooperated," Drake remarked.

"As am I." Salazar gave a reflective sigh. "I have not spent nearly enough time cultivating proper relationships amongst the magistrate's people. It's the minor players in a game who often make the vital difference. That is a lesson my father tried to teach me when I was young, and why he insisted you and I become friends. The truth is, it's not the nobility who keep a king in power. It's those who protect him. And I'm not talking about the captains and high-ranking officers. Without their subordinates, they are nothing."

Drake nodded his agreement. "A smart way of thinking."

He had always maintained a close relationship with his men. It was what had made him such an effective leader.

"Take that young lady Linx is holding, for example," the prince continued. "Lowly, ignored, and made to serve in a post that keeps her far removed from her home. Her commander probably doesn't give her a second thought. But show her a bit of kindness and respect – make her feel like she really matters in the overall scheme of things – and you will have earned her undying loyalty. Repeat that enough times, and before long you have yourself a secret army. One that can lurk in shadows, hidden from sight until you need them."

By now, he was talking to himself as much as to Drake. "That's how my father does it. That's why he's king, and I'm..." He nodded his head as if a decision had just been made.

All along the platform, the walls were covered in green tiles with various posters advertising the amenities of the camping park. After a few hundred yards, the rail tracks disappeared into the blackness of a large tunnel. From within this dark void, a constant rush of musty air swept over the platform, and the low rumble of the approaching train could be heard, even though it was still some distance away.

"What will you do once you are home?" asked Salazar.

Drake shrugged. "I haven't really given it much thought.

I suppose I'll need to find work. But what kind, I don't know yet."

Salazar laughed. "You have rescued the Crown Prince of Vale. You cannot seriously believe you will need to work?"

"I don't think I could just sit around doing nothing for the rest of my life." He gave a lopsided grin. "Then again, I suppose it would be nice to relax, at least for a little while."

"No one deserves it more." He paused to look Drake directly in the eye. "Tell me, if you were able to… Would you return to the royal guard?"

Drake lowered his head. "You know, I've thought about that countless times since my exile. During those first years I would have said yes without a second thought. But now… The truth is, I don't think I'm cut out for it anymore. Too much has happened. I'm not the same man I was. In any case, even if Xavier is behind this and arrested, I'm still a convicted murderer. I would never be accepted back."

"I see."

Drake gave the prince's arm a fond squeeze. "Hey. Don't you worry about me. I'll be fine. If you really want to give me a reward, just make sure I live somewhere near a manga juice shop."

Salazar chuckled. "I had almost forgotten your love for that dreadful stuff. But if it is manga juice you want, then manga juice you shall have." He spread his arms wide and threw back his head. "Do you hear that everyone? I, Prince Salazar, heir to the throne of Vale, hereby decree that Drake Sharazi is to receive all the manga juice his heart desires, even though it is vile tasting and will likely send him to an early grave. In fact, I also hereby decree him to be the new Minister of Manga Juice."

Drake bowed with exaggerated formality. "I accept the position with all due humility and gratitude, Your Highness."

At this, both men burst into uncontrollable laughter. Drake hadn't felt this good in a very long time. It was if the years had melted away and they were young again; transported to a time before the weight of adulthood had come crashing down on their lives.

They were still laughing when the rush of air from the tunnel began to increase, the approaching rumble grew significantly louder, and a light appeared in the darkness.

A minute later there was an ear-piercing screech of brakes as the train began to slow. The first car appeared, silver and polished with a thin red stripe down the center of both sides. The conical nose of the first car shimmered and sparkled from the tiny streams of mana dancing along its surface. There were ten cars in all, each one with an oblong door that rose outward the very moment the train came to a complete stop.

Only two people got out: a middle-aged couple, both of them carrying sizeable packs on their shoulders. Drake and the prince stepped quickly into the first car before the approaching pair had an opportunity to get a close look at them. There was no point in risking recognition.

Inside were rows of plush seats, two per side, with an ample aisle down the center. Small screens were set into the backs of the headrests so that passengers could watch holovids to pass the time if they wished. A door at the rear led through to the other cars, while at the front was a large panel with myriad buttons and flashing lights, though a clear screen was fastened over this to prevent anyone from touching the controls.

The two of them settled in and waited. The train was on a timer and would leave precisely ten minutes after its arrival. If you missed it, then you would be stuck there until the following day. Drake recalled one occasion when he and his father had been racing full tilt to make the train. They'd jumped onboard literally as the doors were closing. Time always went by so quickly then, and he'd never wanted to leave. This time, ten minutes felt like ten hours before there was a soft chime and the door eventually closed.

"There's no turning back now," said the prince, a slight tremor in his voice.

The engine hummed to life. It reminded Drake of Cal. But not even she could match the speed that this train was capable of. Five hours; that was all the time it took to travel a distance it would take at least two days to complete by any other means. His body pressed into the cushion of his seat as the train began accelerating. He shut his eyes, enjoying the sensation.

After a minute, he cracked open one eye and turned his head. The prince was watching the holovid.

"You should try to sleep," Drake suggested.

"I was just checking to see if there was any mention of my absence."

"There won't be."

The king would not allow it. And those out to kill Salazar would not risk exposing themselves. As far as anyone knew, the prince was still safe and sound in the palace.

For now, that was an advantage.

CHAPTER FOURTEEN

rake tried to take his own advice and get some sleep. Not that he was successful; his mind was racing far too much. Once they stepped from the train, they would be exposed and vulnerable. If Linx were unsuccessful, or if someone recognized the prince, they would have to decide very quickly indeed how to react. On one hand, it was possible that they could simply enlist the aid of whoever was on duty at the gate. But that would be risky. Those after the prince would almost certainly be watching every point of entry, and to be caught by them without enough witnesses to ensure that the king would be made aware of their arrival back in Troi could easily spell a death sentence.

Of course, all this subterfuge and caution might be for nothing. He only had the word of the treacherous Bane that the device installed inside Cal had indeed been a bomb. For that matter, he only had the man's word for it that he was even Dorn's son. Drake sighed. None of this could be allowed to change things. He'd damn sure rather look stupid by acting overly cautious than end up getting himself – and the prince – killed.

Resigned to the fact that sleep would not come, he went over the different possible courses of action in his head. They would need to steal a vehicle. But that might not be so easy. The lot was guarded, and to start a vehicle without the proper codes or being mana linked would take a fair bit of time.

He was still going over this in his mind when he felt the train beginning to slow. The prince was already awake.

"Are you ready?" Drake asked.

Salazar gave him a nervous grin. "Of course. I have every confidence in your ability to get me home safely."

"That makes one of us, then."

They gathered their packs so they'd look as if they had just returned from a camping trip. These were cumbersome, but would only need to be carried as far as the gate.

The chimes sounded to indicate that the train had almost reached its destination. Both of the men moved to the door. Drake's heart was pounding furiously. This was it. The final obstacle to overcome. After this he could return home to his former life; the very thing he had yearned for during all those lost years.

The brakes suddenly screeched, forcing them both to grab at the headrest of the nearest seat in order to stay on their feet. Drake took several deep breaths. He should have known this was about to happen; why hadn't they stayed in their seats until the train stopped? Was the tension of the moment affecting his thinking?

As the braking eased, he held out his hands. Yes, they were trembling. *Pull yourself together*, he told himself sternly. After a few seconds of deep breathing, the shaking subsided.

The door hissed open and a rush of air blew over them. It carried a familiar scent: that of Troi. They stepped onto the platform. It was quiet; only the rumble of the tunnel and the echoes of the guards' voices could be heard.

The checkpoint booth was encased in a steel mesh, with just a thin slot through which to pass your ID card. Just beside the booth, two guards were standing at a tall table eating their dinner. A third man was inside, staring at a holoscreen with a bored look on his face.

Drake approached the booth first in order to shield the prince's face for as long as possible from the guard inside. The men at the table showed little interest in them as they slid their cards through the slot. It seemed like their disguise was working and they were being taken for nothing more than campers returning home. For the men eating, their mealtime chat was far more interesting.

But the guard on duty inside the booth was a different matter. It felt like an eternity waiting while he entered their ID's. Throughout this, without making it too obvious, Drake continued doing his best to shield the prince from the guard's gaze. If this didn't work, they would need to move quickly. He was barely able to prevent a sigh of relief from slipping out as the cards were passed back through and the door buzzed open.

On the other side was a large concourse with a ramp going up to the parking area and a set of stairs leading to a mana carriage. He wished it were possible for them to take one of these. They could climb the mana stream directly to upper Troi, and once there, it would be a simple matter to alert the king. The only drawback was, it would mean undergoing another identification check. So frustratingly, that route was out of the question.

While ascending the ramp, Drake could hear the prince breathing in shallow gasps. He looked back and gave him a reassuring nod.

"We're almost there," he said in a whisper.

Upon reaching the top, Drake took note of the scant

vehicles scattered about. A few other facilities were nearby, but most were closed at this time. Only the custodial staff and a few security personnel would be still be around.

He chose a beat-up old compact, hoping the condition meant that the owner hadn't bothered keeping up with its security maintenance. He took a long look around as casually as he could before moving in. There were cameras, but vehicle theft here was rare. In all likelihood, the vids were unwatched most of the time. There would be a guard wandering around somewhere, but at present he was nowhere to be seen.

The door was unlocked, though it wasn't this that would be the challenge. The two of them tossed their packs onto the back seat and climbed in. Drake immediately set to work trying to remove the steering columns casing, eventually banging at it with his fist until it simply fell apart.

So focused was he on his task that he didn't hear the figure approaching from behind. Nor did he see the guard until drew he his gun and pointed it his head through the window glass.

"Don't move," the man roared in a deep imposing voice.

Drake froze. Salazar's face was etched with fear.

"Get out of the vehicle."

"What do we do?" whispered the prince.

"We do what he says," Drake replied. He had hoped it would not come to this.

He opened the door and got out with slow measured movements. "Have I done something wrong?"

This was a young officer, but he did not appear in the least bit unsure of himself. His weapon was trained on Drake's chest. "Face the vehicle and place your hands on the hood. You, in the car – get out slowly and let me see your hands."

The prince did as instructed. Then, the moment his

hands rose above the roof of the car and his face came clearly into view, the officer's eyes shot wide. In a flash, he swung his weapon over in Salazar's direction. Without thinking, Drake spun and made a grab for the gun. The shot sounded loud but flew harmlessly into the air as, still clutching the man's wrist, he rammed his shoulder forward. They stumbled backward, though somehow the guard kept his footing and then thrust an elbow hard into Drake's jaw. The impact was jarring, but after holding on for a second or two, he was able to counter with a savage fist to the gut. This should have doubled his opponent over. Instead, as proof of his toughness, he jerked up a knee with a strike hard enough to lift Drake completely from his feet. Pain tore through him. The knee had hit precisely where the Exodus man's bullet had penetrated. He could feel his legs giving way. Another blow to the back of his head then sent him crumbling all the way down.

In desperation, Drake was reaching for his weapon when the sizzle of mana told him it would not be needed. He looked up to see the officer clutching at his chest, his face twisted in agony. A moment later he fell to the ground, groaning and unable to move.

Drake was still down himself, but he could tell that whatever spell the prince had used, it had not been fatal. Whether or not it had been intended to be was another matter. In an odd turn, the very cloth his father had invented had likely saved the man's life.

From the corner of his eye he then saw the prince moving in to finish the job, hands glowing and crackling with mana. "Don't," he croaked. "Don't kill him."

Salazar glared down at the guard, his eyes still blazing with vengeance.

"We might need him," Drake pressed on. The fact was, he had seen enough death during this mission. The guard had done nothing to deserve being killed. Salazar was loosing his rage at the wrong man.

Gradually the vengeance faded from the prince's expression. With a nod of acceptance, he released the mana and helped Drake to his feet. "Very well. If we're not going to kill him, what do you suggest?"

The officer was now curled up in a ball, moaning. Drake knelt down to examine his wound. The cloth was melted away, and there was a severe burn nearly six inches in diameter just above his heart. There would definitely be a scar. But he would live.

"Help me get him into the car," he said.

"You're taking him with us?"

Drake nodded. "Like I said, we might need him."

The lights above them suddenly turned red, and the ear-splitting wail of a siren filled the lot. Drake cursed under his breath. It looked like someone was watching the vid after all. Rapidly, the two of them bundled the guard into the back seat beside the packs. Drake passed the officer's weapon over to Salazar and then finished overriding the mana pad. The engine rattled into a fitful start, sputtering several times before settling down to a rough whir.

Slamming the car into gear, he pressed down hard on the accelerator. But this was not Cal. This vehicle felt as if it was barely moving by comparison. It was all they had, though, so it would have to do. Winding their way around the support columns, they raced for the exit. On arriving, two men were waiting, weapons trained and ready.

He lowered the window and drew his P37. One quick shot was enough. The ball of white light exploded outward, temporarily blinding the men. In spite of this, one of their shots went straight through the windshield, missing the prince by mere inches.

Drake pulled out on the road and urged the car to move faster. "Do you recognize who this is, sitting next to me?" he shouted over his shoulder to the officer.

The prince turned around in his seat, allowing the man to see his face clearly. Though still in considerable pain, he was now able to move a tiny bit. His expression said he knew perfectly well what the prince looked like. At the same time, though, there was doubt on his face.

"If you really are the prince," he said, sucking his teeth, "why are you stealing a car?"

"There are people who might be trying to kill me," he explained. "I need to get to the magistrate's office as quickly as possible."

"Who would try to kill you?"

"If I knew that, I wouldn't be stealing a car, now, would I?"

"We need your help," added Drake.

The road to the main highway was practically abandoned. No one lived in this area, and nothing but empty offices and closed shops lined either side of the street. Knowing it would take the guards only a minute or so to call for help, Drake was pushing the car as fast as it could go. In traffic he would stand a chance, but here it would be easy for a magistrate's vehicle to outrun him and pin them in.

"How do I know you're really the prince?" the officer asked.

"Does it matter? I'm going to the magistrate's office. You're an officer of the magistrate. So I'm either a criminal or the prince. Either way, you win."

The officer looked as if he was weighing his options – although in truth he had none. He gave Salazar another long look. "If you're not the prince, then you're sure as hell his twin. What do you need from me?"

Drake saw the ramp about two hundred and fifty yards ahead. A glance in his mirror showed several sets of flashing lights closing in rapidly from behind. "I'll tell you in a minute," he told the man. "Right now, just hang on."

He pulled onto the ramp, foot planted firmly to the floorboard. Traffic was much heavier here, and he clipped the front end of a truck as he wove across into the outer lane. An angry horn blasted, but he barely heard it. All his concentration was on the road ahead. He only needed to make it for one mile before reaching the exit.

"Good thing the office is on level one," he muttered. In the mirror, he could see that their pursuers were drawing ever closer. Cars were shifting over to give them room. He cursed under his breath. There was no way they would get there in time. "Take the wheel," he told Salazar.

Leaning out of the window with his P37, he channeled a small amount of mana. The drivers close behind saw the weapon and immediately slammed on their brakes. *Perfect*, Drake thought. In the gap created, he let loose a series of three shots that erupted into pillars of flame the moment they struck the ground. Satisfied that this should gain them a little time, he slid back into the seat and took the wheel again, turning it hard right to avoid colliding with a long cargo van. They continued on, darting into lane after lane until he was in position for the ramp.

"Did that slow them?" he asked.

"Yes," replied Salazar, looking back. "But they're getting around it now."

"That's fine," he said.

They pulled onto the off-ramp for level one at full speed, the car threatening to roll as they descended. Ahead he could see more flashing lights racing across to cut them off.

"You said you wanted to help?" Drake asked the officer in the back.

"Yes," he replied.

Drake grinned and eased up on the accelerator.

❧

The cars trying to intercept them were not magistrate; they were royal guard. This would definitely complicate matters. Drake made it to the bottom of the ramp and took a hard left. The magistrate's office was to their right. He passed one car, but it made no attempt to pull across and stop him. Instead, it spun around and joined four more that were coming up from behind. What they were doing became obvious. They were herding him: taking them to a place where prying eyes would not see what happened next. Away from the one place in lower Troi where the prince would be secure.

He turned hard right, his offside tire clipping the curb as he did so. Instantly, he felt it going flat. The royal guard were now closing in with relative ease, their vastly superior vehicles much better at handling the tight twists and turns. This was it. Drake knew it was just a matter of time. One of the pursuers tried to pull up alongside him, but an oncoming vehicle forced him to back off. Drake wanted to take another right, but a line of flashing lights was bearing down from that direction, so he turned left instead. Another tire blew halfway around, forcing him into side swiping a parked car and tearing his own driver's door free from its hinges.

His head snapped back as the lead vehicle rammed him. With two flat tires, it was almost impossible to maintain control. He saw more headlights growing in the mirror and veered left, but it did no good. The pursuer thudded into his right rear corner, this time flipping him completely over.

Time froze for a moment as their vehicle crashed onto its roof. Glass flew about the interior, and the grating of steel on concrete said that the chase was definitely over.

"Are you okay?" Drake asked the moment their wrecked car had settled.

"Yeah, I think so," he was assured.

Drake smiled weakly and then unbuckled his belt. The pair of them crawled out as fast as they could. They'd been hoping to run, but the royal guard had already stepped from their cars and were pointing P37s at their heads.

After struggling to his knees, Drake clasped his hands behind his head. "Sorry," he apologized. "I really thought we'd make it further." Blood was pouring from multiple cuts on his face and brow.

"What were you thinking?" a familiar voice called out. "Did you really think we wouldn't be able to catch you?"

From out of the glare of the headlights, Xavier was approaching.

"I thought you'd be too busy committing treason to worry about me," Drake responded. "I guess I was wrong."

"You haven't lost your sense of humor, I see. I am not the traitor here. Or hasn't the prince told you why the king issued the warrant in the first place?" He bent down. "Yes, I found out all about what the magistrate was hiding." He clicked his tongue and cocked his head. "What's wrong, Your Highness? Nothing to say?"

"Who are you talking to?" asked Drake, the hint of a smile forming.

The man kneeling beside him looked up.

Xavier's jaw sagged, and for a second he appeared completely incapable of speech. "Who in the hell are you?" he then demanded.

"I am Vernon Molaris," the man replied, wincing through

the pain in his wounded chest. "Officer of the magistrate."

Xavier grabbed Drake by the collar. "Where is Prince Salazar? I know he entered the city with you. Tell me where he is, damn you."

Drake grinned. "Right about now he should be walking into the magistrate's office."

A stunned Xavier was still trying to take in this piece of news when his driver called over from beside their car. "Captain! There's a message just come through for you."

"I think you had better get that," Drake suggested, his grin becoming wider than ever.

All of the color drained from Xavier's face as he released his hold on Drake. Looking every inch like an utterly defeated man on the way to his own execution, with labored steps he turned and crossed over to the car.

࿎

Salazar limped as fast as he could toward where Drake had said the magistrate's office was located. The jump from the car while going down the off-ramp had very nearly killed him. And even if it hadn't, the pains in his leg and shoulder certainly made it feel as if it had.

Every car that passed by had him jumping. Drake couldn't hold them off very long, not in that piece of junk he was driving. But the light shining onto the sidewalk up ahead told him that he didn't need to. One more block...that was all. It felt like one hundred.

Reaching the front entrance was like arriving at his own salvation. With a massive sigh of relief, he pushed open the door and strode directly up to the main reception desk. The officer on duty glanced up without a flicker of recognition and promptly returned his attention to the book he was reading.

"I need you to call the magistrate at once," Salazar demanded.

"I'm sure you do," he replied, not bothering to looking up. "Why don't you tell me what the problem is first?"

With barely contained anger, the prince placed his hands on the desktop and leaned in close. "You will call the magistrate this instant. And you will address me as Your Highness."

This time the officer raised his eyes, though his expression one of irritation. "Look, friend. I don't have time for any of your stupid –"

His words came to an abrupt stop as recognition finally struck him like a hammer.

"Y…Your Highness. What are you… I mean… How did you…?"

"Close your mouth and do as I told you. Then take me somewhere I can wash up."

The man leapt up and showed the prince through to the back rooms.

"The royal guard is pursuing a vehicle a few blocks away from here," Salazar said. "If any of the occupants are hurt in this chase, I will hold each man personally responsible. Convey this to them, then send word to my father that I am home."

"Yes, Your Highness. I will send the messages right away."

By the time he reached a washroom, half of those working on the first floor had already come out to see him. He could hear the whispers about his bruised and battered condition. Not that it mattered. The main point was, enough people had now seen him to ensure his ongoing safety.

While looking at himself in the mirror, he started laughing. They were right; he really was in one hell of a state. The healers would take care of the cuts and bruises soon enough, but something else was different about him. Though it was something inside and hidden from the world, he could see it clearly as if it was right in front of him.

"It is time to move forward," he said. "It is time to make a difference."

Yes, it is, came a reply. One that only he could hear.

CHAPTER FIFTEEN

Drake settled down onto his couch with the lights dimmed and music playing softly on the vibraplayer. There was only one tiny cloud on his horizon; one thing that was troubling him. Two weeks had passed, and there had still been no word regarding the investigation into Xavier's involvement. Not even a hint of one. He knew it was petty, but he dearly wanted to be there when they finally put the man on trial for treason. He wanted to look into his fear-filled eyes, see that smug expression replaced by one of utter defeat, as they handed down his sentence.

There was, however, word on more hellspawn attacks springing up throughout the outer provinces. But that wasn't his problem. The royal guard would handle it. He took a sip of his manga juice and let out a contented sigh. All that hardship and death...all those years of chasing runners...they were now a fading memory, consigned to the past like an unhappy dream.

He would liked to have spoken to the prince one more time, but hadn't yet heard a thing from him. Shortly after Salazar was taken away, Drake had been spirited off to a holding facility, while the officer who had helped them was taken directly to a hospital. As for his wounds, he had been treated on site. Which was fine. Thanks to the vex crystal in his chest, most of them were healing on their own anyway.

He cast a gaze around the small apartment. It was perfect. Though not lavish, it was more than comfortable and possessed every amenity he might need. A sudden urge to jump into the shower came over him. This was his favorite feature of all; he must have used it at least fifty times already in the fortnight since moving in. Only manga juice held a more special place in his heart. And though he hadn't heard directly from Salazar, the prince had indeed been true to his word – his apartment was situated right next door to a manga juice shop. What's more, the owner had been instructed to provide Drake with all the juice he desired, free of charge. With his reward money, he could well afford to purchase it for himself, but it was a kind gesture all the same.

He was not one to be idle; sooner or later he knew he would need to find work. All the same, it was surprising how easily he had settled into a life of pure relaxation. He kicked his feet up onto the table. Perhaps a job could wait a little bit longer. Besides, he had no idea yet of what he wanted to do.

He shut his eyes and listened to the music playing. "One more week," he muttered. "I think I've earned that much."

A knock at the door drew a grumble. He wanted to ignore it, but the sound became ever more persistent.

"Come in, Linx!" he called out.

The door cracked open and she stepped inside, her face beaming with excitement. "Good. You're up."

"Of course I'm up. It's only... What time *is* it exactly?"

"Past your bedtime, old man." She skipped over to the couch, then jumped into his lap.

Drake almost dropped his juice. "Careful. I just cleaned up in here. Anyhow, what's got you so chipper?"

"I'm moving!"

He cocked his head. "Moving? You've just got here." The prince had arranged for Linx to have an apartment in the next building down.

"I'm keeping my place," she explained. "But they're giving me a room in the dormitory at the Royal College as well."

"You're moving to upper Troi?"

She straightened her back and nodded sharply, her smile wide. "The prince recommended me. I'm to get proper instruction on the mana terminals."

Drake smiled back. "That's wonderful. You know my father went there."

"I won't be allowed off the grounds like he was," she said. "But it's still upper Troi."

"It is, and it's very nice. Congratulations. I'm sure you'll do well."

"Of course I will. I'm Linx, after all." She slid from his lap and sat beside him, bouncing several times on the cushion and kicking her feet onto the table.

Drake noticed her confidant expression crack slightly. "You really will be fine," he said in a reassuring tone.

"Yeah, I know. But most of the people I'll be learning with have already been at it for years. I haven't had all their classes and special training."

"You'll be fine. Anyone who can learn what you did on your own definitely belongs there. Don't let anyone tell you differently."

"Thanks. I guess I am just a little nervous. It was weird enough when I first came here. I kept thinking everyone would know I was from the provinces."

"There's nothing wrong with being from the provinces," Drake assured her. "Just keep to your studies and you'll do as well as anyone. Most of the students are just as scared as you."

"Yeah? But they're kids. I'm about to be nineteen."

"Does anyone need to know that?"

"The professors will."

Drake eyed her with a grin. "They'll also know who recommended you. I doubt you'll have much trouble from them."

She jumped up. "Anyway, I just wanted to let you know that I was leaving. I have to go pack now." Leaning down, she kissed his forehead. "I'll be back between courses. We can talk more then."

When she reached the door, she paused. "Oh, I almost forgot. The guy in the lobby said someone left a package for you. I told him I'd take it, but for some reason he said you have to collect it yourself."

"Thanks, Linx. And remember, you belong at that college just as much as anyone else."

She squared her shoulders and jutted out her chin. "Yeah. You're damn right I do."

Once she was gone, Drake found himself feeling more than a touch sad. With her irrepressible enthusiasm and curiosity, Linx could be irritating at times: that much was certain. The first day she arrived, she'd insisted on him showing her around what felt like the entire fifth level. And at least once a day she would show up unexpectedly at his apartment to tell him about something new she had discovered in the city. But for all that, he drew pleasure from her company. Her leaving meant that he would now be alone, with no friends or anyone else to talk to. And when he was alone, thoughts of Lenora arose unbidden. Thoughts he had no business having.

He shook his head and blew out a heavy breath. "What the hell is wrong with you?" he muttered. "Since when did you need company?"

After finishing his juice, he went downstairs to the lobby. Chanz, the attendant, was dozing at his desk. He was a nice enough fellow: a man in his early fifties with a quirky sense of humor that Drake rather enjoyed. The fact that Drake was moving in from the provinces didn't seem to bother him at all. To Drake's mind, this was a sign of good character.

He stepped close to the dozing attendant. "Linx said you have something for me."

Chanz snapped to attention, then realizing that it was Drake, relaxed his posture. "Oh, it's you. My god, man, can't you at least take the lift so I can hear you coming?"

"Sorry. I need the exercise."

"Yeah. A life of leisure does that to a man. How in the hell did you manage that, anyway? You rob the king or something?"

"Something like that. So do you have a package for me or not?"

Chanz reached into the desk drawer and retrieved a small box wrapped in brown paper. "Some guy from the royal guard dropped it off. Said I was to hand it only to you. Told me that three times – like I didn't hear him the first two."

Drake took the box and shoved it into his pocket. "Did he say anything else?"

"Nope. I think he expected me to bring it up to you. But I'm no messenger boy. Besides, you come down for your juice three times a day. I figured I'd see you soon enough."

The mention of manga juice brought on a craving. Whatever was in the box could wait. He must have drunk a hundred cups of the stuff already and still wasn't the least bit tired of it.

"You want a juice too?" he asked.

"What I want is a nap," Chanz replied, folding his arms and leaning back in his chair.

Drake took the hint and moved off. As he entered the manga juice shop next door, the man behind the counter grimaced.

"You're going to put me out of business," he grumbled, grabbing a cup from behind the counter.

Drake reached in his pocket and pulled out a twenty note. "Here. That should cover it."

The man, whose name was Kirk, poured the drink and passed it over. A smile then formed. "I appreciate that, but I was only kidding. I send the bill straight to the magistrate's office. You take care, though. Too much of this stuff isn't good for you."

Drake was pleased to hear that the shop was at least getting paid. "You know, I was thinking," he began. "How would you like a partner?"

Kirk coughed a laugh. "What would I need with a partner? There's not much to this. And not enough money in it. You, my friend, enjoy manga juice far more than most folks around here."

"What about if you had more to offer your customers?"

"More? Like what? I don't have the money to build a kitchen, or to buy the licenses. I'm lucky I can keep the doors open as it is."

"But what if you did? Would you be willing to give it a try?"

The man eyed him skeptically. "Now why in Vale would you want to partner up with some old coot like me? You got any idea how much it would take to get this place running right again?"

Drake stepped back and took a long look around. The

interior was certainly showing its age. But overall, it wasn't in such terrible shape. There was plenty of room for a dining area, and he was sure he could put a kitchen in somewhere.

"Why don't you find out and let me know?" he suggested. "That is, if you're interested."

"I suppose it couldn't hurt to find out," Kirk conceded. "Though I still don't get why. If you have that kind of money, why not just open up a new shop of your own?"

"Because I'm lazy. And I have no idea what I'm doing." Drake took a sip of his drink. "Anyhow, you make the best manga juice in lower Troi."

The compliment was sufficient to have Kirk puffing out his chest. "You're damn right I do. And if you're serious, I'll teach you the secret."

"Just get me the numbers, and we'll talk."

Drake left the shop feeling better than he had since being made captain of the royal guard. He finally had something to look forward to, something beyond sheer survival or finding a way to return home. He had a direction. A purpose. If someone had asked him years ago if he could be happy as a lowly shop owner, he would have told them that the idea was insane. But now...right now, he felt almost giddy with excitement.

Back in his apartment, he jumped in the shower and got himself ready for bed. The name of the shop would have to change, of course. Kirk's Manga was not catchy enough. Kirk and Drake's, maybe? Manga and More? No...Manga Drake's. Kirk wouldn't mind. By the time he was drying his hair, he realized that his face was sore from smiling at all the possibilities.

It was only when he went to hang up his jacket that he felt the box Chanz had given him. In his excitement, he had completely forgotten about it. He ripped away the paper and found a tin box with a hinged lid. Inside this was a holodisk marked ***Prince Salazar, Confidential***.

Moving over to the holoplayer in front of the couch, he inserted the disk. After just a few seconds, the screen came to life. There stood Lord Malcoy, the man whom he had been convicted of murdering. Drake was standing directly in front of him, dressed in his finest uniform and his face a mask of utter fury. Even without the volume, he could hear the words that had been spoken between them all too clearly in his head.

Drake sat heavily on the floor as the video played out the scene.

"How dare you accuse the princess," he fumed.

Lord Malcoy was dressed in a white silk shirt and black jacket. His fingers and neck dripped with gold and jewels, and his chestnut curls were heavily oiled and pushed straight back. The disdain he held for Drake was reflected clearly in his expression. He was a man of high status and wanted everyone to be fully aware of that in a single glance.

"Mind how you address me, Captain," he replied. Though also angry, his voice carried the measured, even tones of the nobility. "The princess has sullied herself by her association with you. Do you imagine I will simply turn a blind eye?"

"What proof do you have?"

"I have my word as a noble. That is sufficient. I saw you together; do not try to deny it. And when I tell people of what I know, they too will see her for the whore that she is."

Drake knew what was coming next and almost couldn't bear to watch. His fist shot out, connecting solidly with Malcoy's jaw. The lord dropped to the floor and then scampered back.

Shock soon turned to rage as Malcoy rose to one knee.

"I'll see you expelled from the city for this. You hear me? You'll be living in the provinces by the end of the day. I swear it!"

Drake loomed over him for a long moment. His hand drifted to the P37 at his side.

Here it comes, he thought, forcing himself to keep watching. But to his astonishment, nothing happened. At least, not what he was expecting to happen. Not what had convicted him.

"Do what you must," he growled, then turned and stormed from the room.

Drake could not believe what he was watching. He had always known that the video used to convict him had been manipulated. He had searched everywhere for the original without success. And yet here it was now, delivered right to his door.

He was about to replay the entire scene when he saw another figure appear; one that he recognized instantly.

"Your Highness," said Malcoy, pushing himself to his feet. "I was just about to come speak with you."

Salazar was wearing the red one-piece jumpsuit that he used when exercising. The towel thrown over his shoulder said that he had just finished. "Is that right?" he asked. "Please tell me why. Was it to inform me that my sister is sleeping with the captain of the royal guard?"

Lord Malcoy's mouth opened in astonishment. "You knew? And you allowed it to continue?"

"Of course I knew. Drake is my best friend. You couldn't possibly imagine a thing like that could be kept from me." The prince paused ominously. "But it isn't my sister's indiscretion that concerns me right now. It's yours."

"Mine?" Malcoy managed to gasp out. "I'm sure I do not know what you are talking about. What have I done wrong? It is the princess who –"

Salazar's hand shot up. "You will be quiet. If you were more of a man – or maybe if Drake were less of one – you would not have this problem. As it is, the only reason you are being permitted to wed my sister is that you are both a noble and a high mage. Only two families can boast of such a distinction, and the Halvershans have no children of suitable age. Be that as it may, do go ahead and express your outrage to the whole of Vale if it pleases you. Then watch as another marries the princess in your stead. You have a cousin, if I am not mistaken. I'm sure he would be quite willing to see past my sister's shortcomings."

Lord Malcoy fumed. "I will not be made a fool of," he snapped, turning to leave.

Salazar caught his arm. "You are not dismissed...my lord. There is another matter I must take up with you. One that I find most disturbing."

Malcoy wrenched his arm away. "If you think to humiliate me further..."

"Hrashast."

Lord Malcoy froze. "Where did you hear that word?"

"Does it matter?"

"Where?" he repeated, his voice a mere whisper.

"So it's true," mused Salazar. "I had hoped I was wrong. But it *is* true."

"Whatever you think you have discovered, I suggest you forget it."

Salazar's face hardened. "Forget it? Are you mad? And once my father hears of this..."

The smile creeping up on Malcoy's face silenced him. Slowly, the smile turned to laughter.

"You had better tell me what is so amusing about this," the prince demanded.

"You think the king does not know already? Of course he

does. And the fact that he keeps his royal tongue behind his teeth is why he remains king. So if you think to threaten me, or the high mages, I would indeed speak to your father first if I were you. Otherwise, I think you might find yourself in quite a sticky situation."

Salazar stared at Malcoy, his air of confidence draining away. "Why would you do this?"

"Why? You can't be serious. It's control, Your Highness. Control over the people of Vale. Control over Troi. And yes, control over you as well. You see, even being aware of such knowledge is punishable by death. Unless, of course, you are a high mage or the king."

"I don't believe you. You're a liar!"

"Frankly, Your Highness, given the current situation, I couldn't care less what you believe. All you need do is go to your father and look into his eyes. Watch as the horror of what he knows could happen to his only son sinks into his royal head."

With a sneer, he turned to leave. "One more thing," he said over his shoulder. "I want Captain Sharazi driven from the city today. After that, have your sister prepare for our wedding. Oh, and do be sure she is scrubbed clean."

Salazar watched helplessly as Lord Malcoy strode toward the door. Then, as if a flood had burst forth from somewhere deep inside him, he spread his arms wide.

"Malcoy!" he shouted, his hands glowing a vivid red.

The lord turned, a stunned expression suddenly appearing on his face. "What are you doing? Are you mad?"

These were his last words. A stream of mana leaped from the prince's hands, striking him in the center of his chest and throwing him hard against the wall. He slumped down to the floor, with smoke rising from his flesh and clothing.

The prince staggered backwards, gazing in horror at

what he had done for several seconds before finally spinning on his heels and running wildly from the room.

The moment he was gone, the screen went dark.

Drake felt as if a knife had been driven into his heart. *All these years, and now it turns out that it was Salazar who killed Malcoy.* And what was worse...much worse...was that his best friend had framed him by altering the video. He had been betrayed by someone he trusted implicitly.

Even as he was still trying to come to terms with this devastating discovery, he saw smoke beginning to rise from the holovid. With a cry of anguish he jumped to his feet and raced over to the machine in an attempt to remove the disk. It was melting away into nothing but smoke and dust.

"No!" he cried. But it was too late. Whoever had sent it had installed a safeguard. Once played, it would automatically destroy itself.

Drake's legs felt limp. For several minutes he could do nothing but sit on the floor staring at the blank screen. Why? What had he done to deserve this? And why tell him the truth now, after all these years?

He wanted to feel anger, hatred, rage...anything at all. But it was as if all emotion had been sucked out of him, leaving him an empty shell. He could neither shout nor weep, only sit there feeling wholly dead inside.

He was still sitting like this when the door burst open and four members of the royal guard rushed in, P37's drawn. Even now, he did not move. Such was the depth of his despair that he'd barely noticed them entering. It wasn't until they lifted him to his feet and began to cuff his hands that he eventually spoke. Just one word came out.

"Salazar."

CHAPTER SIXTEEN

They led him from his apartment to a waiting car in front of the block. Only then did Drake slowly begin to recover his wits.

"Why am I being arrested?" he demanded. He was sure it must have something to do with the video.

"You're being charged with murder," came the curt reply. These were elite guards, he noted. Deadly and efficient. They discharged their duty with complete indifference as to the crime or the perpetrator. Someone very important must have been killed.

"Who am I accused of killing? I have the right to know."

Drake caught a glint of anger in the guard's eyes. Typical for a standard guard, but not one of the elites. These men were rumored to lack any kind of human feeling at all. Not true, of course. But they did maintain absolute control over any emotion. Generally, they were sent out to deal with matters when a noble ran afoul of the law.

"The king," Drake was told. "You are accused of murdering the king."

The words hit him like a punch in the face. "What? No!

That's impossible. I've been at home. I can prove it."

As he already knew they would, his protests fell on deaf ears. They had been ordered to bring him in, and that was what they would do. Nothing else mattered. That it was the king who'd been murdered explained why the elites had been dispatched rather than normal guards or officers of the magistrate.

Utter despair washed over Drake. This couldn't be happening to him. Not again.

A blindfold was placed over his eyes, and he could feel the car moving forward. Questions raced through his mind. Not that there would be any answers forthcoming. Not from these men. He would have to wait.

He tried to reconcile in his mind how the prince could possibly be involved in this new development. Framing him for Lord Malcoy's death had been bad enough, but since then he had risked his own life to rescue Salazar from the clutches of a truly dangerous enemy. Was this how he was to be repaid? By being set up again, this time for a crime for which he was sure to be executed? How could his boyhood friend be so cruel? No. *Cruel* wasn't the word. Evil.

Calm down and try to stay rational, Drake told himself. *The only thing you know for sure is that Salazar killed Malcoy. Anything else is just speculation. You don't know that he altered the video. Or why he said nothing at your trial. And you certainly don't know that he is the one framing you for murdering the king. Just wait and see.*

An image of the old monarch flashed through his mind. Where numbness had gripped Drake, feeling began to return. He had loved the king like a father. And now someone had killed him. But who? Surely not Salazar? No, it had to be one of the nobles, one with sufficient cunning to frame him for the crime. Frustration caused him to grind his teeth. Without knowing what kind of evidence had been stacked up against him, he could not even begin to work on a plan of defense.

After an hour, the car stopped. When the door opened, Drake knew immediately that he was in upper Troi. The scent of the air was unmistakable, and he could almost feel the mana streams flowing above him. Where they were taking him was now obvious; he'd suspected as much the moment they blindfolded him.

A strong pair of hands held his arms and guided him up a long ramp then into a lift. It took them three minutes to reach the level where the high security holding cells were located. This was usually the only place in upper Troi that a person from the lower city would ever get to see. And to enjoy this dubious privilege, you would first need to kill a noble or high-ranking official. Even then, all you ever got to see was a very small part of the building's interior.

After making several turns, he heard a door hiss open, and he was pushed down into a hard, upright chair. His blindfold and cuffs were then removed.

It took a moment for his eyes to adjust. But as they did, the surroundings were just as he remembered: white walls with black doors, six on either side. Each had a one-foot-square barred window and a slot in the middle through which food could be passed. A double door at the end led through the kitchen, and two more chairs were facing him for the guards' use.

"Is Daryl still the cook?" Drake asked.

The two men standing in front of him were not elite guards; the fury on their faces was enough to tell him that. One was standing near the rear wall with his P37 drawn, the other positioned just a few feet in front of him.

Drake glanced at the guard nearest. "I suppose you

uncuffed me hoping I'll try to escape. Sorry to disappoint you, but I know this place too well to think I could get away. So if you're going to shoot me, go ahead." Upon receiving no reply, he asked: "Will you at least tell me why anyone would think I killed the king? I was at my apartment. People saw me there."

"We have nothing to say to you," the guard said. "Not unless you'd like to save us some trouble and confess."

Drake sniffed. "Just tell me which cell is mine."

The guard turned to his left and touched the mana pad of the second door along. Drake waited until he'd backed away before rising and entering.

When the door slammed shut, he felt an overwhelming sense of desperation creeping in. This was exactly how it had been the last time. Hell, even the cell was identical: a single metal chair and small round table set at the foot of the cot, and on the other side a sink, shower, and toilet, along with a curtain that could be drawn across for privacy. These cells usually housed nobles or officials, so the comfort level was a bit higher than one normally found in a jail. The food wasn't bad, either. In fact, as a guard himself, he used to come here to eat on the days they served beef stew and bread. He remembered that as being particularly good, though how it might taste to him under his current circumstances was a different matter entirely.

He plopped down on the cot and laid back, hands behind his head. How in the hell had this happened to him? All he wanted to do was to live in peace. He should have known that whatever dark cloud was hanging over him had not moved on.

It was probably too late to eat, and he certainly wasn't about to ask the guards for any food. They already looked as if they were ready to give him a beating at the slightest excuse. With their P37s, they could cause him quite a bit of pain as well. He closed his eyes and tried to still his mind. There was absolutely nothing he could do but wait and see what happened next.

It took time, but eventually the steady hum of the lights droned him into an uneasy sleep.

❧

The sharp opening of the door outside snapped him awake. It was impossible to know how long he'd drifted in and out of consciousness, but at least a few hours.

"I need a few minutes alone with him."

That voice. Surely it couldn't be? But as Drake sat up in his bed, he could not fail to recognize the familiar face smiling in at him through the bars.

"I see they are taking good care of you," Xavier remarked, his triumphant smile beaming. "I suppose you're wondering how it is I'm walking around free and not in one of the cells."

"The thought did cross my mind." Drake leaned his elbows on his knees. "Let me guess. You somehow convinced the king of your innocence."

"Yes, in a manner of speaking."

"So *you* killed him?"

"Now, why would I do that? No, my old friend, I had nothing to do with it. In fact, I had nothing to do with what happened to the prince either."

"Then who?"

"Haven't you figured it out yet?"

Drake seethed. "I know Salazar killed Lord Malcoy, if that's what you're trying to say."

Xavier chuckled. "Of course you do. Who do you think sent you the video?"

"You?" Drake stared at him, not wanting to believe it. But the man's confident smile said that he was telling the truth. "Why?"

"Because I don't like you," he replied. "It's that simple, really. I just wanted you to know who had done this to you." He paused in order for his words to sink in. "However, before you blame me completely, though I admit I may have altered the original video, Salazar and the king both knew of this and chose to say nothing. The truth is, I just wanted you out of the way. And with the leverage I had over them, that was easy to accomplish."

"I don't understand. You have what you want now. Why try to frame me again?"

"Oh, I'm doing more than trying, Drake. Unfortunately, all those people who claim to have seen you at your apartment have since unfortunately gone missing. And seeing as how it was Salazar who killed his own father, he was more than willing to let me help him out of a considerable mess...again. Let's be honest, who better than you to take the fall?"

"But if you didn't try to kill Salazar, who did?"

"That, my friend, remains a mystery for now. But I have my suspicions."

"So all this is simply because you don't like me?" Anger was building. "You're pathetic. You know that?"

Xavier puffed a breath. "Seeing you get what you deserve is merely a bonus. You see, Prince Salazar and I have plans. Big plans. And I can't have someone like you around mucking things up."

"And I suppose these plans involved murdering his own father?"

"I'm afraid so. Sadly, the old man just couldn't see how a little bad can be used to produce a much greater good. He was like you, in a way...sentimental."

Drake wanted to reach through the bars and strangle him. But he needed to know more. "So what is this grand plan of yours?" he asked.

"Still thinking to save the day, are you?" Xavier sneered. "Do you really believe you can escape from here and turn the tables on me? Or perhaps you are planning to expose us and tell all of Vale about our evil plots?" He shook his head. "To think you called me pathetic. Feel free to tell whoever you wish. Of course, as you know nothing, it might all sound a bit insane. Rather more like a desperate man trying anything he can to save himself from execution."

There was no way around it. Drake knew he was beaten. Xavier had played it perfectly.

"We'll see," was all he could think to say. And even that came out sounding more like weak bluster than anything else.

"Indeed we will," Xavier smiled. "But I don't want you to worry. I won't make you languish in this cell for very long. Even *my* cruelty has its limits." He bowed his head ever so slightly. "Farewell…captain."

Drake wanted to say something more, but prolonging the conversation would have only compounded Xavier's victory. With enormous effort, he waited until hearing his tormentor pass through the door and it close behind him before letting out a feral scream. Though this provided a brief release of all the anger and frustration raging inside, it elicited only laughter from the two guards who by now had returned to their places.

He had counted on there being a trial. At least then he would have the chance to do or say something in his defense. But Xavier had made it perfectly clear that he would never be allowed to leave this cell alive.

Think, Drake. Calm the hell down and think. What do you know?

Xavier framed you for killing Lord Malcoy, presumably to become captain of the royal guard and gain leverage over the king and the prince.

He forced the fact that his best friend had allowed this to happen from his mind. It raised up far too much anger, and there was enough of that burning inside him already. He needed to keep his head as clear as possible.

Salazar ran, and someone was determined not to let him return. But if that someone wasn't Xavier, then who? And why? Whoever it was had also involved Bane. And then there was the holovid. What had Salazar found out? And why would he kill his own father?

Lying back on his cot, Drake closed his eyes. Again and again he went over everything he could remember. Try as he might, he couldn't put it all together in a way that made any sense. He needed more. He also needed a way out of here. Not that this was likely to materialize. In all probability he would die quite soon, never knowing the full story. He would be left only with the mocking knowledge that Xavier had beaten him.

He wanted to scream again, but could only lie there staring at the ceiling, feeling totally defeated.

CHAPTER SEVENTEEN

The dull thud of a body striking the ground roused Drake from his stupor. He drew a sharp breath. Was this how they planned to do it? Knock out the guards and kill him from outside the bars? Hell, the guards weren't exactly his friends either. They'd probably allowed themselves to be knocked out.

He stood beside his cot, determined to look his killer in the eye. He almost hoped it was Xavier. He wanted the man to see that, though he had lost, he was far from cowed or beaten.

The cell door clicked and hissed, then swung open a few inches. Drake's muscles tensed. Better to die fighting, and this fool was giving him the chance to do that. He crouched low, ready to spring.

"Drake," a voice called. A woman's voice.

Slender fingers pulled the door fully open. He was unable to believe his eyes.

"Lenora," he whispered.

She was dressed in the orange and black robes of a high mage, and the hood was thrown back, revealing her delicate features. "Hurry," she said. "We don't have much time." She tossed a bundle at him.

"What are you doing?"

"Saving your life," she replied.

Drake unwrapped the bundle to find a novice's robes and a mechanic's coveralls. "You can't. They'll –"

"My father is dead," she snapped. "Killed by my brother. They'll be coming for me once you are taken care of. Now, for the love of Vale, hurry. Put the robes on over the coveralls."

Without any more delay, Drake stripped off his clothes and did as she instructed. The robe was baggy and cumbersome, but the hood would hide his face.

"Where are we going?" he asked.

"One thing at a time." She regarded him for a brief moment, then pulled her hood up.

The two guards were lying on the floor, though he could see that they were still breathing. Drake paused long enough to take one of their P37s. It was lighter than his own; a newer model and without the alterations he had made over the years.

Lenora peered outside before waving for Drake to follow. "If we're approached, let me do the talking," she told him.

Drake felt as if he were a leaf being carried against his will on a strong wind. Nothing was making any sense at all. Even the few answers Xavier had provided only spawned further questions. But as much as he needed answers, now was definitely not the time.

They walked at an even, deliberate pace. Even the halls leading to the holding cells gleamed and pulsed with mana. Not a speck of dirt or hint of age touched a single surface. At the higher levels, mana radiated and drifted in the very air. At night, everything glowed in a kaleidoscope of color, the mana flowing and swirling freely like thin mist.

Drake caught his breath on seeing two royal guards exiting a side door directly ahead. He need not have worried. The pair simply saluted and went about their business. One did not speak to a high mage unless spoken to, and a royal guard assigned to upper Troi would never dream of breaking with decorum.

They exited through a small atrium and then down a long ramp. At the end of this was a lift that would take them to the gardens at ground level. Once inside this and descending, Lenora immediately set about stripping off the robes, beneath which she wore a simple pair of tan trousers and a blue button-down – typical attire for a laborer. Drake followed suit. When the lift opened a minute or so later, he saw three men standing just outside, all of them wearing magistrate's uniforms. Drake's hand shot to his weapon, but Lenora caught his arm.

"They're with me," she said.

"Are you sure about this, Your Highness?" asked an older man with narrow-set blue eyes.

"Absolutely," she replied. The man opened his mouth to speak, but she cut him off. "The king is murdered, and I am to be the next to share his fate. So either help me or turn me in."

"You know I would never do that, Your Highness. But I must ask, why are you taking…*him* with you? Please. Let me come too. I will protect you."

Lenora smiled sweetly. "I know you would, Karl. However, I need you here. I need you and your men to be my eyes and ears. As for my companion, do not worry. All is not as it seems."

The man gave Drake a suspicious look, but nodded his acceptance. "Very well, Your Highness. You can count on us." He took a quick look around. "Now hurry. We can't be seen."

The path they were standing on only skirted the edge of the enormous garden, yet even on this fringe, the variety of flowers and trees was spectacular. It was possible to wander for days on end and never see them all. A spider's web of cobbled trails threaded their way between many species of plants that it was claimed grew nowhere else but here. A few nobles even kept small private gardens yielding vegetables and fruits reputed to be so delicious that one would feel as if they were cleansing their entire body with each juicy bite.

The group descended a flight of stairs into a narrow alley, at the end of which was a service lift. They took this down two levels to where an open lot housed several dozen magistrate vehicles.

"There's a van near the exit," Karl told them. "Can you make it to level six from here?"

Drake nodded. "Where on level six?"

"Sewage treatment. You'll find a shaft there that will take you to just outside the city."

"Then what?"

"That's taken care of," Lenora told him. "I have a friend already waiting for us." She bowed to the officers. "Thank you for your help, all of you. I will not forget it."

"Just stay safe, Your Highness," Karl said.

Each man bowed and then turned back toward the lift.

"Are you sure they can be trusted?" Drake asked, once they were gone.

"I'm not sure of anything," she responded. "But I think if they were going to betray me, they would have done so already." They started toward the far end of the lot. "My father taught me to cultivate relationships among the rank and file. He said that one day it could prove to be useful."

Drake recalled Salazar remarking on the very same thing. "Are you sure it's your brother who is behind this?" he asked.

239

Lenora looked over to him, her eyes barely holding back tears. "I'm sure."

They reached the van and Drake surveyed the area. "It looks clear," he said. "Are you certain you still want to go through with this? Last chance to change your mind."

Lenora offered no reply. Though she was trembling, he could see a determined set to her face that told him all he needed to know. He simply fired the van to life and pulled from the lot.

He'd been unaware of the shaft that the officer had described. Troi was an old city, built and rebuilt over thousands of years, and the royal guard was pretty thorough about sealing off any old tunnels and passages leading in or out. This one must have been deliberately kept off any schematics, he realized.

Drake glanced across at Lenora. He wanted to speak to her – to somehow bring her at least a measure of comfort – but could not find anything remotely like the right words. From the look of her face, she might burst into tears at any moment. And who could blame her? Very soon she was going to be hunted by her own brother, who had just murdered their father. What could he possibly say to make things better?

After they pulled onto the main highway, it was Lenora who broke the silence.

"I don't want you to worry about me. I'm not as weak as I might appear."

"I don't think you're weak at all," Drake told her. "After what has happened, I think you're handling it pretty well."

She closed her eyes and a tear rolled down her cheek. "Am I? I don't feel like I am."

"Believe me, I've seen people fall completely apart after suffering much less than you have."

She gave him a fragile smile and took his hand. "Thank you."

"For what? It was *you* who saved *me*, remember."

"Just…thank you."

They drove the rest of the way in silence. Drake could feel the firmness of her grip, the warmth of her skin pressing against his. Even with everything else going on around them, it made his heart race. His love for her had not diminished, not even by a small fraction.

The foul air heralded their approach to the sewage facility, and Lenora instinctively covered her nose. "The shaft is just half a mile east of the plant," she said.

"Is it guarded?"

"It's how my brother escaped, so I don't think so."

That would explain why it was kept from the records – a secret way out for the royals, just in case. But that meant Salazar would be aware of it and possibly have it watched.

She directed him to a narrow street that came to a dead-end. Here they parked in front of a three-story warehouse. A few people were about, but no one took any particular interest in them as they exited the vehicle. All the same, Drake made sure he kept his hand in the pocket where he had shoved the P37.

They entered the building where a small unoccupied office was set off to the right and a flight of stairs led to the main floor. Aside from a few scattered crates, it appeared to be empty.

"My brother bought this place years back when he first discovered the passage," Lenora said. "Not even my father knew about it." She pointed to a door on the right-hand side of the room. "The tunnel is just through there."

As they moved toward this, Drake caught a movement in the corner of his eye. Without thinking, he shoved Lenora to his back and drew his weapon.

"Would you really shoot me?" a voice said from several yards away.

Standing beside a stack of empty crates was Salazar. He was wearing a loose-fitting black shirt and pants, together with a long red satin jacket.

Drake channeled mana into the weapon, a vicious snarl on his lips. "You think I won't?"

The prince's body shimmered from a protection spell. He took a single pace closer. "To save my sister? In an instant; I know you would. But that is why I am here as well – to save her."

"You murdered our father," Lenora snapped at him.

Drake sensed the mana surging through her body with ever-increasing force.

Salazar nodded. "And I am sorry about that. I didn't want it to be this way, but he wouldn't listen to reason. He refused to see that what I am trying to do will actually save us in the years to come."

"And what is it you are trying to do...other than kill your sister?" asked Drake.

Salazar looked hurt. "Kill her? Is that what she told you? No, never! I love her."

"Like you loved father?" Her voice quivered with rage.

"I know you must hate me right now. But it will pass in time. Please. Come home. Don't force me to hunt you. You know full well there is nowhere you can go. That's why you didn't leave with Drake the first time."

"Before we go any further, I have to know something," Drake interjected.

Salazar nodded understandingly. "Of course you do. You want to know why I betrayed you. And the truth is, you have no idea how much that pained me. Unfortunately, Xavier was insistent. He refused to allow you to run freely through Vale. He was afraid that if you found out what we were doing, you would cause problems."

By now, Lenora's power had built to an almost critical level. Drake could feel it begging to be released. This situation was about to come to a head. "And what exactly is it you are doing?" he asked. "Does it have to do with Hrashast?"

Salazar smiled. "Yes. He told me you had seen the holovid. And in a way, I suppose it does connect. But as you do not know what Hrashast is, explaining would be pointless."

"*I* know what it is," said Lenora.

His smile vanished. "And that, dear sister, is what has put us both in this unfortunate situation. Your admission has left me without options. Now, enough of this. Come home and I will allow Drake to go free. He can return to his life in the provinces. It might be harsh, but at least he'll be alive. Isn't that what you want?"

"Let me show you what it is I want, brother." Her voice was hard as iron. She leaned over quickly to whisper into Drake's ear. "Together."

"Together," he agreed.

The word had barely left his mouth when both simultaneously let loose a ferocious blast of mana. Clearly prepared for such an attack, Salazar quickly waved both hands to bring a disk of white light springing up a few feet in front of him. Normally, this would be a more than adequate shield, and together with the protective spell already cast make him virtually invulnerable. But this was not a normal attack. The prince could never have anticipated the sheer strength of his sister's rage. The combined power of Drake's P37 and Lenora's magic scattered his shield like dust. The streams of mana smashed into his chest, sending him sprawling.

Drake glared down at the prince, who was moaning and clutching at his chest. Though injured, the protection spell had managed to keep him alive...for the moment. He took aim for another shot, but Lenora grabbed at his arm.

"No," she pleaded. "Please don't."

After a second, he lowered the weapon.

"Thank you," she breathed.

Drake was trembling with fury. In the heat of that moment, she was almost certainly the only person in Vale who could have stopped him.

Without another word, Lenora set off toward the door, Drake on her heels. Beyond was a short corridor, at the end of which was a steel trapdoor. Drake lifted this up on its hinges to reveal a narrow shaft with a ladder fixed to the wall. He waited for Lenora to enter and reach the bottom before following, closing the door behind him. Dim lights from mana bulbs lit the tunnel. Tubes and wires were fastened to the walls and ceiling. From the look of things, this was an old utility tunnel.

"Do you think he'll follow us?" he asked.

"No. Salazar wouldn't want anyone knowing about this place, especially Xavier. If we hurry, we can reach the end before he thinks to send the royal guard for us."

"How far is it?"

"Quite a long way. It will take us at least six hours."

"And you are sure your friend will be waiting there?"

She touched his arm. "I'm sure. You are the only person I trust more."

CHAPTER EIGHTEEN

The trek was grueling, with uneven ground and steep inclines slowing their progress considerably. Further adding to their difficulties, the air was thick with moisture, making every breath labored and forcing several brief halts.

"You told Salazar you knew what Hrashast means," Drake said, as they squatted down for their latest stop.

"Yes, it's a spell known only to the high mages," she told him. "They use it to keep the land sick. They infuse it into the mana streams."

"Sick? What are you talking about? I thought the high mages were trying to heal the land, not destroy it?"

Lenora sniffed. "The only thing they care about is holding onto power. *They* are the ones keeping the land infertile and the people starving. They know that so long as they control the power and food supply, they control Vale."

"And your father knew of this?"

There was a brief pause, as if she were loath to speak the words. "All kings are told of it once they ascend to the throne. I only found out by accident. If the high mages knew I was aware of their secret, they would have me killed immediately."

Drake could barely believe what he was hearing. "Your father was a good man. Surely he would have done something about it?"

"Like what? Shut down the power station? Can you imagine what would happen if Vale went dark? Only the high mages understand how it works. They control the mana streams; so they control Vale. The king is little more than a figurehead."

"But why keep the people hungry?"

"Everything is about dependence and control. If you keep food and resources limited, that keeps the minds of the people focused almost entirely on survival. That way, they cannot see beyond the next day. They do as they are told, never questioning anything."

Drake considered what he had learned for a moment. Was this the secret that Exodus knew? If so, why hadn't they already broadcast it to everyone? The answer came to him quickly: no one would ever believe such a story. The people couldn't allow themselves to. Without the power station, everything they depended on would be plunged into darkness. Utter chaos would quickly follow.

"Is this why your brother ran?" he asked.

"No. He ran because my father discovered what he was planning to do."

"What was that?"

"After you were exiled, Salazar began conducting studies. I helped him at first because..."

She hesitated awkwardly before adding: "Because I hoped to get word about what you were doing."

This made him smile despite the terrible things he was learning. "What kind of studies?"

"Food supply, population growth, demographics, things like that. The more Salazar learned, the more depressed he became. I think it finally broke his mind. He started saying to me that the only way for the people to live properly was to empty the provinces. He wanted to kill the entire population outside of Troi. I told father about this."

"Kill *everyone*? Are you serious?"

"Quite serious. I don't know how he was intending to achieve it, but Father must have found out. He told me Salazar had gone completely mad and was planning something truly horrific. Unfortunately, he didn't give me any details."

"Well, we need to find out about them soon. He's king now."

Drake's mind was buzzing as they rose to their feet and set off again. Kill everyone? It was completely insane. How could Salazar be considering such a thing? There had to be more. He was sure of it. Something else was behind this. The man he knew would never have contemplated such a foul deed, not in a million years.

He sighed. Then again, he never would have believed that Salazar might betray him, either.

By the time they reached the door to the surface, Drake's legs felt as though they were on fire. Lenora seemed to be faring better, though he noticed her posture had become slightly bent. After stopping, he reminded himself that Salazar would have recovered some time ago, and if he chose to, had enough time to send royal guards to intercept them. But would the prince be willing to divulge the location of the passage to anyone? That was the key question. They would know the answer to that soon enough.

He gestured for Lenora to wait while he climbed the stairs and listened at the door. It was a pointless exercise. They were still very close to the city, and nothing short of weapons fire would have risen above the ever-present roar and hum of Troi.

Easing the door open, he stepped outside. The tunnel had left them roughly two miles west of the city. Troi's barrier wall loomed high, behind which its magnificent spires could be seen rising even higher, all the way up to where the mana streams sparkled. Drake saw a service road a few hundred yards ahead. Other than this, just a few small buildings were scattered about, most of them used to store materials for maintenance.

Lenora climbed out behind him, her hands glowing with mana and ready to strike if necessary. Drake scanned the area, but could see no one about.

"Your friend is late," he remarked sourly.

"I'm not late," a voice replied almost immediately. It came from behind a stack of cables next to one of the buildings. "I just didn't want to get shot."

Drake's eyes popped wide as Bane stepped into view, a wide smile on his face. He was clad in a blue suede jacket and black shirt. A broad brimmed hat rested casually on his head.

Drake instantly took aim, but was prevented from firing only by Lenora leaping in front of him. "Drake, no!" she shouted. "Samuel is with me."

He cocked his head. "You know him?"

"Of course she does," Bane said. He strode up with arms held wide. "I am so very pleased to see you, Lenora. I was just about to come looking."

Such was Drake's confusion that for a moment he was unable to speak.

"It would appear our friend is in need of some convincing," Bane continued. "That's my fault, I suppose. Our last encounter was a bit...unpleasant. Though I can truthfully say that I never intended to harm you in any way."

He turned his attention to Lenora to give a sweeping formal bow. "Now, how may I serve you, Your Highness?"

"You can start by explaining to me why you tried to kill Salazar," Lenora responded. "That was not what I asked of you."

Bane averted his eyes. "I know. And I apologize. But when I heard about his plan, I knew it had to be done. And I knew you would never give me permission."

Drake turned to face Lenora, his anger reaching its limit. "Someone had better tell me what the hell is going on. Who is he to you?"

Lenora smiled. "I am truly sorry. I've kept Samuel's secret for so long, it didn't feel right to say anything before."

"So he works for you?"

"Works? No, far from it." She placed her hand on his cheek. "Samuel Freidman – the man you know as Bane – is my cousin."

Drake glared at Bane, whose smile had grown wider than ever. "Your cousin? This low-life murderer is actually related to you?"

"Drake Sharazi!" Lenora snapped. "That's enough. Do you hear me?"

Bane raised a hand. "It's all right. He has good reason to think like that. I wasn't exactly forthcoming on our first encounter, but hopefully we can now start anew." He glanced over his shoulder as a trucked passed by. "But not here. I have made arrangements, so if you don't mind…"

He started toward one of the buildings. "I think you'll be pleased with our mode of travel."

As they rounded the corner, Drake stopped short. Waiting there for them was Cal.

"How did you get your hands on her?" he asked, unable to hide his approval.

"The man you sent her to at Grim Lake let me have her," Bane explained

"Vic just handed Cal over to you?" He had sent her to him for repairs. There were more than ample resources in Troi, and of course there was Dorn, but knowing the situation in Grim Lake, he'd been trying to help the old man out.

"Well, *handed over* isn't exactly the way I would put it," he admitted.

"So you stole her?"

Bane opened the door and slid into the back seat. "I would think you'd be grateful for the trouble I took. It was damn risky for me to go there. Crews are still cleaning up the rubble from our last visit."

Drake fired the ignition and ran his hands along the wheel. The engine hummed perfectly. He had missed driving her; the exhilaration of feeling the power as he pushed her faster and faster down long stretches of open road was a unique joy.

Lenora cleared her throat. "If you don't mind, I think we should be going."

He gave her a self-conscious grin. "Sorry." Then, just as he started to pull out, he heard Bane chuckling in the back. "What?" he demanded.

"I was thinking how angry Father would be if he knew you had sent her to Grim Lake for repairs."

"Yes. Your father." He shot Lenora a sideways look. "I'd like to hear more about that. How in the hell is Bane your cousin?"

She looked back to Bane, who nodded his consent. "Samuel's father had an affair with my mother's sister."

"Dorn? How would he have even met her?"

"My father taught engineering and mechanics at the university," Bane told him.

That, at least, made sense to Drake. Dorn's knowledge and skills were way beyond your typical mechanic. He had built Cal from the frame up; made her into a machine of unparalleled speed and installed features found in no other vehicle. There were times she seemed to have a life of her own.

Lenora continued with the story. "When my aunt became pregnant and it was discovered who the father was, Dorn was immediately exiled. My mother was disgusted by the whole affair, and insisted that Samuel be sent to live with him as soon as he was old enough to leave my aunt's care."

"And how old was that?"

"Let's just say that I doubt I was ever breastfed for more than a few days," said Bane.

"As soon as I found out about him, I kept in touch," Lenora added.

Bane leaned closer to her. "She's being more than a little modest," he said. "She financed my father's business, and later on saw to it that I was accepted into the College of Mages. Though to my shame, I disappointed her by getting myself kicked out. Even though Lenora was just a young girl, she was still kind and thoughtful enough to help us. Not to mention clever enough to keep it secret."

He gave her shoulder a tender squeeze. "We were on the brink of starvation. I owe her my life. I only wish I could repay the debt under better circumstances."

Drake considered their tale for several minutes. At least it tied together one more thread of this tangled web. "Okay. I'll buy it," he said. "But what prompted you to try and kill Salazar. He's your cousin too, right?"

"He is, though in name only. The truth is, he's never held anything but disdain for me and my father. But that's not the reason I wanted him dead. As you know, I worked for

Fisk from time to time. And before you give me a scolding, I was *not* his hired killer. I was the one who cultivated that particular aspect of my reputation. In truth, you've probably killed more men than I."

Drake doubted that very much, though he made no attempt to argue.

"During one of my assignments, I ran across a letter I was definitely not meant to see. It said that Prince Salazar was planning to wipe out all life in the provinces. He was offering Fisk sanctuary within Troi, as well as governorship of the provinces after it was over in exchange for his help."

He paused before turning back to Lenora: "But you knew this too. Why didn't you expose him?"

"I did," she responded. "That's how Father found out his plan."

"And that's why you tried to kill him," Drake said to Bane.

He shook his head. "No, not entirely. The letter also expressed the need to eliminate Lenora. She was deemed to be a threat, as was the king. That's when I knew for certain that I had to act. Lenora knew nothing of this."

"Why didn't you tell me?" Drake asked.

"You were Salazar's best friend. I couldn't risk that you would turn against me. I feared you would think to change his mind rather than do what really needed to be done. Unfortunately, my father discovered the trap I had set. After he'd disconnected it, I didn't have time to put it back in."

Drake's jaw tightened. "*You* put the bomb inside Cal?"

"I didn't ignore everything my father tried to teach me," Bane said, smiling. "But rest assured, it would not have harmed you in the slightest. It was designed to kill only whoever was sitting in the front passenger seat."

"And what if someone else had been sitting there at the time?"

Bane sighed. "That was a small flaw in the plan, I admit. But after my father disabled the bomb, I intended to be with you. I thought perhaps I could use its presence to gain your trust."

A pair of approaching headlamps halted the conversation. Another cargo truck blew by. Drake turned on Cal's camouflage and called up the map.

"Where are we going?" he asked.

"The College of Mages," Bane replied.

This produced shocked looks from both Drake and Lenora.

"Don't worry," Bane added quickly. "We're not going inside. I have a friend there who is willing to help. We'll be safe with him for a while."

"Not a chance," said Drake.

Lenora touched his hand. "I think we should do as he says. Whatever you might think, he's my cousin, and I trust him completely."

The College of Mages was only a few hours to the southeast. From its location, it was still possible to see the lights of Troi – far closer than Drake had intended to be. Nevertheless, Lenora's touch was enough to bend him to her will. It always had been.

"Fine," he huffed. "But if they find us, I swear he'll be the first one I shoot."

Bane burst into laughter. "I could not ask for a fairer deal. Oh, and you'll be happy to know that your sword is still in the trunk, along with almost everything else."

"Almost?"

"I figured the only reason you sent Cal to Grim Lake must have been to help out that poor old fellow, Vic. So I took some of the money and left it where he could find it."

Drake nodded his acceptance. "Thank you. He's a good guy."

"Can't say I ever saw you as the kind and caring type before, though."

Lenora reacted in a flash. "I'll have you know that Drake is one of the kindest men I've ever known," she told her cousin.

Drake felt a sudden desire to wrap his arms around her and pull her close. On the other hand, he felt awkward and unsure about making such a move. She had just lost her father; her brother wanted her killed; and she was running for her life. This was not exactly the best of times for rekindling a romance. All the same, he was sharply aware that every second he spent with her was fueling his passion and love to an even greater level. He had no idea how to best deal with this.

As it turned out, she solved his dilemma a few minutes later when she leaned her head on his shoulder and shut her eyes. An enormously grateful Drake put his arm around her, and she snuggled in tight.

"Wake me before we get there," she said.

She was asleep in a matter of minutes.

Drake nearly wept for joy. He had almost forgotten what it felt like to hold her in his arms. He had thought that returning home would be enough. And perhaps it might have been before. But now, looking at her tiny smile – the kind that only feeling safe and loved could bring forth – he knew he had to have more. He had never believed in fate. Now, though, with the warmth of her body and the way the simple sound of her breathing was making him feel, he was beginning to change his mind. It certainly felt as if they were meant to be together.

"I'm relieved to see it," said Bane. His voice was a half whisper, so not to wake his cousin.

Drake had almost forgotten he was there. "Relieved to see what?"

"That you love her as much as she does you," he replied. "But I need to know one thing. Are you willing to let her go?"

Drake creased his brow. "Let her go?"

"Yes. Like it or not, she is the princess. And this is a war. One that I have no intention of losing. Prince Salazar must die. I know Lenora refuses to accept it at this point, but you and I both understand that things have gone way too far for there to be any other outcome. It's either Lenora or Salazar. When the prince is gone, she will inherit the throne. Once that happens, she will need all the support she can gather. And I think you know what that means."

Drake did indeed, and a crushing sense of reality washed over him. For her to stay in power, alliances would have to be forged. She would need the support of the nobles, and they would never give her that if she were with him. He gave Bane a look that said he understood.

"Good. Because I know her. I know how much she cares for you. She would risk everything to follow her heart. You cannot allow her to do that."

"I won't. When the time comes, I'll leave."

The words tore at his spirit. Fate was indeed playing its part. But fate had never promised anyone a happy ending. Only a certainty that what must be would inevitably come about.

"I'm sorry," Bane said, his tone sounding genuine. "As much as I want her to be happy, I want her to stay alive even more. But for now, you have time. Don't waste it."

I won't, he silently swore.

Despite the millions of mana streams overhead, the night suddenly felt empty and dark. He pressed down on the accelerator, pushing Cal faster. He imagined he could feel fate closing in from behind, reaching out with clawed fingers. He went faster still, all the time knowing there was no possibility of escape. Like Bane, he was determined to win, even though his victory would cost him everything he loved. He looked down at Lenora's sleeping form. In that tender moment, all doubt left him.

Yes. If it cost him his very soul, he would see her safe and sitting on the throne of Vale.

CHAPTER NINETEEN

Salazar winced as he dropped heavily into his chair. His father's private study was always so cold. The books and dark wood furnishings had seemed out of place in the palace, to his eyes. The desk was hundreds of years old, as were the chairs and side tables. The carpet was reputed to have been woven the day after the barrier was erected as a gift for the very first king. Or was it a queen? He couldn't recall. The past three rulers had all been men, a fortune of the order of birth. Now, as the eldest child and with his father gone, this was to be *his* study.

He thought to cross over to the door and warm up the room a bit, but a wave of pain kept him where he was. He cursed under his breath. He had been foolish to go after them alone. He'd had little choice, though; the secret of the tunnel was far too valuable to risk its discovery. He should never have told Lenora of its existence.

Reaching into his pocket, he retrieved the crystal. This, at least, was warm. He cupped it in his hands and closed his eyes, allowing the power radiating from its core to rush through him.

"If only I'd had you with me," he muttered. "But then she would have known his secret. That must never be allowed to happen."

"What would she have known, Your Highness?"

He hadn't heard Captain Xavier enter. He quickly placed the crystal back in his pocket. "What do you want, Captain? Shouldn't you be out looking for my sister?"

He waved a dismissive hand. "Oh, I wouldn't worry about that. Now that Mister Fisk has agreed to our terms, it won't be long."

"And you are sure you can rely on him?"

"No. But I am more than sure he understands the price of failure. The Exodus base that Drake Sharazi destroyed was but one. Once we find the others, all will be ready. That is, assuming you still want to go through with it."

Yes. It must be done. There is no other way.

Salazar shook his head. *Not now. Be quiet.*

"Are you all right?" Xavier asked.

"Yes, I'm fine." Though the massive burn on his chest was covered by a new shirt, it was taking a great effort not to twist his face from the pain.

"I only came to tell you that the funeral arrangements are all going well. As are those for your coronation."

"Is that all?"

"No. There is one more minor detail." Xavier reached into his coat and produced an envelope. "This is the letter of consent."

Salazar looked at the envelope as if it were poisoned. "Do we have to do this now?"

"The sooner the other nobles know of this change, the easier it will be for them to accept it." He placed the envelope on the desk. "That is, unless you do not intend to honor our agreement."

Salazar longed with all his heart to roast Xavier alive, but to do so would spell disaster. The man knew far too much; he was also extremely well prepared to expose everything if he were to die. Picking up the envelope, Salazar removed a letter that he read slowly and carefully several times. Eventually, after a contemptuous glance at the captain and allowing a deep sigh to slip out, he signed and stamped the document with the royal seal.

"There," he said, tossing it across the desk. "You are now officially *Lord* Xavier Mortimer."

The captain examined the signature and seal thoroughly before returning the document to its envelope and storing it safely away in his pocket. "Thank you, Your Highness. Now if you will excuse me?" He bowed low, his smile vicious and confident. He paused at the door. "Oh, I nearly forgot. The Grand Mage wishes to see you. She's waiting just outside."

The whispers in Salazar's mind had become too numerous to make out. This always happened when a high mage was near. He pressed his fingers to his temples and leaned his elbows on the desk. "I see. Tell her to come in."

He heard the Grand Mage's footsteps treading ever so softly on the carpet. The light scraping of silk was like a scream raking at his ears.

"You are not well, Your Highness."

Salazar opened his eyes and looked up. The Grand Mage was not as old as her title suggested. At a guess, he would say no more than forty years. Rather than the orange and black robes her order typically wore, she chose attire suited to a noblewoman: an elegant red dress with gold stitching, together with a silver veil draped over her head that she wrapped around to cover her mouth.

"What do you want?" he asked. Reaching into his pocket, he gripped the crystal. As if a mist had lifted, he felt his strength returning.

"In a foul mood, I see," she responded. Her tone was that of a mother scolding a child. "I came to tell you that you should refrain from further visits to the power station for a time."

No. Don't let her. She wants to keep you from us.

"Why is that?" he demanded.

He could see her frown through the veil.

"Do not play the fool. I know what you have been doing. You cannot imagine how dangerous it is. You are the king now. We cannot permit you to endanger yourself."

"There is no danger," he protested. "Look at me. I'm fine."

"You are not fine," she told him firmly. "And if this plan is to succeed, we need you to keep your wits about you."

He felt a flash of rage. "Everything is going according to plan."

Calm. Patience. She cannot suspect.

"It had better be. It was difficult enough for me to convince the others. Should this fail, you will not like what comes next."

"Do not threaten me, Grand Mage. I am the king, and you will speak to me with respect."

Unmoved by this royal demand, she gave a sniff of contempt. "You are king only because I allow it. As it was with your father before you. Test this assertion and you will quickly find yourself walking the same path as he. Do you not realize that we could have stopped you at any time?"

Salazar rose from his seat, fists balled and face crimson.

Do not act rashly. Your time will come soon.

The voice cut through his anger. Taking a deep breath, he relaxed his posture. "You are correct, of course. I would not want to jeopardize our plans."

"Good. I knew you would see reason. Now, as to your sister. She must be found quickly. Her voice carries much weight. If she moves against us, it could be...problematic."

"I will find her," he assured the woman.

"And what will you do then?"

"That, Grand Mage, truly is none of your affair."

She bowed her head. "Of course. So long as she is out of the way, the high mages will be satisfied. Now, if you will pardon me, Your Highness." Turning away, she seemed to almost float across the carpet to the door.

Salazar returned to his seat and continued fingering the crystal. His anger was boiling. Only the calming tone of the voices kept him from flying into a rage. He had missed them. He hadn't realized how much until his return. The high mages were fools. They had the power to reshape Vale at their very fingertips, yet still they did nothing. Too dangerous? Bah! Cowards, the whole lot of them. Not one possessed the courage of their convictions. They sought to rule in petty, cruel ways. Even when faced with the obvious truth, they hesitated to do the right thing.

A culling was required if Vale was to endure.

CHAPTER TWENTY

D rake pulled into the drive and around to the back of a modest dwelling. It was a single-story home built from wood and brick, with a porch that wrapped almost all the way around. The yard was well kept, and the grass unusually healthy and lush. There were even a few flower bushes planted at the border. Only one light shone through the window, and from the way it flickered and danced, it was not from a mana bulb.

"Max fancies himself a practitioner of natural magic," Bane told them. "You can't imagine how much time he spends keeping his place green."

"Natural magic?" repeated Drake. "What does that mean?

"He believes all living things have their own particular properties of mana. He's been trying to learn how to extract them individually in the hope of curing the land."

"From what I'm seeing, it appears to be working."

"Not really. This is a result of Max spending nearly everything he earns on fertilizers. Most of the other mages at the college think he's wasting his time."

"Do you?" asked Lenora.

Bane shrugged. "Who knows? Max is an idealist. In my experience, that often blinds one to reality."

As they climbed out of the car, the back door opened, and a man in a blue nightshirt and with a candle in his hand came out onto the porch. He was quite old, with a thin head of gray hair and a careworn face. On seeing Bane, he shook his head and frowned.

"What have you done this time, Samuel?" he asked in a sleepy voice. "And who have you brought with you?"

"This is Drake Sharazi," Bane replied. "And this is –"

"Dear god!" the old man gasped. "Is that…Princess Lenora?"

Lenora bowed. "It's a pleasure to meet you."

Max began to wave them inside frantically. "Come. Quickly now, before someone sees you."

He ushered them through a small kitchen into what looked like a study, although it was hard to tell, given the mountains of books and papers stacked all over the floor and on practically every other flat surface available. Short on seats, Max disappeared and returned a moment later dragging a rather large square cushion, which he handed to Bane.

"What the hell are you doing here, Samuel?" he demanded while clearing papers away from the chairs. "And with the princess, no less." He glanced over to Lenora. "Please forgive my rudeness, Your Highness."

"There is nothing to forgive," she responded. "I thank you for allowing us in."

"We need your help, Max," said Bane.

"*My* help?"

Once they were all seated, Max retrieved a bottle of wine and poured each of them a glass. Drake could see that the man was nervous, though being in the presence of royalty could certainly account for that.

Max plopped down into the one remaining chair and took a long drink. "Ah, much better," he sighed. "Now then, how can an old fool of a mage help the Princess of Vale?" When Bane opened his mouth to answer, Max's hand shot up. "I was not speaking to you, Samuel."

Lenora smiled warmly. "Aside from what you have already done, I am not sure. We are fleeing and have nowhere else to turn."

The already deep lines in Max's face deepened. "Fleeing? From whom?"

"My brother," she replied.

"Prince Salazar?" He shot Bane an accusing stare. "What have you done, boy?"

"This has nothing to do with Samuel, master mage," said Lenora. "He is my cousin, and he's put himself in grave danger to help me."

His eyes darted from Lenora to Bane and back again. After a long moment, he began chuckling softly. "Your cousin, you say? Well, doesn't that beat all? I always knew there was something different about him."

"As I recall, you said there was something *wrong* with me," Bane corrected.

"After you became a professor, yes, there was. As a student you were definitely special. But that didn't prevent you from turning into the worst damn teacher I ever saw."

Lenora laughed. "I heard all about that. You challenged the headmaster to a fight, I believe?"

Bane spread his hands. "What can I say? The man was an ass."

"That may be, but you were a mere junior professor. You should have kept your mouth shut." Max shook his head. "Keeping his mouth shut was one skill Samuel never managed to learn." He looked over to Drake. "And you, sir. I've heard your name. You wouldn't be the same Drake Sharazi convicted of killing Lord Malcoy, by any chance?"

"I am," he affirmed.

"Did you do it?"

"No. You have my word."

Drake left it at that. He didn't want to divulge details about what had happened or why they were there. The less the old mage knew, the better it would be for him should they be discovered.

Max regarded him for a moment before turning to Bane. "I can tell that your companions are trying to conceal what is going on from me. I assume that's out of concern for my safety. You, on the other hand, Samuel, know better. Which is why you've come here. So out with it."

"We've endangered you enough already just by being here," Lenora cut in. "We only need a place to stay until we figure out what to do next."

Max smiled and took a sip of wine. "Your Highness, I am an old man. And the one thing about old men is, there's very little you can take away from them. I've lived my life, so they can have whatever is left, including my house and profession, if that is to be the way of things. But what they cannot take is my honor. If the Princess of Vale is in need of my help, it shall be hers. Even if she doesn't want to accept it."

"And if it means finding out you've been believing a lie for your entire life?" asked Drake. "Would you still want to know then?"

"My boy, I would rather die knowing a terrible truth than live on believing a pleasing lie."

Lenora eyed the old man with open admiration. "Then I

will tell you all I know. After that, you can decide what help you are willing to offer."

Lenora recounted the events leading up to their arrival, Drake and Bane adding their own parts of the story as they came up. Throughout, Max simply sat back in his chair staring at them, his hands steepled beneath his nose.

When they were finished, Max rose and poured himself another glass of wine. This was consumed in a single gulp. After pouring another, he lowered his head, closed his eyes, and spoke softly to himself.

"To think of all those innocent people starving. And for what? To fulfill the petty ambitions of a powerful few."

He reflected in silence for another few seconds before suddenly looking up at Lenora. "And should you find a way to stop your brother, what then?"

"I honestly don't know," she replied. "I wish I did. Even if I succeed, the high mages will still be in control. The land will remain plagued by their tainted magic, and the people will continue to starve."

Max returned to his seat. "You know, I saw that study your brother did. The headmaster gave me a copy. He thought it would keep me busy and out of his hair. The dimwit didn't understand a thing about it. He didn't see what I saw."

"And what was that?" asked Drake.

"That Vale *will* soon starve. Not just the outer provinces; all of it. There are simply too many people to feed, and the population is still growing."

"So you think Salazar really *is* trying to save Vale?" Drake was horrified at the thought.

"That's what it looks like to me," the old mage replied. "And in a twisted way, he's right. A massive reduction in population would indeed save those left alive from starvation."

"But the cost…" said Lenora. "All of those people…"

Bane sniffed. "I know it sounds terrible. But ask yourself this: How would he actually go about it? He simply doesn't have the manpower to succeed. People in the provinces outnumber those in Troi by at least fifty to one. Even if he send out every member of the royal guard, they still couldn't kill that many. And that's assuming they're all as insane as Salazar himself and were prepared to go along with his idea in the first place. I know people can be selfish, but to think they would simply stand by while the king engages in genocide…" He shook his head. "I refuse to believe it."

"My brother has a plan. That much you can count on."

"Is there anything at all you can think of that might tell us what that plan is?" asked Drake.

Lenora shook her head. "Nothing. He never spoke of it to me. Nor did my father, beyond saying it was something terrible that must be stopped."

"Well, we need to figure it out somehow. Or find someone else who knows."

"Like who?" said Bane. "Short of sneaking back into Troi and kidnapping the king, there's nothing we can do."

Max spoke up. "There is someone I can think of who might be able to help. But you're not going to like it very much."

"At this point, who cares?" remarked Drake.

"Exodus."

"What? Have you lost your mind?"

"You said they held Prince Salazar prisoner for several weeks. Surely they interrogated him."

"That's true," said Bane. "But I doubt they'd be willing to help us. Not after Drake destroyed their base and killed their people. Oh, yes…and rescued the very man who intends to wipe out practically all of Vale."

"There is an old saying about a common enemy," Max pointed out.

"How would we even contact them?" Drake asked.

The old mage cleared his throat and rubbed the back of his neck. "Well...I actually know one of them."

Bane raised an eyebrow. "You? Since when do you associate with such dangerous types?"

"It was unintentional, I assure you. One came to me for help a couple of years ago. He was a student of mine, but the magistrate discovered he was part of Exodus. I let him hide out here until he could find a way to get to his people."

"And you have a way of contacting him?" asked Drake.

"I think so," he replied. "He left instructions should I ever need him. It will take a few days. But I can try."

"What do you think?" Drake asked Lenora.

She thought for a lengthy moment. "I see no other option. As Samuel pointed out, unless we try to capture my brother, we need help from others."

Max drained his glass. "Then it's settled. I'll leave in the morning, and you three will wait here until I return."

"You should let one of us come with you," said Drake.

He laughed. "Which one do you suggest? Of the three of you, Samuel is the only one not being hunted. And with his reputation, I'd be far better off alone."

Drake was not sure how good an idea this was. Lenora was right, though; they had no other options. They could only hide for so long. And hiding would do nothing to stop Salazar.

After showing Lenora to the spare bedroom, Max brought out blankets and pillows for the other two to use in the living room.

"You can use my bed tomorrow after I leave," he told them.

Drake thanked him and then walked out onto the back porch. The night air carried a slight chill. He took several deep breaths, allowing it to fill his lungs while thinking back on his short time with Salazar after his rescue. He had not seemed unbalanced; though equally, he *had* appeared to be more than a bit preoccupied with the welfare of the people. Small things he'd said now sprang to mind. At the time, they hadn't seemed particularly important; just a word here and there. Had Drake understood more, though, they would have surely served to tell him of Salazar's mental state. He sighed. Even now, knowing full well of his once best friend's crazed plan, he still could not reconcile it with the man he thought he knew.

He heard the door open, and the pleasing scent of lilacs drifted on the air.

"I should have brought more things with me," said Lenora. "Max was kind enough to lend me a robe, but it's really a bit on the large side."

This was hardly an exaggeration. The white cotton robe hung loosely about her, and the sleeves swallowed up her hands. Her hair was wrapped in a towel, with a stray curl peeking out pressed against her brow.

Drake smiled. "You could wear a suit made from mechanic's rags and still look beautiful." Almost at once, he winced at his own words. But corny or not, Lenora blushed anyway.

"You have always been so generous," she replied. "Even when you are lying."

"Lying? Me? Never."

She touched his cheek, the robe's sleeve rolling up over her slender wrist as she did so. "It's good to see that the hard years did not kill the man I knew," she whispered. "I had feared that life in the provinces might change you."

The warmth of her touch had him shutting his eyes involuntarily. "They did. I'm a much different person from the one that left Troi." Suddenly, he was keenly aware of the lines and cracks on his face that nearly a decade of life as a hawker had added.

"I know. But not in the ways that matter to me. You are still kind and thoughtful. Even after all the horrors you have seen, your heart remains the same."

Drake took hold of her hand and met her eyes. "I need to ask you something, Lenora. Did you know it was your brother who killed Lord Malcoy?"

"Eventually. Yes."

The words stabbed at his heart. Still he could not summon even a hint of anger. Not for her.

"When?"

"He told me about a year ago. He said that someone had changed the video to incriminate you, but he wouldn't tell me who it was. I wanted to go to Father, but Salazar assured me he didn't have the original recording. And without proof, there was nothing I could do. Please believe me, I was desperate to do something…anything…"

"Don't be upset," he told her. "I believe you. I truly do. And I don't want you thinking about my time in the provinces. It wasn't all bad. The worst part was not seeing you."

She smiled. "And now here we are."

Drake could no longer control himself. Taking Lenora in his arms, he pulled her close. Her body yielded instantly, and for the first time in what felt like an eternity, their lips met.

The kiss was gentle at first, almost shy. Then, as the years melted away, the intensity grew. Their breaths started coming in short gasps. Desperately they tugged and pulled at one another as if seeking to make their bodies into one.

Drake's passion was a raging storm of lust and desire, tempered only by the deep love and respect he felt for the woman in his arms. He wanted her. And there was no doubt that she wanted him. And he was on the verge of giving in to his yearnings...

The porch door opened.

Even after this most public of interruptions, it was still almost painful to part.

"I see the two of you are getting reacquainted," Bane remarked, looking at them with an impish grin. "I do hate to interrupt, but Max has asked me to come and get you. He says he'll be leaving at dawn and wants to go over some things that we'll need to know while he's not here."

Lenora's face was flushed as she pulled her robe tight. "Yes. Of course."

Drake watched her hurry inside. He wanted to throttle Bane. "Perfect timing," he growled.

Bane spread his hands, clearly enjoying the awkward moment his arrival had caused. "What can I say? Max sent me. What was I supposed to tell him? It's not my fault you thought right now might be the perfect time to revive your romance."

He was right. Drake was aware of that. Not that this knowledge helped very much.

We still have time, he told himself. But did they? In fact, was it even a good idea to be doing any of this? Was it fair... to either of them? It was difficult enough knowing that, even if they succeeded in stopping Salazar, they would once again be forced apart. Maybe they should just stop now? But of course, there was always the small matter of self-control; and with Lenora, he had none.

He could hear Max complaining inside that he was taking too long.

"Come," said Bane. "Old men get grumpy at night. Max more than most."

"You go. I'll be right behind you."

With the taste of Lenora's lips still lingering on his, Drake took a moment longer to calm himself before following.

CHAPTER TWENTY-ONE

Max told them that he would be back in three days. The few neighbors were not close enough to have a clear view of his house, but he said they should remain indoors except after sundown anyway, and even then only venture as far as the back porch.

Though not exactly becoming distant, Lenora's affection toward Drake did not continue as he hoped it might. Every time he drew close, her eyes fell on Bane and she immediately shied away. Of course, when they'd first become involved, it had been necessary for them to be constantly discreet. Drake could understand that, after having lived such a guarded life, even now it was uncomfortable for Lenora to make any public displays of affection. He tried a few times to catch her alone, but Bane was always nearby. After the second day, he began to suspect it was intentional. Probably protecting his cousin from future heartbreak and pain, he decided.

They spent most of their time listening to music or watching the holovids, and Bane occupied himself by rummaging through a few of Max's books.

"Did you really challenge the headmaster to a fight?"

Drake asked on the second night, while they were all lazing about in the living room.

Bane smiled and shrugged, wearing his best innocent face. "What can I tell you? I was impulsive, and he baited me. He found out that my father is, in his words: 'Nothing but a lowly mechanic.' After that, he kept on at me until I'd finally had enough. He's one of those lower Troi fools who thinks he's better than everyone else. I had to put him in his place. You should have seen him when I reacted. I think the man actually shat himself."

"Sounds to me like you won the battle but lost the war," remarked Drake, disapprovingly.

"You could say that," he agreed. "I was young. The youngest professor there, in fact. If I had it to do over… well…" He paused and then started laughing. "Hell, I think I'd probably do the same thing all over again. I get a bit touchy when it comes to my father."

"Your father was quite upset with you at the time," Lenora chipped in.

"My father is always upset with me. He's never forgiven me for not wanting to follow in his footsteps"

"No," she retorted. "He was upset because you refuse to live up to your potential."

Bane's face twisted into a frown. "And what potential could I live up to in this hell of a world? I didn't want to end up fixing cars and gadgets. And the idea of ending up like Max was…" He feigned a shudder. "The life of a hawker seemed far more appealing."

"But at least fixing gadgets doesn't require that you kill people," Drake added.

"Then *you* go work with him."

"If I had an ounce of talent for such things, I would have."

274

Bane threw up his hands. "A killer with a conscience. Splendid. Let's hope your delicate sensibilities don't bother you too much when it's time to kill Salazar."

Lenora reacted instantly, springing up and glaring at Bane with lips trembling and hands balled into fists. Such was her anger that for a moment it looked as if she might actually strike him. Instead, she spun on her heels and stormed from the room.

Bane's expression immediately became one of regret.

"What the hell is wrong with you?" snapped Drake, in a hushed tone.

"I'm...I'm sorry. I don't know why I said that."

"Because you're an arrogant jackass who tries to pretend he knows everything. You want to know the real reason you got kicked out of the mages' college? It wasn't because the headmaster thought you weren't good enough. It's because deep down, *you* don't think you are."

A sneer formed on Bane's face. "I don't need a lecture from you. What the hell do you know about me?"

"Not much. But enough to know that you're self-destructive. I can see that as clear as day. You're constantly trying to prove how good you are, while all the time you really believe you're not worth a damn. Look how you talked just now about your father and Max. You should be so lucky as to end up like either one of them. At least they know who they are." He noticed a dim glow radiating from Bane's hands. "Right there. You see? No self-control whatsoever."

Bane jumped to his feet. "You've got a damn nerve preaching to me about self-control. You know perfectly well how this thing must end. Yet you still continue to pursue Lenora as if the two of you have the rest of your lives together."

This struck hard and deep. "What's between Lenora and me is our own business."

"No. It's mine as well. You are not the only one who loves her."

The two men glared at one another, tension crackling between them. It was Drake who finally allowed himself to give a little ground.

He held up a calming hand. "Look, I'm sorry. I was out of line. Whatever our differences, we both care deeply for Lenora. That's understood. And we've a long road to travel together if we're going to make sure she's safe. It's no good for us to be at each other's throats."

Very gradually, Bane released his mana and nodded in agreement. "You're right. I apologize too. When you spend as much time alone as I do, you tend to forget about other people's feelings."

Drake smiled. "I know what you mean. We just have to remember that neither of us are hawkers anymore."

"Yes. And at least that should please Father." He gave a short laugh. "I suppose, in a funny kind of way, we're both royal guards now. Imagine that."

Drake smiled. "I suppose we are."

Bane turned to the door. "I should go speak with her."

He paused at the doorway and looked over his shoulder. "I did mean what I said. I won't try to stand in your way. But I do hope you'll leave whatever was between the two of you in the past."

Drake considered this after he was gone. Did he have the strength to resist being selfish? Because right now, that was precisely what he was being. No answer to this disturbing question was forthcoming, even though he wanted to believe that he would always act solely out of care for Lenora's feelings and the security of her future.

He wanted to do what was right...but still wasn't sure if he would have the willpower to do so.

Lenora and Bane returned a short while later, both smiling. Lenora had always been the forgiving sort, though too often people mistook her kindness for weakness; a mistake many learned to regret. She could be as hard as stone and fierce as mana fire when the need arose.

Bane was the first to retire, leaving Drake and Lenora alone – though he did flash Drake a warning look on his way out. They talked for a time, mostly about when they were children, with Drake taking great care to avoid making any mention whatsoever of Salazar.

Finally, a reflective silence developed. After a minute or so of this, a change seemed to come over Lenora. No longer was she simply reminiscing over past times; her mind was now very much on the present. Rising to her feet, she crossed over to where he was seated, her hand outstretched. Every movement she made was slow and seductive, and the fire of passion in her eyes was an open invitation. Suddenly, Drake felt his willpower being tested to the full.

Before he knew what he was doing, he was on his feet and being led to the spare bedroom. It was if his desires and love were carrying him along rather than his legs. It was only when they reached the bedroom door that he somehow managed to stop.

"I...I think we should wait."

Even after the words were out, he still wasn't sure if they had actually passed his lips or if they were mere thoughts in his head.

Turning to face him, she draped her arms over his shoulders. "Wait? I *have* waited. I've waited nine years for this."

"I know. So have I." His will was crumbling. The scent

of her perfume and the intimate closeness of her lips were almost overwhelming.

"Then why must we wait any longer?" She moved in even closer, brushing those tantalizing lips lightly over his ear and cheek. "All I know is that tomorrow could be our last day. Who can tell what will happen once we meet with Exodus?"

He took a step back. "You know that I love you, Lenora. I always will. But I just can't do this. I'm so sorry."

He fully expected to see a look of hurt and rejection appear on her face. Even anger. But instead...astonishingly...all he saw was gentle understanding.

She touched his cheek. "It's all right."

"It's not that I don't want to," he added quickly and rather awkwardly. "It's just…"

He wanted to explain; he yearned to tell her that he simply couldn't bear the pain of losing her once this was over. If this happened between them now, how could he ever let her go? He knew what she would say to reassure him. And if he heard those words, he would surely give in.

She kissed him lightly on the lips. "Don't think about it. It's my fault." She cast an eye over their surroundings and let out a soft laugh. "Besides, this isn't exactly how I pictured our first night together after so long, anyway."

Drake smiled back. "Me either."

With a sigh, she slipped her arms around him and buried her head in his chest. "You know, I never imagined I would be happy again. And with all the terrible things that have happened, I know it's not right for me to be. But I am anyway."

Drake kissed the top of her head. "So am I."

They stood there locked together for some time before Lenora reluctantly backed away. A wistful smile then formed, and she simply said: "Good night, Drake."

The pain in his heart was almost unbearable as she slowly

closed the bedroom door. He wanted to scream out at the top of his voice. That...or to smash something into a million pieces. Most of all, he just wanted to burst into the room and ignore what his mind was telling him.

He walked outside onto the porch, all the time cursing himself for being a fool. The woman he loved, who still clearly loved him in return, was not a dozen yards away from where he was standing. "And what do you do about it?" he muttered. "Not a damn thing."

He stood there staring into the night, watching the mana streams overhead as they delivered both lifesaving power and life-draining sickness to the whole of Vale.

He tried to think about the immediate future. They would be meeting with Exodus soon, but would they really be able to help? He doubted it. The group was likely no more able to rid Vale of the new king and the high mages than he was. If their interrogation of Salazar had yielded something that could turn the tide, surely they would have made use of it already. He had a sinking feeling that this had all been for nothing. They would continue to run until they were either caught or forced into a suicidal attempt to re-enter Troi and kill Salazar.

He imagined his former friend at the coronation, the crown atop his brow bought with the blood of his father. And all the while, Xavier would be hiding in the shadows, a smug expression on his wretched face. Drake wasn't sure which one of them he despised the most.

Eventually he returned inside and lay on the sofa. It was late, and tomorrow would come soon. If he were to protect Lenora, he would need to be at his best.

A sharp bang startled him awake. He scrambled up, eyes

searching for his P37. Then he remembered that it was in the bedroom. Urgent voices carried in from down the hall, followed by a woman's scream.

"Lenora!"

Barely had he called her name when two men dressed in black kicked in the front door. Both carried large caliber rifles that were pointing directly at him. These were not magistrate officers, nor were they royal guard.

"Don't move!" barked one of the men.

From where he was standing he could see down the hallway to where Bane had been sleeping. Three men were already leading him out, weapons pressed to his head.

"On your knees," the man ordered.

There was nothing he could do but comply. He dropped down as instructed, with arms raised. While one man kept his weapon trained, the other quickly cuffed his hands behind his back and then pulled him to his feet.

"Where is Lenora?" he demanded.

"Do as you're told and she'll be fine."

Drake was led through the house and onto the back porch. Bane and Lenora were already there, their hands cuffed as well. A perfectly timed raid, he thought. In all, he counted a dozen men. A truck was being backed into the yard in front of Cal, and a windowless van was parked a few yards beyond.

Lenora was in her nightgown, her face expressionless as she glanced over to Drake.

By contrast, Bane was bright red with fury. "Where is Max?" he shouted. "What have you done to him?"

No answer was given. They were pushed roughly from the porch and over to the van. After being bundled into the back, they were chained individually to bench seats fixed along either side – Drake and Bane to the left, and Lenora on the right.

The door closed, and the vehicle instantly lurched forward. The entire operation had taken less than a minute. These guys were no amateurs. They knew what they were doing.

"Do you think Max betrayed us?" he whispered.

Bane shook his head. "No! Max wouldn't do that."

"Are you sure?" he pressed. "I know he's your friend, but —"

"I *said* he wouldn't do that."

Drake could see that Bane was boiling over with fury. He'd expressed his admiration for the old mage on several occasions, telling them that Max had been the only professor to defend him when he'd been expelled from the college.

"Can you get free?" he asked the other two.

Both of them shook their heads.

"The cuffs have mana suppressors," Bane told him.

He looked over to Lenora. "Are you all right?"

She forced a smile. "Well, I was hoping for a more cordial introduction. But I'm fine."

If this *was* just an introduction, Drake considered. On the positive side, if Exodus really wanted them dead, it was unlikely they would have gone through all this trouble to capture them, particularly considering the fact that they would have known all three could be highly dangerous in a fight. If he hadn't been so foolish as to leave his weapon in the other room, things might have gone very differently indeed.

They rode on for hours, making a few turns from time to time. He guessed that they were headed north. Bane tried to find out how long it would be before they arrived, but the two men in the front were unwilling to speak. This only served to fuel his anger.

By the time they pulled up, Drake was both sore and

hungry, and he knew the other two would be feeling the same way. After several minutes, the back doors opened, and they were unshackled from the bench by a young woman wearing gray coveralls. Six men stood immediately outside, all of them holding rifles.

"If you'll be patient, this will all be over soon," said the girl, in a friendly voice.

"Where are you taking us?" Drake asked.

"To see Zara," she replied.

He recognized the name from the briefing in the magistrate's office – she was the purported leader of Exodus.

The girl helped Lenora from the van first. "If you will come with me," she said. "I'm sure you would all like something to eat."

Two men leaned in to pull Drake and Bane outside. They were in an empty field surrounded by thin pines on all sides. Even so, Drake could feel the ground vibrating through his boots. Another underground facility, he told himself.

This was confirmed when he heard a thin hiss, and a thick steel door rose up from within the grass. A long flight of stairs leading down ended in a series of corridors. The walls were bare and dull gray, and every door along the way was shut, though he could hear voices coming from inside the rooms as they passed.

They were taken to a large chamber that, judging from the numerous tables scattered about, looked to be a dining hall.

"Just so you know," the girl said. "This entire wing is rigged to release gas into the corridors. So please behave. No one here has any intention of hurting you."

"And what about Max?" Bane asked.

"The mage from the college? He's here. Don't worry; we're not animals. We wouldn't hurt an old man, and we'll be taking him home soon. All the same, he's not too pleased with us right now. He thought it would be better if we simply asked you to come."

"Why didn't you?" asked Drake.

"After what you did to our refinery, I'm afraid that was a risk we weren't prepared to take."

It was at that moment he noticed a slight twitch at the corner of the girl's mouth. She was hiding something.

"At the time, I didn't know the truth," he explained. "I was only doing what I thought I had to do."

"Yes. I'm sure." The girl turned to Lenora. "Once I uncuff you, I advise you not to try anything. Even were you to kill me and all the men here, the halls will be filled with gas before you can make it more than fifty yards."

"We did not come to fight," Lenora assured her. "We need your help."

The girl's eyes darted over to Drake. "Yes. That's what we've been told."

She uncuffed each of them. Just as she was finishing, three guards entered carrying trays and glasses filled with water. These were placed on one of the tables.

"Once you've eaten, you'll be taken to where you can freshen up a bit before seeing Zara," the girl said. She then exited along with all but two of the guards.

The trio sat down, each taking a plate filled with beans and a small portion of stewed meat. "Not exactly palace food," Lenora remarked, grinning. "But it will do for now."

"I don't like this," remarked Bane. "There's something going here."

Drake didn't like it much either, particularly the way the girl had looked at him. However, not wanting to alarm Lenora any more than necessary, he kept this to himself.

"At least we know Max is all right," he said.

"I'll know that when I get to see him," Bane retorted.

Lenora picked up her spoon. "Well, given the fact that we are prisoners, I say we eat our food and make the best of it. I really don't think they would go to all this trouble just to kill us."

"Agreed," Bane said. "They could have simply blown up the house or come in shooting."

Or they could be getting ready to torture us for information, Drake reflected. This was another thought he felt best kept to himself.

After they finished their meal, the two guards led them out and along yet more hallways. The same girl was waiting for them in front of an open door.

"Your Highness," she said. "If you would step this way? I'm sure you would like a bit of privacy." She nodded over to another door opposite. "You two can bathe and change in there."

Although loath to be separated, Drake could hardly take issue with this arrangement.

Inside their room were two bunks and a metal table, while off to the right were a bathroom and a small closet. On opening this, they found their belongings had been brought.

"That was considerate," said Bane, showing the first flicker of a smile since their abduction had started. "Walking around in my night shirt and pants *was* becoming a bit awkward."

"Too bad they didn't leave my P37 as well," Drake responded, trying to further lighten the mood.

"If what she said about the gas is true, I doubt it would do us much good." Bane held up his finger and a tiny flame danced on the tip. "But if it comes to it, I think I will not go alone."

Drake flashed him a stern look. "Don't do anything like

that unless I do it first. Understand?"

The flame vanished and Bane paused for a moment before speaking. "If they hurt Lenora –"

"They won't," Drake said, cutting him off. He paused a moment before adding: "Me, on the other hand..."

"Yes, I saw how that girl looked at you. She's holding a grudge about something, that's for sure." Like Drake, Bane's experience as a hawker gave him an exceptional eye for reading emotions.

"Nothing to be done about it now. If she tries to kill me, I guess I'll just have to deal with it then."

They both showered and changed into their clothes. After about three hours of waiting, Drake was becoming restless, and he could tell that Bane was feeling the same way. Both of them sat on their cots, eyes fixed on the door.

Another half hour passed. An exasperated Drake was on the verge of leaving the room to check on Lenora for himself when their door swung open. The girl entered, with Lenora walking just behind her. She had a worried look.

"What's wrong?" Drake asked.

She forced a smile. "Nothing. Teri here is taking us to see Zara now."

Drake and Bane followed her through the corridor and down another stairway. After a few more turns he showed them to a small office. The door to this was guarded by two men; inside, at the far end, an olive-skinned woman of about forty was sitting behind a desk. Her black hair fell loosely about her shoulders. She was wearing a simple green cotton blouse and a set of diamond earrings. Her dark eyes bore down on them for a long moment before dismissing the girl and the guards with a brief wave of her hand.

She gestured to the chairs against the wall. Drake grabbed two of these, pulling them up in front of the desk, and Bane took a third. Once all were seated, the woman looked them over one by one.

"So you are Drake Sharazi," she said finally. "The man who rescued Prince Salazar."

"At the time –"

"I'm not finished," she snapped. "By rescuing him, you not only destroyed a key facility, you also killed more than four hundred innocent men and women."

"What?" Drake could barely believe she had said the words. The number didn't seem real. "That's impossible."

"When you ruptured the vex chambers, most of my people were on the second level. So yes. It was very possible. Only a handful escaped alive."

He glanced over to Lenora, who by now was staring down at the floor, clearly already aware of this. The girl, Teri, must have told her.

"I didn't know," was all he could think to say.

"And if you did? What would have changed?"

"I…I'm not sure."

Bane leapt to his defense. "What would you have the man do? Call in the royal guard instead? At least Drake did what he did unintentionally. But the royal guard...they would have simply slaughtered every last one of you without mercy."

"Ah, yes," she sneered. "Bane. Outcast mage and hawker. How is it you are still alive? Is there anyone in Vale who doesn't want to see you dead? I take it you know that Fisk has put out a bounty of fifty thousand notes on your head. And to be honest, we could use the money."

"Samuel is my cousin," said Lenora. "And whatever you might think, he is a good man."

"And then there's you," said Zara. "Princess Lenora. What is it exactly you are running from? Oh, yes. Your brother wants you dead. Or at least, he did. It seems that the illustrious captain...actually, it's *Lord* Xavier now... has found a way for you to make amends. Are you aware of this yet?"

"Teri told me about it only a few minutes ago."

Drake's eyes shifted rapidly in her direction. "Told you about what?"

Zara spoke first. "It seems that her brother has given his permission for Xavier to wed the princess," she told him. "He claims you kidnapped her, and has offered a fortune for her safe return."

"So is that it?" said Bane. "You captured us for bounty money?"

"There's no doubt it would help our cause," she replied, leaning back in her chair. "And it would be ironic that the very man who wants to destroy us would be funding his adversaries."

Drake noticed Bane's hands glowing faintly.

"But no. I have no intention of turning you over. You are far too valuable to us for that."

"Then what do you want from us?" asked Lenora. She reached over and touched Bane's leg. Gradually, he released his mana.

"It is my understanding that you want to know what we learned from your brother while he was in our custody." Rising from her chair, she crossed over to the door and dimmed the lights. "The fact is, we learned quite a lot. We already knew about the high mages' corruption of the mana streams. But what we learned from the prince..."

She eyed Lenora with clear suspicion. "It makes me wonder exactly how much you know, and if you are a part of his plan as well."

"I learned of my brother's mad schemes some time ago," she admitted. "But I am not a part of it all. Quite the opposite

– I hope to prevent it from happening."

"The old mage from the college says that you need to know how he intends to carry out his plan. Is that right?"

Lenora nodded. "None of us have any idea how he might be able to accomplish such a seemingly impossible task. I'm sure he must have a way. But if we don't know what it is, how are we to stop him?"

Zara resumed her seat, her gaze still fixed upon the princess. There was a long pause before she spoke again. "Tell me, what do you know about hellspawn?"

Lenora knitted her brow. "Hellspawn? Nothing at all, really. Only that they're monsters from the outer world."

"You've never heard your father or brother speak of them?"

"Only once or twice. When they found a way into Vale."

"What does this have to do with us?" demanded Drake.

Zara's eyes shifted across to bore into him. "Absolutely everything," she replied.

CHAPTER TWENTY-TWO

The holoprojector came to life, and the image of a hellspawn appeared on the wall to their left. As it moved closer, its black soulless eyes seemed to be staring directly at them. The creature's pale green flesh was literally covered in blood, much of it likely from the horrifically mutilated corpse it was dragging along with one of its taloned claws.

"This was taken a week ago," Zara told them. "It killed twelve people before the royal guard was able to take it down." She looked to Drake. "You were a royal guard. Did you ever find out how they were getting into Vale?"

"No," he replied. "We looked for weeks, but we were never able to find a point of entry."

"That's because you were looking in the wrong places."

Drake stiffened. "Are you saying that you know how they got in?"

"What if I told you they didn't come from beyond the barrier at all? That they were here in Vale the whole time?"

Drake coughed a laugh. "Then I'd say you've lost your mind."

She made no immediate reply, choosing instead to merely push the mana pad in her hand. In response, a massive steel building came up on the screen. It bore no markings, though the exterior was well maintained, and the entrance was being watched by two royal guards.

"Do you recognize this place?" she asked.

"Yes, of course I do," Drake said. "It's a research facility. We kept men there around the clock. But we were never given access to the interior. Only the people who worked there were allowed beyond the door."

She regarded him for a moment. "Were you never curious as to what they were doing?"

He spread his hands. "It was none of my affair. The royal guard was charged with security, that's all. You don't question orders from the king. You just obey."

"So would it surprise you to learn that this is where the hellspawn come from? Or at least, those that you have seen."

Drake didn't like where this was going. "Are you suggesting…?"

"That hellspawn are not from the outer world. They are created right here in Vale."

"That's not possible," Lenora blurted out. "My father would have never allowed such a thing."

A flash of annoyance at her outburst showed on Zara's face. "Your father, your grandfather before him – in fact, every king and queen for as long as we have records of hellspawn have known about them. Your brother knows as well. How do you think we found out?"

"I don't believe you," Lenora insisted, her face taut.

"Why not? The high mages allow people to starve. The king was complicit in that. Would this be worse than the crimes they already have committed?"

"But it makes no sense," Drake said. "What's the point?"

"What is the point to anything the ruling class does? To maintain control, of course." Her eyes fell on Lenora. "If it makes you feel any better, we don't believe that it was the king who ordered these beasts to be set loose. According to your brother, it's the high mages who do this. They use them to instill fear in the people and keep them from becoming curious."

"Curious about what?" asked Drake.

"You'll find out in due course."

Zara touched the mana pad again, this time bringing up the image of a large glass tank. Though the picture was blurry, there could be no denying that the creature inside was a hellspawn. A woman in a white coat was standing beside the tank, giving it a sense of scale. The creature wasn't anywhere near as large as the one he and Bane had fought. If anything, it was closer to the size of those he had seen in the secret room at the nightclub in Narsil.

"This picture was taken at great personal risk by one of our people," she continued. "As you can see, the hellspawn isn't yet fully grown."

Drake hesitated before telling her about his own experience.

"So you believe her?" asked Lenora, mortified.

"I'm not sure," he admitted. "I still don't see what this has to do with Salazar."

"We think he intends to use hellspawn to wipe out the population."

Drake blew out a derisive breath. "That's just stupid. Say you're right. Say that hellspawn are grown in Vale. Do you realize how many of them it would take to do the job? And even if they had enough, what good would releasing them do? These creatures wouldn't stop at the provinces. They would destroy all of Vale. Even Troi."

Zara turned up the lights and then returned to her desk. "Unfortunately, you came along and interfered before we could learn the entire plan."

"I have to ask," Bane interjected. "How are they made?"

Zara's face darkened. "We don't know the process. But we do know what they are." Her gaze fixed on Lenora. "I should say, what they *used* to be. They were people: just ordinary people."

The dawning implications of this could easily be read in Lenora's expression. How could her father have known and done nothing to stop it? Within seconds, her bearing began to crumble.

Bane touched her arm. "Even if it's true, it's not your fault."

Tears were spilling down her cheeks. "It's true. I just know it. This is what my brother was hiding. This is how he intends to slaughter the people."

Drake felt helpless. To learn that your entire family was guilty of murdering innocent people so as to create monsters out of them...it was unimaginable. He wanted to comfort her, but no words would salve this kind of wound.

Zara's features softened. "I am sorry, Your Highness. I can see quite clearly now that you were not a part of this. But I need to know...will you help us stop it?"

It was as if something inside Lenora suddenly switched off her tears. Her face became hard as steel and her eyes narrowed. "What can I do?"

A thin smile crept up from the corners of Zara's mouth. "Quite a bit. I'll explain more shortly."

"Are you planning to attack this place?" Drake asked her.

"I could," she replied. "But it wouldn't do any good. That particular facility is much too small to house the kind of numbers Salazar would need. And if we attack now, we'll be exposing our intentions prematurely. When we strike, everything has to be in place. Which means the power station has to be destroyed."

"Destroy the power station!" This was the craziest thing Drake had heard yet. "You'll never get close enough," he stated. "Not with a thousand men. Not even with five thousand. The magistrate's men and the royal guard, not to mention the mages, would cut you down before you made it to lower Troi."

Zara smirked. "You think so?"

"I know so. Have you ever seen what five guards armed with P37s can do? Well, imagine a thousand of them. Then imagine the hell the high mages would unleash. And that's always assuming you could get past the hundreds of magistrate officers." He shook his head. "No, it's impossible."

"Perhaps we could sneak in," suggested Bane.

"Into the city, yes," Drake agreed. "But you'd never make it to the power station. The royal guard runs drills three times a year trying to break in. No one has ever succeeded."

"There has to be a way," Bane said, stubbornly.

"No, Drake is right," Lenora told him. "Unless you're already in the palace, it's impossible. And even then, you'd need a special code. One wrong step and you'd be incinerated."

She folded her hands and closed her eyes for a second. "However, I think I might know a way around this." She looked up at Zara. "That's what you meant by me helping you, right?"

Realization struck Drake like a hammer. It was too awful a thing to even think about. "Not a chance!" he shouted. "I won't let you do it."

"There is no other way," she said, weakly.

"What are you talking about?" asked Bane.

"She intends to return to Troi and marry Xavier."

Bane's eyes shot wide. "Are you crazy? I'm with Drake on this one. No chance. More likely than not, he'll just kill you."

Zara began laughing softly. "You are indeed a brave woman, Your Highness. More so than I would have thought possible. And in spite of my feelings about your choice in companions, I can see that they're loyal to you. But set your mind at ease. I'm not asking you to suffer such a fate."

Lenora looked confused. "Then what do you need me to do?"

"Salazar isn't ready to initiate his plan just yet. We have time. Our spies tell us that he has engaged Fisk, along with a few others scattered throughout the provinces, to aid him. Though what they're getting them to do, we're still trying to find out."

"I could help you with that," said Bane.

"That was our intention," she told him.

"What about me?" asked Drake.

Zara let out a long breath. "You, I'm afraid, are a difficult matter. You killed a large number of our people, and nothing I can say will change that. If you remain here, sooner or later someone will try to take revenge."

"If Drake goes, I go too," Lenora said flatly.

"As it happens, that's truer than you think."

She rose from her seat. "I need you both to come with me. I have something to show you. Then you can decide if you really do want to help us." When Bane stood as well, she held up her hand. "You should stay here. Someone will be along in a minute to go over with you in detail everything that we've learned so far."

Bane's objections to this were quickly quelled by Lenora. She took his hand. "Don't worry. We'll be fine. Stay here and gather all the information you can. That would be most useful."

With Bane seated once more, Zara led the other two out. After a few turns, they entered a large room with a number of evenly spaced round tables. Two holovid players were in the far corner, and several game boards and books were scattered about. A door was situated on the left wall, through which music could be heard drifting out.

Once they were seated, Zara folded her hands on the table and regarded them both closely. "What you are about to see is known only to a very few of us. I have to ask that you do not tell your cousin about it."

"I will not hide anything from him," Lenora responded quickly.

"You must. At least for now. I promise that it's nothing he needs to know."

Lenora looked to Drake, who gestured that it should be her decision. After several seconds of thought, she slowly nodded her acceptance.

Zara smiled. "That's good. But before I reveal our secret, tell me what you know about the world beyond the barrier?"

"It's a wasteland," Lenora replied. "Nothing grows there, and it is filled with ravenous, twisted beasts. They say it was once a garden, devastated by the war of the ancients."

"Yes," said Zara. "That's what we're all told. But what if that was a lie?"

"I've seen beyond the barrier," Drake said. "It's not."

"Have you? Have you really? How far in did you go?"

Drake shrugged. "Not far. Just to the other side. All new recruits of the royal guard are taken there so they can see for themselves what they're protecting the people from."

"So you didn't venture out at all?"

"No. Why would I wish to? There was nothing there but black earth and dust as far as the eye could see."

"And you, Your Highness?"

"I've never been. But I've seen the images."

Zara nodded while digesting their answers for a moment, then called out: "Maliel! Can you come in here, please?"

The door to their left opened almost at once, and a tall thin figure emerged. At first, Drake was confused as to what he was seeing. Clad in a tan cloth robe and leather shoes, the new arrival had long silver hair that fell to the middle of his back. His deep bronze skin seemed to shimmer in the mana light, while his eyes were widely spaced and tilted slightly upward, giving him a striking appearance. But it was the newcomer's ears that had Drake jumping to his feet. Long, thin, and pointed at the tip, they were clearly not those of any human.

"What the hell is that?" he demanded, placing his body directly in front of Lenora. "Some sort of hellspawn?"

The figure halted, eyes fixed on Drake.

"He is not a hellspawn," Zara insisted firmly.

"He?" Drake repeated. "That's a he?"

"Yes, I am most certainly male." His voice was surprisingly deep, yet in a way light and musical. "If indeed, that is your question."

His accent was unlike anything Drake had heard before, with rolling r's and elongated vowels.

"This is Maliel," said Zara. "And he is how we will defeat Salazar and save the people of Vale."

CHAPTER TWENTY-THREE

Maliel sat next to Zara, across from Drake and Lenora. His movements were fluid and graceful, and his emerald green eyes darted between the pair of them repeatedly.

"What...what are you?" Lenora's voice was a mere whisper.

He glanced over to Zara, who nodded her approval.

"We call ourselves Nelwyn. Beyond that description, I can tell you nothing more."

"We found him two years ago," Zara added. "Just beyond the barrier, severely injured and unconscious. He's been living here ever since."

"You are actually from beyond the barrier?" asked Lenora.

"I am."

"How is that possible?" she pressed.

"Life outside your world is not what it seems," he explained. "There is tall land..." He paused to give an embarrassed smile. "Forgive me. I sometimes confuse your words. There is much you do not see. The world outside is vast and green. Not like here." He looked as if he had tasted something disgusting. "Here, the solas tastes foul. It makes people ill."

"*Solas* is what they call mana," Zara explained. "He can feel the taint of the high mages."

"Then why have you stayed?" asked Drake.

"Outside is dangerous for my kind. The Bomar have cut me off from my people. They hunt us down whenever they can find us. Here I am sick, but at least I am alive."

Lenora creased her brow. "What are the Bomar?"

"Human…like you. But not like you. They cannot feel the touch of solas in their hearts. They are fire and smoke. Ash and blood."

"As best we can understand, Maliel's people are at war with the Bomar," Zara said.

"Yes," he said, emphatically. "They make war on us. Drive us from our homes. Slaughter us for sport."

"That's terrible," said Lenora. "But if they have no mana, can't you fight back?"

"Solas is a spirit for bringing life, not death."

"They have no aggressive magic," said Zara. "They have no concept of how to use it for defense."

"I am truly sorry about all this," Drake said. "And forgive me if I sound insensitive. But you said he could be our way of defeating Salazar. How does any of this help?"

Reaching into her pocket, Zara pulled out Drake's P37 and across the table. "Perhaps it's best if I show you." She took Maliel's hand she said, "He has to see for himself."

Maliel nodded. "As you wish." He stood up and backed away a few paces.

Drake took his weapon and examined it carefully. It appeared unaltered.

"Shoot him," Zara instructed.

Drake sat straight up. "What? I'm not shooting him."

She grinned. "Trust me. Just do it."

He looked to Lenora, who was appeared to be just as confused and unsure.

"You cannot harm me," assured Maliel.

After nearly a minute of consideration, Drake stepped away from the table and channeled a small amount of mana into the chamber. "Are you sure about this?"

"Absolutely," Zara replied.

Without giving himself time to think on it any longer, Drake aimed at Maliel's leg and fired. He staggered back a pace, a hole burned into his robe. But otherwise, he seemed completely unhurt.

"That is all?" he taunted. "Zara said your weapon was powerful."

Drake knew the shot would not be lethal, but it should have at least put him to the floor. He readied a more powerful shot, this time aiming it at his chest. "You asked for it," he muttered.

The sizzle of mana cut through the air, sending Maliel sprawling onto his back. Smoke rose from where the shot struck.

Both Drake and Lenora rushed to his side. Drake could only look in slack-jawed astonishment. Though like before the robe was burned away, there was not so much as a blemish on Maliel's flesh.

"Is that the extent of your weapon's strength?" he groaned, clutching at the point of impact. He was hurt, but not severely.

"That shot should have killed you," Drake told him, still not believing his eyes. "Are you using some sort of ward or cloak?"

"No, he is not," Zara said. "His people are just highly resistant to mana. You could charge your weapon fully and it still might not kill him."

Drake and Lenora helped Maliel to his feet.

"Thank you," he said. "But I am fine. There is no need for concern."

Drake gazed at his weapon, then back to Maliel, still struggling to accept what had just happened. Zara gestured for them to sit.

"I think I understand," said Drake, placing his weapon on the table in front of him. "With that kind of power, nothing could stop them. But there is only one of you, right?"

"In Vale, yes," Zara affirmed. "But outside, there are thousands just like him."

"So you intend to enlist them to our cause?" asked Lenora.

"That is my hope. And Maliel has agreed to speak to them on our behalf."

"Forgive me for asking," Drake chipped in, turning to Maliel. "But why would your people be interested in helping us?"

"As things are, they would not," he replied. "They are being chased by our enemies. Our numbers dwindle."

"So what do you plan to do?" Lenora asked Zara.

"The Nelwyn have no offensive magic," she said. "But that is not because they cannot wield it. They simply don't know how to. We can give them that ability. Or more to the point, *you* can, Your Highness."

"Me? You want me to teach them how to fight?"

"We are strong," said Maliel, his tone prideful. "Teach us to use fire and storm. Give us what we need to save ourselves from the Bomar."

"I'm not that sort of mage," she protested. "I work mostly with healing magic. Bane is much better suited to this kind of thing than I am."

Zara nodded. "Yes, we are well aware of his powers. But

given the fact that you are currently being hunted by Salazar and he is not, where better for you to hide than beyond the barrier? And the task should not be a difficult one, even for a healing mage. I'm sure you were also taught how to protect yourself. All you need to do is pass that knowledge on to the Nelwyn. They will develop quickly from there."

"Please," said Maliel. "Help us, and I promise I will bring my kin to cleanse your world for you. We can save each other."

"And what am I supposed to do?" asked Drake. "If you think I'm staying behind…"

"I wouldn't send our only hope without protection," Zara told him. "And being that you killed the only mage we had among us, the job is yours."

He looked to Lenora. "What do *you* want to do?"

She drew a long breath. "If his people can stop my brother, then I see no other choice."

Her agreement produced a sigh of gratitude from Maliel. "Thank you," he said.

"You do realize what this will mean," Drake said. "If we succeed in destroying the power station, all mana will cease to flow. Vale will be plunged into darkness."

"There is a solution to that," said Zara, "one we have been working on for many years. Though thanks to you, we've suffered quite a setback to our research."

Drake nodded. "The vex crystals. One of your people thought I was there to steal them. I really am sorry for what happened. I hope you know that."

His apology was ignored. "We've been working on ways to stabilize them. In fact, that entire facility was run on mana from vex crystals."

"Could that be what runs the power station?" mused Lenora, more to herself than to Zara.

"It's possible. But if so, then the high mages must have found a way of projecting the mana many times further then we can. For now, we can only build small stations capable of providing power to an area of just a few hundred square yards. It would take years for us to complete enough of those to cover all of Vale."

Drake looked at her closely. "You think you can find the knowledge you need in Troi, don't you?"

"That is our hope, yes."

He furrowed his brow. "And if you don't?"

"Then Vale will be no worse off than it is now. And at least the land will be able to heal. What would be better – spending a few years in the dark, but with enough food for everyone? Or letting the people die?" She set her jaw, her eyes burning with resolve. "No. This farce must end. It may take time. But we *will* make things better…for all of us."

The thought of Troi being cast into darkness disturbed Drake greatly. The city had been a beacon of hope to him his entire life. And though he now knew that everything it stood for was one massive lie, he still could not help the way he felt.

"When would you want us to leave?" asked Lenora.

"Right away," Zara told her. "Every moment we wait, Salazar is moving closer to his objective."

"And what about Samuel?"

"He has to make his own choice. We won't force him to help us."

Of course he'll want to help you, thought Drake. How could anyone not want to after discovering what Salazar intended?

"I'm sure he'll make the right decision," said Lenora.

"I hope you're right." She touched Maliel's hand. "You should get rested. It's almost time."

Maliel rose and said farewell then returned to his room. His expression was difficult to read. It was so very different

– inhuman. But Drake thought he noticed a sign of relief in his peculiarly shaped eyes.

Zara led them back to the chambers where they had bathed and changed, telling them that they would be departing just before dawn. Until then, two men would be placed outside the door to keep any vengeance-minded people away from Drake.

He was still reeling over the number of people who had perished during Salazar's rescue. But he had to put that out of his mind for now. Protecting Lenora must be his only focus.

Something the Nelwyn had said was troubling him. He'd described the Bomar as human. If that were so, was it even right for them to be doing this? Then again, how did he know Maliel was telling the truth about anything?

"You don't," he muttered while lying down on his bunk. "And it doesn't matter."

What mattered was defeating Salazar. If there was a possibility that the Nelwyn might be willing to help, they had to try.

Lenora seemed to believe what Maliel had said. As for himself, he would just have to trust her instincts.

CHAPTER TWENTY-FOUR

S alazar threw open the door to his bedchamber. He could still feel the weight of the ceremonial crown on his brow and the loathsome touch of the Grand Mage on his cheeks. Her voice continued to ring in his head, calling out the words of ascension for the assembled nobles and high mages to hear. He could still see the smirks on some of their faces, as well as the looks of suspicion. They knew – or they suspected – what he had done.

As fast as he could, he stripped off the cumbersome clothes he'd been compelled to wear and flung them into the corner. He needed to wash off the stink of the day.

You are king now.

The voice was kindly and filled with pride. So unlike his father's.

"I know," he responded. "But they think I'm a pretender. They don't respect me."

What does it matter? You are king. And soon you shall be the savior of Vale. Let them laugh and scheme. In time, they will beg you for forgiveness.

He crossed over to his desk and retrieved the crystal

from a drawer. It felt warm to the touch...soothing. "But I'm not ready. The hellspawn are still growing. What if we are discovered?"

By whom? No one can stop us. You are strong and wise. You will shepherd the people into a new age. One of plenty and prosperity.

He pressed the crystal to his breast. "Thank you. Where all others are against me, you are my only ally."

Salazar could feel its power seeping into him. Each day he became stronger and more powerful. But this crystal was nearly spent. He needed more if his true ambition was to be realized. And when the high mages finally understood, he would laugh at the fools while crushing them to dust.

Then you will be loved by all.

Placing the crystal back inside the desk, he made his way to the shower. Though it was still early, as the hot water washed away the invisible layer of filth he imagined the day had laid upon him, he felt fatigue setting in. All business could wait. He would sleep first.

While donning his silk nightshirt, he noticed the painting of his father hanging on the wall near a tall bookcase. The eyes were staring at him accusingly, as if watching his every move. Salazar stood in front of it for a time, lips curled into a snarl.

"This is all your fault," he growled. "You knew what they were doing. You let me believe that you were helpless to change things. But that was a lie. Wasn't it?"

He waited, as if expecting the image to respond. Unwanted memories flooded in: memories of his father walking with him in their garden; telling him stories of the ancients; teaching him magic; holding him in his arms when he was afraid, wakened by nightmares.

"No!" he shouted. "You won't trick me. You won't make me weak like you."

A knock at the door snapped him into the moment. Grabbing hold of the painting, he jerked it from the wall and quickly shoved it underneath his bed. Only then did he push the mana pad on his nightstand. The door clacked open to reveal a royal guard still dressed in his full ceremonial uniform.

The guard bowed low. "Forgive the intrusion, Your Majesty. There is a young girl here to see you. She bears your seal."

Salazar realized that he was perspiring. He dabbed his brow with his sleeve and smoothed down his shirt. "Yes, of course. Show her in."

The guard bowed again and then ushered a young girl inside. She was wearing the blue and white uniform of the university. Her hair was tied into a topknot, kept in place by two white pins, and she was holding a leather book in one hand.

Salazar smiled broadly. "Linx! I am so happy to see you."

She did not smile in return. "I did what you asked, Your Majesty."

He felt an overwhelming sense of relief. "I knew I could count on you." He gestured over to a small table near a window overlooking a private garden. "Please sit."

Linx hesitated for a second before complying. "How long have you known?" she asked, sliding the book across the table.

Salazar cocked his head. "Known what, my dear?"

"About the power station. About the high mages."

"That all depends." Salazar's eyes drifted to the book. "What is it *you* know?"

"I know a vex crystal when I see one," she replied coldly. "That's what really powers Vale. Not the high mages."

Salazar took the book and opened it cautiously. Nestling

inside a small recess was what he had been yearning for. His desire to touch it was unbearable. What Linx had said only seconds before faded from memory.

"Your Majesty?"

He blinked hard and closed the book.

"Yes...the high mages. Well, Linx, things aren't quite as simple as you might think. While it is true that the vex crystals provide the mana, it's the high mages who know how to stabilize the crystals. They're the only ones who know how the station works...for now."

He could see that there was more than just the power station troubling her. He had taken a great risk in sending her there during the coronation, but she was the only person he could trust to complete the task. A thought then occurred.

"You didn't touch the crystal, did you?"

"No."

He breathed a sigh of relief. "That's good. It would be very dangerous for someone like you, with no magical abilities." He regarded her for a long moment. "You have something to say?"

"Yes, I do." She met Salazar's gaze. "Is it true what they're saying about Drake?"

Salazar leaned back in his chair and lowered his eyes. "Can I trust you, Linx? I mean, *really* trust you?"

"You know you can," she answered. "I broke into the power station for you, didn't I?"

"Yes, you did. And you have no idea how grateful I am. However, there are things happening that you could not possibly fathom. And I need people I can trust by my side."

"That doesn't answer my question."

"No, it doesn't," he agreed. "Are you sure you want to know the answer?"

"If you're asking me if I would still be loyal to you if I

discovered that Drake is innocent, then the answer is yes. Look, my life before was nothing but stealing, running, and trying not to starve to death. Much as I like Drake, it was you who brought me here to Troi. It is you I owe the most to. So you can trust me or not; tell me or not. It won't change a thing."

Salazar smiled. "You are a unique individual, Linx. I feel fortunate to know you. Of all those around me, I trust you the most. For that reason, I am going to share something with you, something only a handful of people know. But you must understand, once you have been told, there can be no turning back. Your fate will inescapably be bound to mine. So I will ask you one more time: Do you want to know the answers? All of them?"

Linx's expression hardened. It was clear that she would not be dissuaded. After a long moment of stone silence, she nodded. "Tell me."

CHAPTER TWENTY-FIVE

I t took three days to reach the point in the barrier where they could cross over, during which time Drake's apprehension continued to build. Maliel had gone over with them a rough estimate of the path they would need to take, but as it had been two years, he was not entirely sure of his accuracy.

The way the Nelwyn had described the outer world was wholly unbelievable to Drake. He could still see ruined land as clearly as the day he'd stepped onto its barren soil, with not so much as a dried twig lying upon the ground; still smell the odor of ash; still feel the complete lack of any moisture in the air.

Bane had nearly become violent when first being told that they were to be separated. This was exacerbated by the fact he was not allowed to know where they would be going or what their mission was. It took Lenora more than an hour of talking to him before he calmed down. In the end, he reluctantly accepted the situation and vowed to be ready to strike by the time they returned.

Maliel told them of how his people had first met the Bomar.

"They claimed to come to us in peace," he began. "They said they only wanted to trade with us – machines in exchange for food, cloth, jewelry, and other things we make. Our artisans are quite skilled, and our fields are rich with bounty. Though we had very little use for what they offered, we could see their need. They were starving. Without solas, their fields withered. The only thing they had was their industry, and even this had polluted their rivers and lakes.

"At first they appeared grateful and eager to be friends. Then the winter came. We did our best to help them, but their need was far greater than our resources could bear. When we could give no more, they simply took what they wanted instead. When we protested, that was when the killing began. Since then they have spread like a disease, driving us farther and farther from our homes. Now we have almost nowhere else to retreat. Our backs are pressed against the mountains, and now it is we who are dying of hunger and thirst."

Maliel was almost in tears by the end.

Lenora placed a hand on his shoulder. "We will do what we can."

He smiled weakly. "With your help, I am sure we'll have victory. You are not like them. The soul of the world is within you, as it is with my people. Even your machines use its essence for strength. I am sure it was the Mother who sent me to you. I had wondered why…but looking at you, I think I understand."

"The mother?" asked Drake.

"The creator and keeper of all things. She was here in the beginning. She molded my people from the earth and breathed into us the spirit of life. I do not think your people hold such beliefs."

Drake nodded. It was said that the people of Vale had

once worshipped a creator. But that was long ago. "And the Bomar?" he asked. "What do they believe in?"

"Who knows? What god could create such people and deserve worship?"

"So you don't think your *Mother* made them?"

"I have asked myself that many times," he admitted, "and have yet to come to an answer. Some of us think they must be descendants of the Amarizians, those who came before."

Drake gave him a lopsided frown. "Before what? Creation?"

"Of this world, yes. We believe the world has been destroyed and created many times. There is proof of this in the mountains, and in the icy lands beyond. I have seen with my own eyes the remains of the old world."

The ancients, thought Drake. Maybe the stories were true after all, or at least some of them.

On arriving at the barrier, he could see that Lenora was genuinely frightened, though she was doing her best to hide it. They had packed only a few days' worth of food and water, but Maliel assured them they would not be needing more.

The man who had driven them to this point called Drake to the back of the van and handed him a long item wrapped in a cloth. Inside was his sword.

"Zara said to make sure you had this," he told him. "She said you might need it."

The other two were busy slinging their packs as Drake drew it from its sheath. Maliel immediately took notice.

"A fine weapon," he remarked. "It is much like what many of the Bomar carry, though I can sense the power of the Mother within its steel. Are you skilled with it?"

Drake gave a casual shrug. "I'm not bad."

His natural caution was making him reluctant to say too much about his own abilities. He wondered what the Nelwyn

311

thought of the vex crystal implanted in his chest. Thus far Maliel hadn't mentioned it at all, though the occasional look from him suggested he knew full well that it was there.

The sun was not quite fully beyond the horizon as they approached the fifty-foot-high tower directly ahead. Humming and sizzling with mana, it was sending a wall of translucent green light shooting off in both directions, spanning gaps of more than twenty miles to where similar towers were doing the same. Maliel looked up at it with genuine wonder.

"Had we this," he remarked, "the Bomar would never have been able to trouble us."

"It shuts the world out," said Lenora. "But if the world beyond is as you have described, it has also become our prison."

Maliel smiled. "Come. You will see. Our land is a wondrous place. The spirit of the Mother is everywhere. It fills you with a warmth the like of which you have never known."

Lenora smiled then took Drake's hand.

"Are you sure you can do this?" he asked.

"I'm sure."

Their driver led the way to the base of the tower. Here, a three-foot-in-diameter portal was set at just above knee level. He pulled hard several times on a handle before it came loose.

"You'll need to kick out the other side," he told them. "Just be sure to put it back after you're all through. Maintenance from Troi checks these from time to time."

Drake grinned and drew his P37. He had modified to it his specifications just before they had departed using the parts still in Cal's trunk. "I think I'll do it the easy way."

The man caught his arm. "No magic this close to the barrier."

With a sigh, he holstered his weapon. "If you say so."

Lowering himself, he crawled inside. Above he could feel the heat of the mana being generated. The tower he'd passed through as a recruit had been different; that one had allowed passage through to the other side via a simple narrow corridor sealed by a steel door. He had known these much smaller portals existed, from his time hunting for where the hellspawn were entering, but they were deemed too small for the creatures to have used, and none had even been found tampered with.

Upon reaching the far side of the tunnel, he twisted his body around to deliver several firm kicks. As the portal fell away, the smell of ash instantly invaded his nostrils, and a hot wind blasted him in the face. He exited the tower and waited until the others were all through before replacing the covering. He could see that the man on the other side had already done this and was making his way back to the van with urgent strides.

Lenora was trembling, and after only a few steps began clutching at Drake's arm.

"What's wrong?"

"I…I don't know."

"Do not worry," said Maliel. "Zara experienced the same thing. It will pass."

"I'll be fine," she said. "Just give me a moment."

She stopped and knelt, taking deep panicky breaths. Drake held her shoulders, helpless to do anything other than watch. After a few minutes, she seemed to regain her composure.

"That was a very strange feeling," she said with an embarrassed smile.

Drake gently helped her to her feet and, taking her hand, continued on. Mile after mile they walked, and still Drake could see no evidence of life, only more of the dead black earth stretching out endlessly.

Maliel seemed not to notice. In fact, a smile was slowly building on his lips. His strides were becoming longer and more sure, as if leaving Vale behind was in some way giving him renewed vigor.

"The air feels better, yes?" he remarked.

"It feels hot and dry to me," replied Drake sourly.

Maliel laughed. "Hot and dry, yes. But cleaner. Filled with the Mother's bounty." He reached out to Lenora. "Take my hand and I will show you."

She hesitated. "What will happen?"

"Nothing painful or foul, I promise."

After a brief hesitation, she did as the Nelwyn asked, though retaining a firm hold on Drake's as well.

The crystal in his chest instantly begin to pulse and fill with mana. Lenora's eyes grew wide and a soft gasp escaped her lips.

"This is incredible," she said, in a half whisper.

Drake could feel the power flowing into him through her touch. All the same, it felt no different to the mana he channeled when in Vale. After a few seconds, Maliel released her.

"This is good," he said. "The other mage could not see as you do. You are indeed strong with the Mother."

She looked to Drake. "Did you feel it too?"

He shrugged. "I felt...something. But I couldn't say what it was."

Maliel sighed. "The thing inside your chest blocks you from truly seeing, I'm afraid. Forgive my rudeness, but why you would do such a thing to yourself?"

"Let's just say that it has its advantages."

Maliel nodded, though did not press the matter further.

"Is that how you see your world all the time?" asked Lenora.

Maliel laughed. "No. Were I to stay that close to the Mother for too long, I would become lost within my own spirit. Though I have at times thought that might not be such a terrible fate."

"What did you see?" Drake asked Lenora.

She smiled, her eyes distant. "It was as if all the colors of the world were dancing around me, filling my eyes with brilliance and magic. It was almost like I had become a mana stream myself."

"Are you sure it's not dangerous?" he asked Maliel.

"Only if she were to remain so connected for days at a time. We use this magic to grow our crops and heal our sick. But perhaps caution *would* be best until you know more of our ways."

"I agree," he said.

It was late into the afternoon before Drake eventually called for a halt. They hadn't eaten, and his legs were aching quite badly. He was sure Lenora was faring little better.

"We should go on," Maliel insisted. "We're not far now."

Drake's irritation was growing. His hand shot out to point at the horizon. "Look! There's nothing there. We've been walking all day, and there's still not a single tree in sight."

"Please, trust me. I would not lead you astray." Maliel moved ahead, waving for them to follow. "There's a cool stream and soft grass close by. We can rest there."

Drake heaved a sigh. "Fine. But we are stopping soon, stream or no stream."

"Yes. Very soon."

In spite of this assurance, after another two miles, everything still looked the same. By now, Drake's frustration was reaching the breaking point. Her head bent and eyes downcast, Lenora had stumbled twice and was holding onto his arm for support. He offered to carry her pack, but she refused outright.

"I imagine this is but the beginning of our trek," she said. "I need to grow accustomed to the travel. I can't have you bearing my burden all the time."

Maliel was several yards ahead. "Wise words," he called over his shoulder. "Yes. Our journey is long. But your body will get stronger. I will show you how."

"Is it me, or does he make less sense with each word?" Drake remarked quietly.

"At least he speaks our language," Lenora whispered back.

Whispered or not, Maliel heard their exchange. "Yes. I speak human. The Bomar…they talk like you. Many of us have learned."

"I suppose those ears aren't just for show," Drake said, smirking.

This comment drew a laugh from the Nelwyn. "My people have keen hearing, yes. Much better than yours. It helps us when we hunt."

Drake was on the point of asking what it was they hunted when he felt a cool breeze wash over him. Lenora tilted back her head and let out a long sigh of relief. A moment later, Drake caught the scent of pine on the air. But how was that possible? He could see nothing other than the same wasteland stretching off into the distance.

Maliel glanced over his shoulder, grinning impishly. "I told you so."

Almost as soon as the words were spoken, the Nelwyn completely vanished from sight. Both Drake and Lenora stopped short, looking at each other in utter confusion and astonishment.

"What the hell?" growled Drake. "Maliel!"

"I am still here," came the reply. "Come see."

He hesitated. "What is this? A cloak of some kind?"

Lenora shrugged. "At this point, if it takes me away from this place, I really don't care what it is."

With no choice other than to move on or return the barrier, they continued forward, albeit with wary steps. When they reached the point at which Maliel had disappeared, they found the light around them suddenly beginning to ripple like the disturbed surface of a pond. After another pace forward, these ripples transformed into great waves of spectacular colors that wrapped and swirled in a frantic tempest. Drake pulled Lenora close, but as quickly as they had appeared, the colors vanished.

It took a moment for them to get their bearings. But once they did, Lenora let out a loud gasp. "It's true."

Drake could not believe what he was seeing. They were standing on the edge of a dense forest, the canopy of which was hundreds of feet high. Flower-laden vines snaked their way up the massive tree trunks, each one reaching across to others nearby to create an unimaginably intricate web of life and color. Birds, the likes of which he had never seen, flitted playfully from branch to branch. The air was cool and refreshing, though far from cold. And where before he had smelled pine, this was now replaced with aromas so sweet and pungent that it made him dizzy.

"How could this be real?" he said, tears forming in his eyes. His legs felt weak and he stumbled back. This time it was Lenora who was there to lend her strength as she wrapped an arm around his waist to steady him as he settled to one knee.

How could a place like this exist? Drake continued to ask himself. *How?* All the lies he had believed his entire life came crashing in on him. The innumerable deaths he had been responsible for while serving in the royal guard and chasing runners; it had all been for nothing. His entire life was nothing more than a clever deception.

So transfixed and awed by the sight, he hadn't even been aware that he was openly weeping, until he felt a gentle touch on his shoulder. Looking up, he saw Maliel standing over him, a kindly expression on his face.

"Zara reacted in much the same way as you," he said. "Aside from her, you are the only humans of your world to see this. I am sorry if it causes you pain."

He could see that Lenora was weeping as well, though still holding her composure.

"I'm sorry, Maliel," Drake said. He was hardly able to phrase the words. "I know you told me…but I never dreamed…"

"It is not all like this," he said. "There are cruel lands of bitter cold and high mountains where great storms rage eternal. And deserts very much like the one we crossed."

Drake was recalling more of what Maliel had described: wide-open plains dotted with lakes that glistened in the sunlight; vast orchards providing bountiful crops of every type of fruit imaginable; rich green fields dissected by a web of tiny brooks of crystal clear water, every one of them pure enough to drink from. They must all be real too. He took several deep breaths before struggling to his feet.

Lenora held his hand firmly, the look of wonderment showing through her still weeping eyes. "It makes the gardens of Troi look common and drab," she said. "And you say the Bomar are destroying it?"

Maliel nodded. "They care nothing for beauty and life." He shook his head as if to banish them from his mind. "But there is time for that talk later. I promised rest and comfort.

I hunger too, and my feet are blistered from the scorched land."

On approaching the edge of the tree line, the sheer scope of the forest became into focus. Its thick canopy nearly blocked out the sun completely, and the vines barred their way at every turn. But even in this dim light, the colors were still breathtaking, their hues subtle and blended as if a celestial hand had run its finger over a canvas of life.

Drake allowed Maliel to continue leading. To his amazement, the Nelwyn easily found gaps in the vines and brush they could pass through when none at first appeared to be there. Some gaps even seemed to open up for him as he approached, though Drake thought this was likely a mere trick of the light.

Even with this expert guidance, Drake and Lenora still found themselves constantly tripping on hidden roots and snagging their clothes on protruding limbs and vines.

"You will learn the forest in time," Maliel assured them.

Drake could swear that the man was now several inches taller than when they had left. The tone of his skin was deeper too, radiating an aura that was only just perceptible.

After only half an hour, the foliage started to thin, and Drake could hear the rushing of water over rocks. Not having eaten since the morning, his stomach growled.

They emerged by the bank of a narrow stream no more than a few yards across. The clear water flowed swiftly over a bed of small pebbles, making it look as if it were no more than an inch or two deep. But when Drake knelt beside it, he could see that it was much deeper – at least a couple of feet.

The ground alongside was covered in a thick grass that simply begged to be laid upon. Lenora was the first to do so. Spreading her arms and legs wide, she closed her eyes.

"Take your ease," Maliel said to Drake. "I will find us some proper food."

Before he could respond, the Nelwyn vanished into the forest.

"Have you ever dreamed of such a thing?" mused Lenora.

Drake stretched out beside her, the grass as comfortable as any bed he had ever slept upon and made even more pleasing by its wholesome scent. Within seconds, he could feel the fatigue being lifted from his body as if syphoned away by the purity of the earth.

"If the people of Vale only knew about this," he said.

Lenora threw an arm over his chest. "I do not think they would believe it. I'm here, and I'm not sure that I do."

"Well, if this is a dream, I hope I never wake up."

They lay there in amiable silence until Maliel returned carrying an armful of fruit and berries, none of which were familiar. "Not enough time for hunting," he said. "But this should satisfy our hunger."

Drake forced himself up and accepted an offering of three pieces of bright yellow, fist-sized fruit and a handful of red berries, each one the size as the tip of his finger. He waited until Maliel had bitten into one of the fruits before doing the same.

A gush of sour juice poured over his tongue, causing him initially to wince, but quickly the taste sweetened as his teeth sank in deeper. The pulp was much like that of an apple, and he soon found himself delighting in each bite. The berries, however, were unusually tart throughout. Drake decided that he preferred the yellow fruit.

"What are these?" asked Lenora, doing her best to contain the juice flowing from her lips.

"Varpa fruit and chen berries," replied Maliel. "Not my

favorites, but they were all that was available nearby."

"It's delicious," said Lenora.

Drake mumbled his agreement through another mouthful of varpa fruit.

Soon the sun was low, prompting them to unpack their blankets. The chirping and squeaking of insects surrounded them, and Drake caught the shadow of several small creatures scurrying through the underbrush.

Maliel assured them that nothing would trouble them in the night. At this point, Drake was inclined to trust him.

"It will be at least a week before we reach my people," he told them, after stretching out on his blanket. "And we will almost certainly see the Bomar along the way."

Drake simply nodded and pulled Lenora close. He'd had so many questions when they started out, but at this moment none of them seemed important. Right now, he was experiencing something he had never felt in his entire life: a sense of complete safety and peace. Even if it was just an illusion, he would enjoy it while it lasted. The troubles of Vale felt so very distant. And from the way Lenora was cradled to his chest, her breathing slow and even, she had managed to leave them far behind as well. If only he could freeze this moment in time, he thought. He could happily live there forever.

Somewhere, the struggle for life raged on. But not here. Not now. For now he would give himself over to a deep and peaceful slumber. Whatever his dreams this night, they could not compare to what his waking eyes were sure to witness. He had seen behind the Vale – and beyond.

Now he could not contain his need to see more.

End of Book One

ABOUT THE AUTHOR

Brian D. Anderson is the indie-bestselling fantasy author of The Godling Chronicles, Dragonvein, and Akiri (with co-author Steven Savile) series. His books have sold more than 500,000 copies worldwide and his audiobooks are perennially popular. After a fifteen year long career in music, he rediscovered his boyhood love of writing. It was soon apparent that this was what he should have been pursuing all along. Currently, he lives in the sleepy southern town of Fairhope, Alabama with his wife and son, who inspire him daily.

CPSIA information can be obtained
at www.ICGtesting.com
Printed in the USA
LVHW110155170921
698041LV00003B/114